Praise for Erin Nicholas's
Anything You Want

"With wonderful writing and a superb complex plot, humor and sentiment a plenty, amazing chemistry and some very erotic scenes, there is everything I could have asked for in *Anything You Want*."
~ *Literary Nymphs Reviews*

"... *Anything You Want* had a playful quality to the story... A wonderful read."
~ *SensualReads.com*

"Erin Nicholas has written an enchanting and hot love story all about coming home again... The characters are well crafted, and the situations are believable and in some cases, heartbreaking."
~ *Long and Short Reviews*

"I did not want to put the book down once I started... I absolutely loved this story and would love to see more from this town and this author."
~ *The Romance Studio*

"One word for Erin Nicholas, *Anything You Want*, is WOW.... I can't wait for more from this talented author."
~ *Fallen Angel Reviews*

Look for these titles by
Erin Nicholas

Now Available:

No Matter What
Anything You Want
Hotblooded

The Bradfords Series
Just Right
Just Like That
Just My Type

Anything You Want

Erin Nicholas

SAMHAIN
PUBLISHING

Samhain Publishing, Ltd.
11821 Mason Montgomery Road, 4B
Cincinnati, OH 45249
www.samhainpublishing.com

Anything You Want
Copyright © 2012 by Erin Nicholas
Print ISBN: 978-1-60928-412-1
Digital ISBN: 978-1-60928-383-4

Editing by Lindsey Faber
Cover by Scott Carpenter

First Samhain Publishing, Ltd. electronic publication: March 2011
First Samhain Publishing, Ltd. print publication: April 2012

Dedication

To Nick, who knows a little something about loving a woman in spite of her (of course, minor) imperfections. Thank goodness.

Chapter One

She blamed the bartender.

Sabrina Cassidy's stomach roiled and she quickly nibbled on the corner of a saltine cracker. She held her breath for about ten seconds and the wave of nausea passed.

Definitely the bartender's fault. Maybe not *just* him, but he certainly had some responsibility in the whole thing.

For one, he'd made the rum taste so good. He was the one who'd mixed it with the orange and pineapple juices, coconut liqueur and club soda. He was the one who'd poured it into to the cute pineapple glass and put in the umbrellas that had made it seem so innocuous.

For another, he should have looked at her skimpy wrap-around skirt and bikini top, her spray-on tan and her hair highlights and known that she was on vacation.

Women on vacation in Jamaica with their girlfriends, sitting at bars on the beach and dancing with cute guys until the sun came up three nights in a row should be limited to two alcoholic drinks. Period.

But no. He'd poured her a fourth and a fifth, never once thinking that he was changing her entire life.

Her stomach pitched again. She wasn't sure if it was in response to the memory of the rum that she used to like and would never again touch, the memory of the last guy she'd danced with—Paul—who she wished she'd never met, or the fact that she'd spent every day for the past ten weeks nauseous between the hours of seven a.m. and two p.m.

Or maybe it was that the whole thing was so cliché. She

should have known better—she *did* know better. She'd never done it before—absolutely cliché. She should have been smart— one-night stands were not smart. She should have been safe— unprotected sex was *not* safe. Or smart.

Ugh.

She started on a third saltine as she watched the mechanic move to the other side of her car, his head still under the hood. She knew next to nothing about cars, but the sound hers had made just before it stopped would have been enough to convince her that it was a lost cause. Then the black smoke had poured out and she knew that she would not be driving the 1996 Toyota home to Justice.

The mechanic—who looked barely old enough to drive a car, not to mention fix one—was still looking at it and not saying a word. That couldn't be a good sign.

It was just one more thing in a long line of things that proved her life was *not* going the way she'd intended. Like Caribbean vacations. Tropical vacations should be fun and relaxing. All she should have gotten from it was a tan and some great pictures. Instead she got morning sickness.

"Well, Miss Cassidy, I hate to tell you, but—"

Sabrina steeled herself.

"—your transmission is shot."

She groaned. She knew what a transmission was and what it did. Sort of. And, as in this case, that it wasn't good when it stopped doing it.

"And then there's the..."

"Never mind," she interrupted, rubbing her forehead. "It doesn't matter." Whatever else was wrong with the car was not going to drive the price down, so there was no point in pursuing the conversation any further.

She didn't even bother to ask how much it would cost to replace or repair or whatever had to be done. She was broke— thank you, Paul—so it didn't really matter. She couldn't afford it.

She resisted the urge to scratch her right buttock. The itch on her rear end was nearly unbearable. The sun beating down on the Wyoming highway had also beaten down on her, making her sweat like she couldn't remember, even at nine in the morning. In fact, she hadn't been aware that the backs of her legs, including the sensitive area where her thigh curved into her buttock, could sweat. But they could. And the denim of her short shorts had rubbed repeatedly as she walked, resulting in the heat rash from hell.

Which was just, what, number seventy-two on the list of things not going her way?

The mechanic wiped his greasy hands on the rag he pulled from the back pocket of his faded blue jeans. "You want me to write up an estimate?"

There was no hope of a second opinion. The car was kaput. She should know. She'd been the one walking along the highway waiting for someone with enough decency to stop and offer to help—and not murder or kidnap her—for half an hour.

She fought the urge to laugh and lost. "Do you think the repair will cost less than nineteen dollars and—" she dug in the front pocket of her jeans and pulled out the change there, "—thirty-six cents?"

The young man frowned, seeming puzzled. "Um, yes, ma'am. I think it will be more than that."

He wasn't even going to joke around with her. "Then, no, I won't be needing an estimate."

He tipped back his greasy cap and scratched his head. "Okay." He seemed more puzzled now.

She sighed, realizing that it was probably the first sigh of many. Her cell phone was dead on the front seat of her dead car, her water bottle was empty, as was her wallet. She was out of options.

"Can I use your phone?"

"Is it a local call?"

She glanced around, looking up and down the Main Street of Muddy Gap, Wyoming, which was even shorter than the one in her tiny hometown. She could walk to anywhere that was local in five minutes. "No. It's not local. I'll add that to what I owe you."

He led her to a tiny, stuffy office inside the shop that smelled of motor oil. She briefly wondered if the station would

11

hire her to pump gas and wash windshields but quickly discarded it. She was sleep deprived and stressed out.

She noticed that the mechanic's shirt had *Dan* stitched over the left chest. He handed her the cordless phone. "Thanks."

She smiled at him and waited for him to leave. He didn't.

"What's up, Dan?" she finally asked.

"Is someone going to come get you?" he asked.

She certainly hoped so. "Yep."

"What do you want me to do with your car?"

The sting of the rash intensified as she shifted her weight and the denim rubbed. She had no idea what to do. She had several hundred miles to go yet. Suddenly she felt like crying.

"Any chance you could use it for parts?"

He looked out the window, puzzled yet again. "I don't know."

One little emotional breakdown, even a few seconds long would be such a welcome release. But that would accomplish nothing.

So she sniffed once and opted *not* to sit down.

"Then I'll have to get back to you."

Another car pulled up in front of the shop and Dan left her alone.

The dial tone buzzed in her ear as she lifted the heavy black mane of hair from the back of her neck. The dark tinted window inside the shop didn't give her a clear reflection of the rest of her face, for which she was grateful. The dark blue of her eyes would bring out the even darker circles that hung underneath, she was sure, and her make-up, what little there had been to start, was a day old.

On the bright side, her stomach seemed to have calmed down.

The dial tone turned to an annoying computerized beeping, signaling she'd been standing holding the receiver without doing anything with it for too long.

She frowned at the phone for its impatience.

A few minute later she frowned at the phone for its inability to deliver what she'd needed—a conversation with someone she knew who would be willing to come and pick her up.

She was closer to Justice than Seattle, so she'd called Nebraska first.

Her best friend, Kat—Dr. Katarina Dayton—was not answering her cell phone and was, according to the receptionist at the clinic, in Kansas City for the next few days at a medical conference. No, the receptionist didn't know how to get a message to her and no, Kat was not answering her pager because Dr. Hanson was on call for her.

Terrific.

Sabrina had never even heard of Dr. Hanson.

Her friend Chase, who was approximately nine hours away in the other direction from Kat, didn't even have his cell on. Chase didn't have another phone at home. Or work. He was a private construction contractor so his cell was for personal and business. And it was off, at least at the moment.

She'd known Lori and Jen, her companions on her ill-fated trip to Jamaica, for a month and getting on the plane with them had been more a spontaneous what-the-hell kind of thing than something borne of a I-can-depend-on-you-for-anything friendship. It wasn't just anyone who would drive nine hours one-way for her.

She didn't have many options for help.

It was times like this when a woman realized not only who her true friends were, but that she didn't have all that many of them.

She mentally weighed how desperate she was.

She *wouldn't* call her father. She'd placed a collect call to him once since she'd left home. He had refused the charges.

Which left her with one option. There was one person she knew would come for her for sure. She held her breath as she started dialing.

"Have you seen Luke?"

Marc turned from the frustrations of the soup recipe that wouldn't come together. "He's interviewing someone for the bartender position."

Josie, the afternoon hostess was holding the wireless phone. "He's got a phone call. Can I interrupt him?"

Marc Sterling and Luke Hamilton owned the restaurant they'd named The Camelot. They were fifty-fifty partners. There weren't any business calls that Luke received that Marc couldn't handle. "I can take it."

"Well..."

Marc quirked an eyebrow. "What's the call about?"

Josie grinned. "I'm not sure. But she said it's important and asked for Luke specifically."

"She?" Marc repeated. He grinned back. "It's a she?"

"It's a she," Josie confirmed. "And she *really* wants to talk to Luke."

"Does she now?" Marc grabbed a towel, wiped his hands and took the phone. "I think I definitely need to take this call."

Josie laughed and headed back for the lobby. Marc took the line off hold. "Hello?"

"Um... Hi."

Nice voice, slightly breathless. Marc smiled.

"Hi."

"It's...um..."

There was a long pause and Marc wondered if she was nervous. That was nice. Luke deserved a woman who was a little nervous about calling him. He usually dated women Kat set him up with, which generally meant professional, polished women with high paying careers and confidence to spare. Physicians, lawyers, professors, women in marketing and PR. None of them would be nervous about calling a guy. None would be breathless on the phone unless they were engaging in phone sex.

Luke deserved a woman who would be nervous—or who would have phone sex with him.

His interest piqued, Marc said, "Who is this, honey?"

A moment's hesitation then, "It's, uh, Sabrina."

He froze. No, it couldn't be. Maybe it was a different Sabrina. It was possible that Luke had met another woman named Sabrina. Sure. There had to be a thousand Sabrinas in the world. Maybe it was...but somehow he knew it was *the* Sabrina.

Sabrina Cassidy.

The love of Luke's life.

The bitch herself.

"Sabrina?" Marc answered, not trusting himself to say more.

"Yeah. I, uh... How are you?"

Seriously? She was asking how he was? They could barely be in a room together for ten minutes without arguing or needling and insulting each other. She'd never in her life asked how he was—or cared.

No, he realized a split second later. She was asking how Luke was. She thought she was talking to Luke. After four years.

After he'd proposed to her and she'd run out on him.

Now she was calling out of the blue. Which meant she needed something. And she was calling Luke about whatever it was. Of course.

Well, he had a few things to say to Miss Sabrina Rose Cassidy too.

And there was no way she was going to get to talk to Luke.

"Fine. What's going on?"

"I'm...traveling." Her voice was cheerful, but he could hear the tension underneath and it snapped him out of his daze.

"What do you need?" he asked bluntly. With his short responses she might not be able to tell that it was Marc and not Luke. He could find out what she wanted from Luke, turn her down and maybe piss her off enough that she'd never call Luke again.

"I hope I'm not interrupting anything."

"No. What do you want?"

There was silence on her end of the line and then he could have sworn he heard a diesel truck engine in the background.

"I didn't know who else to call," she said finally.

She sounded dejected. He tried to be happy about that. But

15

she hadn't called in four years. He supposed it was possible she really was in trouble. God knew she didn't always make the best choices. He wanted her to leave Luke alone. He didn't necessarily want her tortured or dead or anything. Miserable was okay. Unhappy, friendless, broken-hearted were all acceptable. But in danger or hurt probably not.

Dammit.

She had a way of sucking men in. Of all people, he should be immune, but...maybe he needed a booster against her charms. About an hour in her presence had always worked in the past.

"Sabrina, what is going on?"

"I'm...stranded."

He frowned. "Did you say stranded?"

"Yeah."

"What do you mean you're stranded?"

"I'm in Muddy Gap, Wyoming..."

"Muddy Gap?" he interrupted. "Seriously?"

She sighed over the phone. "I don't think I could make that up."

"Why are you there?" Why would anyone be in a place called Muddy Gap?

"My car broke down and I don't have enough money to fix it. I'm...stranded."

Of course she was. She did need something. She always needed something from Luke. And he had never in his life said no to her.

"How can you be stranded?" he asked. "Get on a bus, buy a plane ticket."

"This is a smaller town than Justice," she said. "They don't have an airport or a bus station. I'm not sure they have a grocery store. The closest airport is Laramie or Casper, which is about an hour and a half away. By car. Which I don't have. And I don't have any money, anyway. I'm serious. I'm broke. I called Kat but she didn't answer her cell phone."

This was fantastic. Marc shoved a hand through his hair and dug his fingers into his scalp. Sabrina was stranded in Wyoming with no car and no money and she was calling Luke.

16

Who would jump in the car in thirty seconds and head out to get her. Even to a place called Muddy Gap, Wyoming.

"Kat's at a conference."

"I know. Do you know when she'll be home?"

"No."

"Oh."

He hated that defeated tone in her voice. It wasn't something he'd heard before. She was full of spunk and fight. The more challenging things were, the tougher she got. He'd always grudgingly admired that about her. It was what made her dependence on Luke and his willingness to always jump on her command so damned frustrating...and pathetic. Sabrina didn't need anyone. Except Luke.

Except that she didn't even truly need Luke. But she liked making him jump through hoops for her. It was a ridiculous, sorry excuse for a relationship but it had functioned that way since they were toddlers playing in the backyard together. Luke and Sabrina had grown up as neighbors and had been inseparable.

Marc didn't want to help her. That probably made him a jerk, but he didn't. At least, part of him didn't want to. The part that knew her as the manipulative bitch who'd broken his best friend's heart.

But another part of him, that was evidently bigger, couldn't help but prolong the conversation.

"What are you doing in Wyoming?" he asked.

"Just passing through." According to the post cards she sent to Luke from all over the country, that was all she did anymore. "I was on my way home when the car died."

Home. The word echoed through his head.

"Home?" he asked sharply. "As in Justice?"

"Yeah." Her voice was quiet. "As in Justice."

"You were on your way back *here*?"

"Yes."

"What for?"

His caustic tone obviously took her back. "For... Because... I...need to."

17

It was a vague answer, on purpose. Fine. The less involved he got, the better. Marc stomped into his office and jerked open his middle desk drawer where he'd thrown his wallet.

"How much to get your car fixed?" he asked, pulling a credit card out.

"I'm not sure. Too much. I don't want you to pay for my car, Luke. It's not worth it."

Luke. Right. She thought she was talking to Luke. Marc threw the card down on his desk. "Then what do you want?"

"I...I guess... I was going to ask Kat for...a ride home."

He closed his eyes. She was coming here. This was a disaster just waiting to happen. Luke had been broken-hearted and Marc knew that his friend wasn't over Sabrina, but with her thousands of miles away he could at least *try* to move on, to get a life—the life he wanted and deserved. If she came back here, even temporarily, Luke would be a mess all over again.

"Why are you coming home?" he asked again.

"Things have changed," she said after a pause. "A lot of things."

"And suddenly you want to be back in Justice?" He was sure his skepticism was obvious.

"Yes."

Right. Something was going on. And he needed to know what it was. Sabrina was trouble for the man Marc loved like a brother. The man he would do anything for. Including protecting him from himself. Luke had never realized how bad she was for him and Marc had no delusions that Luke had wised up in the time she'd been gone.

He couldn't hang up on her either. She'd call back anyway. Or she'd finally get a hold of Kat. Or someone else. Somehow she'd make it to Justice and turn Luke inside out.

Marc couldn't let that happen. "How far is it from Muddy Crack to Justice?" he asked.

"Gap," she corrected. But she didn't answer his question.

"How far?"

She hesitated and he braced himself. Where the hell was this place?

"About three hundred and fifty miles, give or take."

"Three hund—" He recovered and quickly figured in his head that it would take him between five and a half to six hours to get to her.

Was he willing to spend, essentially, most of a workday on the road for Sabrina?

And that was one way.

But the answer came quickly. Yes. Not for her so much, but for Luke.

They needed to talk. He needed to make sure she understood a few things—like the fact that he would *never* let her hurt Luke again—and then give her whatever she needed to keep her as far from Justice and Luke as she could get. Money he could give. Transportation he could give. References, a down payment, a fake ID. Whatever it was that she thought she needed to come to Justice for he would find a way to provide.

And then send her off in the *opposite* direction.

"I'm on my way." He tucked his wallet in his back pocket, then grabbed a pen from the middle drawer.

"You're coming to get me?"

She didn't sound as surprised as he would have liked. But then, she knew as well as he did that Luke would have agreed to drive six hours to come and get her.

"Yes. I'm coming to get you." It was nine seventeen in the morning. He'd be there by four o'clock.

"You don't have to," she protested.

"Oh, but I want to." Marc knew his voice sounded ominous.

"Oh."

Was that a touch of nerves that he heard again? He hoped so.

"Where are you, exactly?" he asked, already scribbling instructions for the kitchen staff for that night.

"A mechanic's shop. I'll get the address, hold on."

He stopped writing. "Hold on. You're just sitting in a shop?"

"I don't have anywhere else to go."

He'd dearly love to make her sit in a hot, smelly shop waiting on him for six hours. In fact, he could easily stretch it into seven if he thought she was sitting on the hard pavement

19

by the roadside choking on the dust kicked up by the passing cars.

But he wasn't fooling himself for a moment. He wouldn't do something like that. "Ask the mechanic where the closest motel is."

"Motel?" she repeated.

"Yes, a motel. You know. A place where they let you sleep in their beds and use their showers for a nightly fee."

He knew that she'd been traveling and staying in some low-budget places in the past few years. Kat had kept Luke informed once she found out where Sabrina was and what, precisely, she was doing, even after Marc threatened to never let her drink for free at The Camelot again if she didn't shut up. Kat had ignored him, knowing he'd never follow through on a threat like that. So Luke got to hear regular reports on Sabrina's life. Which kept him thinking about her. Which kept him from totally getting over her.

Marc reigned in his thoughts before he could work up a good, healthy anger. Again. He had time for that later.

"There's only one motel in town," she said a moment later.

"How close?"

"Four blocks."

Four blocks. Hmm.

"You have luggage?"

He could make her walk four blocks dragging her luggage along, probably in high heels. Was it as hot in Wyoming as it was in Nebraska in late June?

"Not a lot. I sold a bunch of stuff before I left."

"You sold your clothes?"

"Some of them."

"Why?"

"For money."

Marc rolled his neck, listening to the cracks and pops. Her situation couldn't be any more pathetic if she'd scripted it. And who knew? Maybe she had. He wouldn't put it past her. Still, the whole thing made it tough to be mean to her.

"Get me the number for the motel. I'm going to call and

make a reservation for you with my credit card. Tell the guy there at the station that I'm on my way and I'll swing by and give him twenty bucks if he'll give you a ride to the motel."

"You don't have to do this, Luke. I know I'm imposing. I know you're surprised to hear from me."

What he was surprised about was that she hadn't realized she wasn't talking to Luke yet. But it had been a long time and maybe the phone reception in BFE, Wyoming wasn't so good.

Besides, the other emotions he had about her calling were much too strong to let something as mild as surprise really surface.

"It's done. Don't worry," he interrupted, thinking that she should worry the whole time she was waiting for him to show up. "Get me the number and get down to the motel."

She sighed. "Okay. Thanks, Luke. You're the best."

Her words sent a jolt through him that literally stopped him in his tracks. He stood in the middle of the hallway outside of his office, his car keys gripped tightly in one palm, the phone in the other.

Anger tightened his chest and his throat.

You're the best, Luke. She always said shit like that to him. That was what kept him holding on, kept him hoping they could be more than friends. But no one walked away from the best. People *wanted* the best, they *demanded* the best. They didn't leave it behind without a look back.

Luke wasn't the best anything in Sabrina's eyes—unless she was in trouble and had nowhere else to turn. Which didn't make him the best at all.

It made him her last resort.

This same scenario had repeated itself too many times. She fell back on Luke because he was there—unassuming, easy, comfortable, totally infatuated with her, whenever she needed him.

Marc didn't want her waltzing back into Luke's life every time she ran out of options. He didn't want any more phone calls out of the blue. Or any other time for that matter. Especially when he couldn't ensure that he would intercept them all. It had been four years and Marc had stupidly begun to believe she might be gone for good.

And now she was on the phone.

If he had anything to say about it, this would be the last time.

And he intended to have everything to say about it.

"I'll be there in a few hours." He disconnected before she could say one single thing more to raise his blood pressure. There was plenty of time for that later too.

Sabrina stood in the doorway to the motel room and felt tears well up. No one was around, so she let the drops fall. It was a simple mom-and-pop roadside motel, but she didn't care about the lack of neon or a chain-name.

It was a clean, comfortable, secure room.

She had no idea that it would mean this much. She was tired. She was fed up. She was scared. She was pregnant and the victim of fraud.

Almost worse, she'd slept the last two nights in her car in truck stop parking lots.

She owed Luke big time.

Nothing new about that.

She tossed her purse on the small round table near the window, lay back on the closest bed and stared at the white textured ceiling.

Luke.

He was an average-sized man, about six-two, muscular and slim, but to Sabrina he'd always seemed large. Some of that was because of her own small frame, but more it had to do with the fact that Luke had always been her hero. Luke did the right thing and he made no excuses or apologies for it.

And now he was on his way to get her. It was ridiculous, of course. But typical. He always wanted to save her and he did a great job at it. Way above and beyond.

They hadn't seen each other in four years. The last time she'd seen him was the night he'd proposed and she'd asked him to run away with her.

They'd both said no.

She pushed herself up to sitting on the edge of the bed. There wasn't anything she could do about it. Luke was on his way and she was going to have to face him...and try to act naturally. Whatever that was.

A shower. That was what she needed before she shared the close confines of a car with her almost-ex-fiancé.

As she started the water and shed her clothes, she hoped that at some point in the next few hours she could stop thinking about Luke as the guy whose heart she'd broken and remember that he was the boy who put dead spiders in her sock drawer when she was eleven.

As she lathered her hair with the complimentary shampoo from the basket by the sink, she thought about dead spiders. That would definitely do it. Dead spiders, *not* gorgeous engagement rings, *not* hopeful smiles. Dead spiders, *not* hopeful smiles drying up like those spider carcasses, replaced by resentment and hurt.

Yeah, this was working just great.

It had been four years and she could still see Luke's smile die as if he were standing in front of her now.

They'd been at the Grand Opening for The Camelot, Luke and Marc's restaurant—Luke's dream. He'd been smiling, laughing, surrounded by family and friends, full of confidence and energy and excitement, and as he'd walked toward her from across the room it struck her that she should be desperately attracted to him.

Not just that he was a great guy. Not just that she really cared about him. But she should *want* him. He knew her—the good and the bad—she could always count on him and he always took care of her. She never worried about making the wrong decision when Luke was around. He'd bailed her out of everything from traffic tickets to bad dates and given her everything from money to advice. He enabled her to feel secure, even brave, because he was always there to catch her if she screwed up.

She needed that. She screwed up a lot.

And he was in love with her. She'd known that for about a

year.

She should want to be with him.

So when he asked her to dance, instead she'd pulled him out on the back patio, lit by moonlight and white twinkle lights in the tall potted plants. She'd looked up into his face for the millionth time in her life, but she said something she'd never said to him before.

"Kiss me, Luke."

She'd shocked him, she knew, but he didn't hesitate. Which told her a lot about his thoughts and feelings for her. He'd cupped her face, tilted her head and kissed her.

And it was good. Really, really good.

"Come home with me," he'd whispered.

She was shaken, but not incredibly surprised, by his request. "It will change everything," she'd answered.

"Good."

She remembered the goose bumps that word, and the accompanying look in his eyes, had caused. He wanted her. *Wanted* her. What woman wouldn't respond to a guy like Luke wanting her?

She wanted to want him like that. She really did. She'd spent years feeling passionate about, committed to, desperate for her music. It was exhausting and frustrating to repeatedly have no return on those emotions. She really wanted to feel that way about something *else*. Something that would love her back.

"If I do..."

"You'll make me the happiest man on the planet."

It was pretty hard to ignore a declaration like that.

So she'd said yes.

They'd left the party immediately. Even four years later, Sabrina could admit that was big. He'd left his restaurant's grand opening party to go home with her.

But Luke had always dropped everything when she needed him.

The sex had been good too. It had been slow and sweet. He took his time, like he was savoring it, making it last. She'd felt *cherished*, almost like he couldn't believe she was really there.

And what woman didn't want to be cherished? What woman didn't want to have a guy so crazy for her that he felt lucky to be with her all the time? What woman didn't want to be the best thing to ever happen to someone?

She didn't regret it the next morning. Or even at lunchtime.

She didn't start feeling nervous until he was getting ready for work and talking about Thanksgiving. It was a stupid thing to panic her. She and her father had spent the last several Thanksgivings with Luke and his family. But she knew, without Luke saying it, that he felt this Thanksgiving would be different. Because she wouldn't just be there—she'd be there *with* him. And their families. On a family-oriented, tradition-packed holiday.

Their first Thanksgiving as a couple. The first Thanksgiving of a lifetime of Thanksgivings.

The doubts and regrets built through the rest of the afternoon, and as she walked into The Camelot for dinner that night she realized she'd made a huge mistake.

The place was packed. Which was great for Luke and Marc's business aspirations. But it also meant that nearly the entire town witnessed Luke greet her in the doorway with a kiss. A kiss. Not a peck on the cheek, not a hug, a *kiss*.

It was obvious that things had changed between them.

She'd noticed Luke's mom and dad were there, sharing a table with her father. All of their friends were too—including Kat.

Kat was home from medical school? On a Thursday night in October? Without telling Sabrina?

And just like that her whole body went cold. She felt like she'd swallowed a chunk of ice. Her throat hurt and she'd started shivering.

She knew what was coming.

He was going to ask her to stay, to stay with him, for good. In front of everyone.

"Come with me for a second," he'd said, holding her hand and tugging her forward. Toward the front of the room near the windows, near where their parents were sitting.

She'd dug her heels in, resisting. "I need a mint."

25

"A mint?" He'd grinned at her. "Later. Just come here for a minute."

"No, now." She'd thrust her hand into the pocket where he always carried Altoids. But instead of a tin of mints, she felt the velvet ring box.

Breathing carefully so she wouldn't freak out, she pulled it out. "What's this?"

He'd looked disappointed, she remembered. Disappointed she wasn't going to be surprised, because he wasn't going to get to do it in front of everyone.

"A ring box."

"For what?"

He'd smiled. "You really don't know?"

She grabbed the sleeve of his jacket and pulled him out of the dining room and down the hallway toward his office. When she opened her mouth, she hadn't been exactly sure what she was going to say. But she couldn't say yes.

She couldn't say no either. Luke had done so much for her, without hesitation or question. How could she possibly hurt him by saying no to the biggest question he'd ever ask someone?

So, she couldn't let him actually ask her to marry him because there was no way she could answer. She loved Luke. He was the most important person in her life. He'd always been there for her.

But she didn't want to spend her life in Justice and Luke did.

She didn't dream about a big house, kids, and neighborhood barbecues. Luke did. She didn't care about fundraising for the new basketball courts at the park. Luke did. She didn't plan on running for the school board and the city council. Luke did.

Her dream was her music. She wanted to sing. Really sing. Not just in the church choir but on stage in front of paying audiences, on the radio, hell, at the Grammys. Big time singing. Not the kind of singing Justice could offer. Maybe if he was willing to consider something else, something beyond Justice, she could imagine being with him forever.

"Come to Seattle with me," she'd blurted.

He'd been clearly confused. "Seattle? What are you talking about?"

She'd gripped the ring box tightly in her hand. She didn't want to open it, see the ring he'd picked out. She didn't want to wonder why he already had a ring picked out, and with him at the restaurant. And she *really* didn't want to think about the fact that twenty-four hours ago when she'd kissed him she'd put a down payment on a small-town Midwestern life with Luke.

"I want to go to Seattle. Ashley and I were talking and—"

"The band." He voice hardened. "You want to go to Seattle with the band."

"Yes. There's a showcase this weekend. If we get there early enough we might get in."

"And you want me to go?" He'd seemed surprised.

"Yes." She'd grabbed his hand. "Come with me. Be with me."

"I want to be with you. But—"

"Here."

His jaw tightened. "Yes. Here."

"Come with me," she'd repeated, looking up into his eyes.

"I can't. I can't leave."

"You *won't* leave."

There had been a long pause. Then he sighed. "That too."

"Not even for me?" Luke had very rarely said no to her. Anything she wanted, he did.

Not this time.

"This is where I belong."

She'd nodded. He was right. Justice was where he belonged. "I'm leaving. I'm going to Seattle." Initially she and the band had planned for the trip to be only a few days. But she couldn't come back here now. Coming back to Justice would mean a mortgage, a joint checking account and Mr. and Mrs. Luke Hamilton on next year's Christmas cards.

There was no in-between anymore.

Her heart ached. She should have known better. Going

27

home with him last night had been the stupidest thing she'd ever done.

His eyes were shuttered when she looked up again. "I thought—"

"I know."

"Dammit, Sabrina, *you* kissed *me*."

"And *you* jumped to conclusions."

"Obvious conclusions."

"Kissing doesn't *obviously* equal a marriage proposal, Luke."

"For us it does," he said bluntly. "And there was a hell of a lot more than kissing."

"Last night was...sex. You're overreacting. You haven't proposed to all the other girls you've slept with, have you?"

"No. This is *us*. It's different. You've never been like all the other girls."

It was true. Sabrina was not like the other girls to him and she'd always known it.

Which meant last night she'd screwed up by finally stepping over that thin invisible boundary between friendship and more. They'd hovered there for a year—probably more if she were really honest—with Luke on one side and her on the other. She knew that at any point all she had to do was say the word and she could have had Luke and been secure and adored for the rest of her life. But she'd stayed firmly on her side—the friendship side—of the line. She loved Luke. She needed Luke. But she didn't want the life he wanted.

She should have stayed on her side of that damned line last night too. Thrown up a brick wall, an electric fence and gotten a mean dog. Because now she couldn't pretend that this was anything other than him dismissing her dreams and her choosing smoky bars, certain repeat rejection and cheap dinners of mac and cheese over life with him in Justice.

The thing was, she wanted to want it. The life he offered was easier, less risky, far less humbling than hitting the road and trying to make it in the music business. That was why she'd kissed him. She wanted something that made her heart race and her mind spin and her nerve endings tingle like when she was on stage. She wanted a rush from something that would *work*.

The auditions hadn't worked so far. The demo tapes hadn't produced anything yet. The trying and hoping and dreaming hadn't turned into anything.

If Luke could give her the same rush, it could turn into something. Something forever, something to be proud of, something that wouldn't let her down.

"Come to Seattle with me," she'd tried one more time.

He'd taken a deep breath. "No."

She knew he meant it. He wasn't going to change his mind. If she left, she was definitely leaving him behind.

An hour later she'd climbed in Ashley's car and headed west.

She'd cried for the first hour of the trip, but finally convinced herself it was for the best and she hadn't felt guilty since. Much.

She'd sent him postcards from whatever city she was in at the time and she always wrote *Thinking of you. Love, S.* Short and sweet. Simple.

But she hadn't heard anything back.

And now he was coming to rescue her. Now she needed him more than ever. Now she was going to be in a car with him, alone, for six hours straight.

She leaned her forehead on the cool white tiles of the shower.

It was going to be a long trip to Justice.

Chapter Two

Sabrina was sound asleep on one of the beds with her back to him when Marc opened the motel room door five hours and forty-eight minutes later.

He didn't know what he'd expected. In fact, he'd purposefully spent most of the trip thinking about anything but the actual reason for his long drive. He'd mentally played with some recipes, listened to talk radio, made some business calls. But it almost felt like he'd been worried about her.

And that irritated him.

He jerked the drapes open, spilling light into the room. That didn't wake her.

He cleared his throat, then coughed, then coughed louder. She didn't even turn.

But as the door met the frame in an angry *smack*, she sat straight up in bed, the sheet clutched to her chin, eyes wide. She found him standing near the door and sucked in a deep breath.

"Let's go, Seattle. I don't have all day."

She opened her mouth to scream, then she narrowed her eyes and peered at him. "*Marc?*"

"Yeah."

"What are you doing here?"

"I told you on the phone I was on my way." He strode toward the bedside lamp and switched it on.

"I thought I was talking to Luke." She scowled at him even as she blinked in the sudden brightly lit room. "I asked for Luke."

"He was busy."

"And you didn't tell him?"

He slammed his hands down on his hips. "No, I didn't tell him that you called, that you were in trouble, or that you needed him. Because this shit is not going to start again. I mean it."

"And you decided to drive six hours to tell me that?"

"Yeah, as a matter of fact I did. Among other things. And you're welcome," he said, towering over where she sat with her back pressed against the headboard of the bed.

"For what? The terror that ripped through me as a man unexpectedly charged into my motel room? Yeah, you bet. Thanks."

"And am I right to assume that you don't have pepper spray or self-defense skills or any other way of protecting yourself if I actually was someone who was here to hurt you?"

"Other than the butcher knife under my pillow, no."

Marc glared at her. "You didn't have to sell all your butcher knives so that you could get across Wyoming before becoming stranded in Dirty Gulch?"

"Muddy Gap."

"Whatever."

"You don't believe me about selling things so I could have money to come home?"

"It doesn't matter. I'm here now so I don't care." Why he was being so mean he couldn't say. Maybe because he'd held back when she'd first called. He'd held back because down in some deep, stupid part of him, he'd been worried about her. She was over three hundred miles away, stranded with no car or money, no friend or even acquaintance nearby, and he'd been worried about her.

Now, however, he was here with her, could see for himself that she was fine, and was here to be sure she stayed fine. There was no need to hold his frustration and bitterness and anger back anymore.

Sabrina swung her legs over the edge of the bed and pulled the sheet tighter around her. "I've been taking care of myself for a long time, by the way," she said, clearly huffy. "So, not that it's any of your business, but the money issue is new. And I didn't even intend to call *you*. I called Luke if you remember. You could have delivered a message. You took it upon yourself to come."

"You had to know that there was no way in hell I was letting him come. Real sorry to foil your plan."

She snorted. "You've never been sorry about anything having to do with me in your life. What plan?"

"The plan to get Luke out here, hundreds of miles from home, feeling sorry for you, coming to your rescue."

"You think I somehow messed my transmission up on purpose?"

"Can't say that the thought didn't occur to me."

She stood and turned to face him, her eyes glinting with her temper. "All I would have had to do was call Luke and ask him to come. I wouldn't even have had to pop the hood."

He scowled at her. She was right and he hated that she knew it and was so in his face with it.

"Let's go already."

"Okay, okay..." She continued muttering something under her breath he couldn't hear and decided that was likely for the best. She scooted to the edge of the bed and pulled the top sheet with her.

She looked at him expectantly.

"What?" he finally asked.

"I need to get dressed."

Automatically his eyes slid over her body. It was hidden under the sheet but he felt his heart speed up.

"You always sleep nude?" That would be a redeeming quality at least.

"I was hot and sweaty when I got here. I showered and rinsed my bra and panties out and laid them out to dry. If you must know."

She pointed in the direction of the air conditioning vent. It was directly over the chair she'd obviously drug into place so she could hang her underwear over the two wooden arms.

Lavender.

Her panties and bra were lavender.

And tiny.

She wasn't a big girl by any stretch, but these things were clearly more for show than support.

"Nice," he commented dryly.

"So glad you like them." For Marc, Sabrina and sarcasm went hand in hand.

"Put them on already and let's go."

She stood, with the sheet wrapped under her arms sarong-style. "Do you mind?"

"Not a bit."

"You want to step outside?" she asked, looking pointedly at the door.

"No I don't. As you pointed out, it's hot out there. I'm starting to cool off now. You don't want to be in the same room with me, *you* step outside."

Her gaze flickered to the bathroom door. That would make sense. She should go in there and change. But, as expected based on history, she wasn't going to let him get away with the last word.

"Fine."

She tucked the sheet in more firmly between her breasts, turned her back and snagged the bra from the arm of the chair where it hung.

Marc took a seat in the chair by the window, facing the room. That should drive her nuts. He would ignore his own traitorous reaction to the whole thing. It was simple—he was a guy and she was a nearly naked woman in a hotel room. Some reaction should be expected. In fact, if he *hadn't* reacted he'd be concerned.

He watched her stick her arms through the straps of the bra and pull the cups into position, then reach behind to fasten the hooks.

Beautiful, pretty, cute, sexy—they were all different terms he used to described women. If he had to choose one for Sabrina he'd definitely go with sexy. But beautiful too. Not drop-dead-gorgeous. She didn't turn *every* head when she walked in a room. There were men who would not, maybe, find her attractive. Guys who liked curvy blondes, for example. Or who were firmly in the redhead camp. Guys who liked major curves also wouldn't find her slim, toned build tempting.

Unfortunately, Marc wasn't one of those guys.

Which annoyed the bejeezus out of him. It had always annoyed the bejeezus out of him.

It seemed that one way or another Sabrina Cassidy was destined to raise his blood pressure. A lot of the time—*most* of the time—she was pissing him off. And most of those times she was doing it on purpose. But he could walk in a room where she was and feel his heart race even before he saw her. He anticipated seeing her. He always searched her out. He used to try to tell himself that it was because he was instantly expecting her to do something to make him mad and it was better to keep an eye on one's enemies. But he hadn't believed that even from the first moment.

He didn't like her. He didn't trust her. Yet his body wanted hers.

The damnedest thing was he was attracted in spite of trying to fight it. For years. He'd never fought it like this with another woman. Only one other woman had been off-limits in his mind and it was because she was the younger sister of a friend.

The thing that really put Sabrina on Marc's do-not-go-there list was the fact that he found her to be the most frustrating person in the entire world. If he said the sky was blue, she would argue it was purple, just to annoy him. He'd once complimented her outfit. She'd asked if his mother knew he was gay. He'd offered to help her study for a calculus test once and she'd asked if everyone else on the planet had been wiped out by a nuclear disaster—because that was the only way she would even think about spending more than ten minutes with him in one stretch.

He supposed that was where it came from. He didn't like her because it had been clear since the day he moved into the neighborhood in fifth grade that she didn't like him.

Of course, it also had a lot to do with the fact that she screwed over Luke Hamilton, the nicest guy on the planet, repeatedly.

She glanced over her shoulder as she pulled the bra straps

into place.

He yawned.

He'd rather die than let her know that she'd created some of the fastest and most painful hard-ons he'd ever had. And today was no exception.

She rolled her eyes and reached for her panties. Somehow she managed to step into them without losing the sheet. It was huge on her, wrapped around more than once, so there was no glimpsing skin as she moved. Until she had the panties in place underneath.

Then she let the sheet drop.

He was glad he was sitting down.

Over the years he'd seen her in a swimming suit, short sundresses and once even in a wet T-shirt, but that was years ago...and he'd quickly distracted himself.

Now she was fully filled out, a woman, and there wasn't a frickin' thing in that hotel room—or county for that matter—that could distract him from the sight of her.

She was thinner than he remembered, but she was still soft in all the right places. Her skin was pale and smooth. Like rich cream. He could practically imagine the texture on his tongue.

She had never been big on the great outdoors and the lack of freckles, tan lines or wrinkles suggested that was still true.

There was however a...

"Nice tat." Right on the dimple above her right butt cheek.

She looked over her shoulder. "I lived with a tattoo artist in training who needed to practice."

He raised an eyebrow. That tattoo was a traffic sign—a yellow diamond shape that said *Proceed with Caution*. He couldn't help the smile. "Not a lot of practice. That's pretty small. But I do like the sentiment."

She turned and smiled. "We thought it was funny."

Marc felt a kick in his gut that had nothing to do with the fact she was standing in her underwear. He'd seen her smile a lot over the years but rarely directly at him.

She tugged down the left edge of her panties, revealing another small picture right on her hip bone. "I wouldn't let him do anything huge so I let him do more than one."

35

Marc's brain seemed unable to process the tattoo—and its location—her words and breathing at the same time. He cleared his throat and shifted in the chair. "He?"

She nodded.

"I thought you said you lived with this person."

"Right." She peered at him, her thumb still hooked under the top edge of her panties. "Stephen. He lived there for about six months. I met him through his sister who bartended with me."

"I didn't ask for your whole life history," Marc said, sounding more irritated than he should feel. Who gave a rat's ass who she'd lived with and for how long? She could have had six male roommates and been sleeping with all of them. At the same time. He didn't care.

"Right," she said after a pause.

Marc looked closer at the tattoo on her hip. The Tasmanian Devil. "Appropriate," he murmured.

She shifted her weight, stuck that hip out and put a hand on it. "Taz is appropriate?"

"Cute at first, but a terror if you get too close. Destruction of everything in his path. All of that."

She regarded him quietly, her eyes narrowed. "You think I'm cute?"

That was what she picked out. She didn't seem shocked he thought she was a terror or offended about the implication she caused destruction. The one kind-of-not-really compliment was what she focused on.

And cute was not the word. Sexy as sin. Able to heat his blood within ten seconds. "From a distance."

"Hmm."

"Any others?"

Not that she could reveal a whole lot more skin, but he was very curious now.

She lifted her right foot. Around the ankle was a something in a script font. He leaned closer. "One Moment?" he read. "What's that?"

"A reminder."

She put her foot down and he tried not to notice how small

and delicate it was, how great the purple sparkly nail polish looked—he never noticed or had an opinion on stuff like that—or how his eyes wanted to follow the arch to the heel and then up the back of the curve of her calf and then continue on up to the curve of...

"A reminder of what?" he forced himself to ask.

"How one single moment can change your whole life," she said softly.

She was looking at the tattoo with a thoughtful, almost sad, expression. Taking a deep breath seemed tough. He wasn't used to Sabrina being soft. He'd seen her cry on Luke's shoulder, but that was all part of her master plan to not let Luke have anything more important in his life than her. As far as Marc had ever experienced, she was tough, spunky, independent with a mouth on her that wouldn't stop—even when she knew better.

He'd rather fight with her, or tease her, than see her vulnerable. That didn't fit the woman he knew.

"Did he do piercings too?" He noticed the glint of the stud in her belly button. Purple again.

"Yep."

"Others?" he asked looking at the gem in the middle of her flat abdomen.

She lifted her hair away from her left ear. Five different studs marched from the earlobe up the curve.

"That's it?"

"There's only so many places you can pierce." The challenging glint was back in her eye and he felt instantly comfortable. Their truth-or-dare relationship was what he knew best. "You want to search for the rest?"

"Kind of."

The flicker of surprise was obvious before she hid it. "Really?" Her tone implied she didn't believe him.

"Hey, I'm a human male."

"Meaning?"

Was she searching for something or just playing along? He'd love to know. "Meaning that I don't have to like you to want to see you naked."

She watched him as if trying to gauge how serious he was. Or wasn't. "Ah," was all she said in the end.

Marc ran his gaze over her from head to toe. "I can't believe the stripper job didn't turn out."

"Thanks."

Of course she took that as a compliment too.

She reached for the rest of her clothes lying on the chair. His attention hadn't made it past the bra and panties.

"My roommate was always trying to get me on stage. But I only bartended there."

"The tattoo artist wanted you to strip?" Nice guy. Just a friend his ass.

"No, Jenny. My roommate before Stephen. She was a stripper at the club."

"You lived with a stripper?"

"Yep. She made a ton of money."

Sabrina would have too, he had no doubt.

"How many roommates have you had?"

She pulled her denim shorts up—wincing slightly he noticed—and seemed to be counting in her head as she buttoned them. "Eleven," she finally told him.

He felt his eyes widen. "I know you're hard to get along with but, wow, eleven roommates in four years?"

She shrugged. "We got along great. They needed a temporary stop. The lease was in my name so they could live there and leave without a penalty."

"You had an extra bedroom you rented or what?"

"A pull-out couch." She grinned. "But they weren't paying rent, so couldn't be too picky."

"You let them all live there for free?" Marc shook his head. She had been a business major in college, for God's sake. "That's not a great way to make extra money."

"They helped pay for groceries and for the phone minutes they used, stuff like that. But I was already paying the rent with or without them. I was doing them a favor."

"Eleven people came, slept on your couch for several months at a time and didn't pay you a dime?"

"They taught me stuff, introduced me to people, took me places. It was a trade-off. A good one." She pulled a tiny tank top over her bra.

She still looked sexy enough to...

"What did they teach you?" he asked, forcing his mind on safer topics.

"Lots of stuff. I learned to fiddle."

"Fiddle."

"Yeah, you know...country music? Fiddle. Oh, and I can speak French."

"Very practical."

"It is if you're going to travel in France."

"Are you going to travel in France?"

She lifted a shoulder. "Maybe some day."

"There's a big call for fiddlers in France?"

"I've fiddled on stage six or seven times. In the US," she informed him. "For money, if you want to know. The band I played with got paid for those gigs. And Tanya—my roommate who taught me—even gave me one of her old fiddles when she moved out."

"How nice."

"And I can read tarot cards."

"Another very handy skill," he drawled.

"And Zumba. I'm a great Zumba dancer."

"Zumba?" he asked. "You learn that at the strip club?"

She shook her head and began moving her hips, rolling her pelvis and moving her arms to some rhythm he couldn't hear. He was entranced.

Holy crap.

She could have made money doing that fully clothed. He'd pay big for her to keep going. Without clothes it would be downright dangerous.

She stopped a moment later and smiled. "Zumba."

Fully distracted, he shifted forward and rested his arms on his thighs. "Did you learn anything useful? Can you cook? Fix a leaky pipe? Change a tire?"

She reached up to pull her hair into a ponytail. "I can

pickpocket a wallet out of a guy's pants. I've never done it for real, but in practice I'm pretty good."

He smiled in spite of himself. She'd taken in a bunch of strays who paid her back with useless and/or illegal knowledge. How great. "I suppose that could be considered practical in desperate circumstances."

"Yeah, too bad there weren't any guys walking the streets of Muddy Gap—too bad there aren't any streets in Muddy Gap—I wouldn't have had to call you."

"Right." He frowned. She wouldn't have called him. She would have waltzed back into Justice without any warning. At least this way he had a chance of preventing some of the Tasmanian destruction she brought with her. "Speaking of which, you ready to go or what?" He stretched to his feet, hoping she'd be too distracted with gathering her things to notice the semi-erection he had going.

Except she didn't seem to have any things to gather.

"Yeah, almost. I need to...go to the bathroom."

"Hurry up." He wasn't going to win any chivalry awards, but what was she going to do? He was her only hope at the moment.

"I don't suppose you could, um, get me some toothpaste?" she asked.

He frowned. "Toothpaste? Is there a store nearby?"

"They have some for sale in the motel office. I noticed a basket of stuff on the counter when I checked in."

He looked at her to see if she was messing with him. "Why didn't you get one on your way up?"

"No money, remember?"

"It's fifty-dollar toothpaste?"

"I think it said a dollar twenty-five."

He gaped at her. "You don't even have a couple of dollars for toothpaste?"

She shrugged, not looking very apologetic. "Nope. I used my last nineteen bucks to pay the guy from the gas station to bring me over here."

His frown deepened. "I thought I told you I would take care of that."

"I had the money. It seemed silly to make the guy wait."

"But you needed toothpaste," Marc pointed out impatiently. She never had listened to him. Or anyone really. "Didn't it occur to you that you might need that money?"

She shrugged again. "Nope. I knew Luke was on his way."

His annoyance level shot up instantly. Luke was willing to do almost anything for her and she knew it. She knew he'd give her anything she needed. Of course, why would she think any differently? It had always been that way.

"But I'm going to pay you back," she told him, picking up the pad of paper with the motel's logo from the bedside table. On it was scribbled a column of numbers.

"What's that?"

"A running tally of what I owe you," she told him, handing the pad to him.

Beside each number was what the amount was for, including the motel room and a tank of gas.

"Did you eat anything on the way?" she asked.

Still distracted by the fact that she intended to pay him back for the gas he'd volunteered to use to come and get her and the motel room he'd practically forced her to get, he said absently, "Some cupcakes and a cup of coffee."

She took the paper from him, added some numbers to the bottom and re-totaled the column.

"You added the cupcakes to the amount?" he asked as he watched her.

"Of course. Those were cupcakes that you wouldn't have needed to buy if it weren't for me."

"I don't..." he stopped short of telling her that he didn't expect re-payment for any of the expenses of the trip, least of all a dollar and twenty-nine cent package of snack cakes, as it occurred to him what was going on.

Sabrina was in debt to him.

"Add toothpaste on the bottom there and I'll be back in a minute," he told her.

"Toothpaste," Marc announced as he re-entered the motel room. "I also took the liberty of buying deodorant. It's close confines in my car."

"Thanks." She already had deodorant, toothbrush, had even had toothpaste until sometime yesterday when she used the last of it. But she wasn't going to confess that to him. She'd use the deodorant he'd bought without hesitation. She was startled by his lighthearted mood and teasing words and didn't want to mess it up. She hadn't even been totally sure he was going to come back.

"We'll stop for something to eat after we get on the road," he called to her as she headed for the bathroom to brush her teeth. "I don't think they even have cupcakes in Dusty Grove."

"Muddy Gap." It sounded great to her. She was starving. She'd been pretty distracted from it since Marc had showed up, but her stomach rumbled now.

She was still in shock from seeing Marc too.

She hadn't seen him in four years and they had never spent much time together alone. In fact, she couldn't come up with more than maybe twenty minutes total in all the time they'd known each other. But apparently it had been enough over the years for her to catalogue things like the fact that his light brown hair was shorter and his face was leaner and his chest was harder than when she'd last seen him.

He was as tall as Luke but broader. He was solid through the chest and shoulders with thick thighs, but a hard, flat stomach and tight butt. In spite of just getting out of the car after a long drive, he looked good. He was sporting a jaw of stubble, but instead of looking disheveled, though, it looked sexy. Unfortunately.

The thing that had always unnerved her about Marc, besides being built like a battle-ready Marine, was his eyes. They were a deep green and when he made direct eye contact with her she had the weirdest feeling that she was on the verge of blurting out all her deepest secrets and desires.

She had never acknowledged an attraction between them, but she'd always been *aware* of him. Like watching a predator. It was always better to know where he was and what he was doing. And then avoid him.

She and Marc had never been what anyone would consider friends. But she knew he wasn't here out of concern for her. It was to keep Luke from coming. And she understood. She could imagine Luke's reaction after she left.

She was going to have to face Luke eventually though.

Still, she could hardly think about that with Marc here. She was amazed by her reaction to him. He'd always rubbed her the wrong way, making her defensive and sarcastic and full of bravado. He hadn't, however, made her tingle deep in her belly.

Until today.

She wasn't sure what exactly had gotten into her with refusing to go into the bathroom to get dressed. She supposed it was his typical cocky attitude, the smugness that seemed to hint that he was absolutely not affected by her in the least and couldn't care less if she was naked in front of him, that made her want to prove him wrong.

She'd never thought about a physical attraction between them. But if *he* was unaffected by her, then she was—by God—going to be unaffected by him. And was going to prove it.

That hadn't happened. She was still vibrating from the whole scene.

"Is the next town bigger than Muddy Gap?" she asked.

Marc chuckled. "I don't think it could get smaller."

It was not fair that his quiet laughter melted her like hot fudge on ice cream. "Do you think they have a drug store?" she asked, determined to ignore all of these stupid feelings.

She was basically homeless, stressed, tired, hungry. Hormonal. Marc was the first familiar face she'd seen in two days. Liking him wouldn't last.

"What for?"

"Some...thing I need."

He didn't answer and she quickly brushed her teeth and rinsed, then stepped back into the main room.

"Why didn't you ask me to get it when I went for the toothpaste?" he asked when she appeared.

"They don't have this in their basket." The plastic basket held the basics—toothbrush and paste, disposable razors, deodorant, combs and ibuprofen.

"What is it, Sabrina?"

It was the first time he'd used her name and the goose bumps that erupted on her skin were very real.

And terrifying. God help her. She couldn't react like this to Marc. Maybe it really was hormones or something.

"It's no big deal," she muttered.

It was too much to ask that Marc leave it at that. He continued to watch her, eyebrow quirked, clearly waiting for her to go on.

"I need some hydrocortisone cream."

"What for?"

Marc never had been particularly tactful where she was concerned.

"I have a rash."

"A rash?" He wrinkled his nose as if she'd announced she had an STD.

"*Heat* rash."

"Heat rash?"

Marc was an intelligent guy but sometimes she wondered how he'd managed to obtain his Master's degree.

"I have heat rash from where the denim of my shorts rubbed on the back and inside of my thighs as I walked down the highway in eighty-seven degree heat, looking for a service station for my damned car."

He stared at her for a full ten seconds. Then his eyes dropped to her thighs. He stared harder, seeming puzzled.

"What?" she finally demanded.

"How'd I miss that?"

"Excuse me?"

"You were standing there in your panties and I thought I looked you over pretty good."

She felt a jolt of heat remembering his eyes on her. If he'd been looking *really* closely he could have seen her heart thumping in her chest. "You were staring at my tattoo."

"And thinking about proceeding with caution."

She froze. Had he meant to say that? Was he teasing her or had it slipped? Or did that even mean what she thought it might mean?

Marc Sterling drove her crazy. That had obviously not changed in four years.

"It's..." She cleared her throat. "It's pretty high up. Probably hard to see."

"Those are damn short shorts."

"Right."

His attention made its way from her thighs to her face. "Where do you buy stuff like that cream?"

"There's got to be a Walmart between here and Justice."

"Well, this is America."

It took forty minutes to get to a city of any size—which only had a tiny airport with a charter service and no bus station. There was also no Walmart, but there was a decent-sized grocery store that had hydrocortisone cream.

Her next problem was how to get the cream on and maintain some dignity. She was contemplating that and wishing she'd gone into the restroom at the grocery store, when Marc said, "Let's find someplace to eat. Are you hungry?"

"You have no idea what I'd do for food right now," she answered without thinking.

Then she felt his eyes on her. And it felt... She glanced at him quickly, hoping to see amusement or teasing. That wasn't how it felt, but that's what she could handle. Instead it was— she swallowed hard—just like it felt.

Hot.

So much so that she stopped walking and turned to face him fully.

"What?" she asked, hands on her hips, wondering if he'd follow up on that look on his face and wondering what she'd do if he did.

"I was reviewing my ideas and trying to decide which to go with."

She licked her lips, unintentionally, but saw his gaze drop to her mouth and follow her tongue. How had this happened?

45

This was *Marc* standing in a grocery store parking lot making her breathe harder just by looking at her mouth. Dammit. Maybe it was the elevation here. Or low blood sugar. Yeah, low blood sugar. That was good. She'd go with that. She needed to eat something fast.

"Are you paying for the food?" she asked, shifting her weight to her other foot.

"I was under the impression that was the only option."

"It's illegal to expect...something like that...in return for payment."

"Something like that? Geez, Seattle, maybe I was thinking about having you do hand stands or wash my car."

"Were you?" she challenged.

One corner of his mouth curled up. "Definitely not."

"Uh-huh. Illegal."

Her stomach rumbled in loud enough that he heard it. He laughed. "I'll let you give me a rain check."

She vowed to *not* think about that. At all. Ever again. He was kidding anyway. Probably. Surely he was kidding. He liked pushing her buttons and maybe it was obvious that he was turning her on a little. If it was, she wouldn't put it past him to take advantage of the chance to make her uncomfortable.

Seven minutes later, it didn't matter a bit. If he asked her to clean his house in a pink bunny costume for the next six months, she'd do it. The diner they found smelled that good.

"I'm going to make a call. Order a cheeseburger, fries and iced tea for me, 'kay?" He slid out of the booth and she nodded.

It was nice to have some space from him. They'd been together constantly and it seemed that the weird, unexpected, what-the-hell-am-I-supposed-to-do-with-this chemistry between them was pressing in on her on from all sides.

It was nice to be able to take a deep breath.

She leaned back and surveyed the restaurant. It was strange that until Marc was gone she hadn't even realized that she'd paid little attention to her surroundings. Why was he so distracting? She'd known him for years and didn't remember being unable to focus on anything else when he was around. She wasn't that starved for male companionship. Male companionship she had plenty of. Besides her band mates, who were all men, she spent time with plenty of men as she bartended from time to time and there were men at school— teachers, administrators, janitors. And she did date. She put a hand against her stomach. In fact, if she'd had less male company she wouldn't be on her way back to Justice.

Butterflies kicked up in her stomach at the thought of her return home. It was really going to happen. Not that she'd expected the car to break down, or any other true barrier to keep her out of Justice, but she hadn't let herself think about where the road was taking her as she drove east. Now that Marc was here, in a car that seemed to be in perfect working order and on the interstate that would take her to Nebraska, there was no reason she wouldn't get to Justice.

She made herself block those thoughts and looked around the restaurant. It was a typical roadside diner with black vinyl booths and white laminate tabletops. It was small and clean, but the faded paint, chipped countertops and menus frayed at the edges all told of a long history. Country music played from the speakers, but it wasn't Tim McGraw or Alan Jackson. Instead it was the good old boys: Waylon Jennings, Willie Nelson and Johnny Cash.

A woman across the room dressed in a bright red T-shirt caught her eye. She was about Sabrina's age and was using sign language to communicate with the man at the table with her. The man was signing back so Sabrina couldn't tell who was deaf, or if they both were, but she felt her cheeks grow warm as she watched them. It was an intimate conversation. The kind that couldn't be had in public out loud. One definite advantage to sign language. The man told her he hoped she wasn't wearing panties. The woman confirmed that she wasn't. Sabrina tried to look away. The woman asked if they should get a motel room. The man said that he couldn't wait and told her to sneak into the men's room with him.

As the woman nodded, the guy pushed his chair back and headed for the restroom. Sabrina caught the woman's eye and blushed. The woman looked suspicious and Sabrina reluctantly signed "Sorry. I didn't mean to eavesdrop." The woman looked startled, likely not used to finding strangers who could

47

communicate with sign language. Then she smiled and signed back, "We haven't seen each other in three weeks." Sabrina smiled and signed again, "Make sure you lock the door." The woman laughed.

Sabrina thought about if she would follow a guy into a public restroom for sex.

Then she thought about if she knew any guys who would suggest it.

Marc's face appeared in her mind. Which was crazy. She didn't know Marc well enough to know if he was the public sex kind of guy or not. And it was even crazier to think that he'd suggest it to her.

But the heat in his eyes in the motel room and the parking lot wouldn't leave her alone. And they certainly had the lack of verbal communication going for them.

In the car, Marc's satellite radio had been tuned to an all-80s channel and had thankfully filled the silence from Muddy Gap to Rawlins. Small talk seemed silly. She and Marc had never spent more than twenty minutes alone in their lives and hadn't seen one another in four years. It wasn't like there were ongoing story lines or memories to talk about. Besides, Marc was Luke's best friend and he'd been there to see all the fallout after she left so he probably didn't have a lot of nice things to say to her anyway. She was glad they'd opted not to talk.

Marc and Luke were more like brothers than friends. Marc had moved to Justice with his parents and younger brother in fifth grade. When his parents and brother were killed in a car accident in April of his seventh grade year, he was put into the foster care system. He'd been on his way to a foster home in Grand Island, almost three hours away.

But Luke had saved him.

He had begged his parents—who had been foster parents since before Luke was born—to take Marc in. Luke was an only child but he'd grown up with a constant parade of needy kids in his home and life. But Luke wanted more than another foster brother. He wanted them to adopt Marc. Three weeks after the accident, Marc moved in with the Hamiltons. To stay.

It had all made disliking him harder and easier for Sabrina. Harder because he'd lost his family and had turned into a pretty nice guy in general—as far as everyone else was concerned. Easier because after that he'd competed for Luke's attention and time and he was living right there, in Luke's house, in his life—in *her* backyard.

Marc returned before she could figure it all out.

"Did you tell Luke where you are?" She knew that he'd called back to Justice.

"Nope."

"He didn't ask?"

"I left a message on his cell."

She glanced at the clock above the cash register. It was shortly after four p.m. in Rawlins, Wyoming which meant after five in Justice. Right in the middle of the dinner rush. "He never has his phone on during lunch or dinner," she said.

"I know."

He hadn't wanted to talk to Luke in person. "You left a message but didn't tell him where you are?"

"I said I was fine, taking care of something and I'd fill him in when I get back."

"You didn't tell him anything about me then either." She didn't have to phrase it as a question.

"Absolutely not."

Got it. Marc was protecting Luke from her. She wondered how that was going to go once she was back in Justice for good. She shifted uncomfortably on the vinyl seat, her heat rash stinging.

The waitress arrived with their food. The aroma of Marc's burger hit her as the waitress placed her order in front of her. Her mouth watered.

"What is *that*?" Marc demanded, pointing with his fork at her food.

"Cereal," she answered.

"Cereal?" he repeated in disbelief. "That's it?"

"Orange juice too." She gestured toward the glass.

"You ordered cereal and orange juice?" he asked, staring at her as if she'd sprouted two heads.

She shrugged. "Yeah."

"Why?"

She looked down at the bowl of corn flakes. "I like cereal."

Marc sat back in the booth, his eyes narrowed. "Did you order that because it's cheap?"

"I..."

"Sabrina," he said warningly. "Don't lie to me."

"You don't have to pay for the motel room, drive to get me *and* feed me. I'm used to eating cereal. I like it, it's got lots of vitamins—"

"Son of a bitch," he cursed and then lifted his arm to wave at the waitress.

"Is there a problem?" she asked, returning immediately to the table.

"I need a cheeseburger, fries, chocolate milkshake and a big slice of apple pie."

The waitress looked at his plate, then shrugged.

Sabrina scowled at him and crossed her arms, her rash burning. "What was that?"

"*That* was how you should have ordered your dinner," he retorted.

"I didn't want a cheeseburger," she protested, ignoring the way her stomach rumbled at the mention of her favorite food.

"You love cheeseburgers," Marc told her as he lifted a fry to his mouth.

She had to swallow the saliva that erupted on her tongue before saying, "How do you know I'm not a vegetarian now?"

"Are you?"

She couldn't lie about something serious like that. "No. But you don't need to order my food for me."

He looked at her bowl of cereal pointedly. "Really?"

She tipped the pitcher of milk over her cereal and then picked up her spoon, digging in with feigned eagerness. She crunched away for a few moments, shifting from one buttock to the other, seeking some relief while watching Marc bite into the thick cheeseburger and crispy fries. That looked good. She was tired, hungry, chapped and basically irritated from head to toe.

She emptied her glass of juice, sipped the last of the milk

from her bowel and sat back, trying to look satisfied.

"Better save room for the burger."

"I don't know if that's possible. Cornflakes are very filling."

"You're eating the damned burger, Sabrina. And the fries, the pie and the milkshake." He looked serious.

"I haven't eaten that much food at one time...ever," she told him, unable to hold back the smile she felt threatening.

"That's about to change."

"You can't force me to eat."

He leaned forward and pinned her with a stare. "Dare me."

The smile died. He *was* serious.

"I'm not that hungry," she tried one more time.

"We have all night. We'll sit right here and I'll keep you company, even if it takes until tomorrow morning."

Marc continued to eat and she tried to ignore him, focusing unsuccessfully on the view out the window. From the corner of her eye she saw him lick ketchup off his bottom lip then suck salt from the tip of his index finger.

She shifted on the seat again, but not so much from the rash now. "Knock it off," she said irritably.

She could *not* find Marc sexy. Not standing in a parking lot, not even completely naked and *not* eating greasy diner food.

"Knock what off?" he asked, his lips still wrapped around the tip of his finger.

"The sucking and moaning."

"I wasn't moaning."

Okay, that might have been in her mind. "But you were sucking. Stop it."

"Why is it bothering you?"

He gave her a knowing little grin that she wanted to slap off his face.

"It's annoying."

"Noted." He didn't look sorry. Or concerned.

Shouldn't he be concerned about this crazy heat between them too? They. Didn't. Like. Each. Other.

"Here you go." The waitress set a plate in front of Sabrina.

Marc slid the ketchup toward her and she tried to frown at

him for being so bossy. She opened her mouth to tell him again that there was no way she was going to be able to eat everything, but the aroma of the cheeseburger and fries and the sight of the milkshake and pie hit her at that exact moment. She stopped with her mouth partway open and her stomach growled loudly. Apparently her body had forgotten the way it had insisted on throwing everything up that morning.

"It—" she swallowed, "—looks fine, I guess."

He took a drag on his tea, then said firmly, "Eat."

He didn't have to twist her arm. She picked up the burger and prayed that she wouldn't embarrass herself by eating it in two bites. She opened her mouth, anticipating the taste of the cheese and toasted bun blending with the sweet ketchup and tangy pickles and... She bit into it and sighed. It was even better than she'd imagined. She almost wanted to cry.

"How is it?"

Until he spoke, she hadn't even realized that she'd closed her eyes. She took a long draw on the straw. Cool, creamy ice cream with real chocolate syrup blended to perfection and garnished with whipped cream... She closed her eyes again. "Fine."

Marc chuckled. "Remember, we'll sit here all night if we have to."

It was going to take her about three minutes to finish everything and she'd probably want more. "I'll eat it all." She tried to sound annoyed. "You're so stubborn."

Marc settled back in his seat. "I'm glad you understand that there's no point in arguing."

That would have normally been enough to get her going. But well, he'd driven six hours one way to pick her up. And frankly it was pretty tough to argue when her mouth was full.

Chapter Three

Marc watched with pleasure as Sabrina devoured her meal.

He loved women who ate and ate real food. He was a chef. It went with the territory to enjoy watching people enjoy good food. But this was more than that. He hadn't even made this food, but being able to help satisfy her in some way...

His smile died. He didn't care one bit about Sabrina or satisfying her in *any* way. In fact, he liked when she was miserable.

Supposedly.

He did, however, like that she was distracted by him sucking salt off his finger.

Stupid.

"I'm going for a walk," he announced. He slid from the booth and stood.

Her mouth was still full, so she didn't reply for a moment. But she stood quickly and reached for him, grabbing his hand. "Marc."

He froze under her touch. Strange since all he felt was heat. "Yeah?"

"Thank you," she said softly. "For trying to save me. For buying me the best meal I've had in a long time. For coming to get me."

"I—"

She rose up on tiptoe and pressed a quick kiss against his lips before he could say whatever it was that he thought he actually had to say. It was a simple, second-long meeting of lip to lip. He barely got a good taste of her. But his whole body reacted.

She was smiling up at him when the lust finally settled full and hot and complete in his gut...and lower.

"Sabrina," he said gruffly, "I..."

"Yeah?"

"I'm...glad you're okay."

She looked up at him and he had to blink. She looked like...she wanted to kiss him...*really* kiss him.

And he really wanted her to. Which was so stupid and so surprising and so the opposite of what he thought he felt about her that he quickly shoved her back. "I'll be back in a few minutes." He stomped out of the diner without looking back.

Sabrina finished her meal, mentally chastising herself. What the *hell* had that been about? Okay, so they'd been teasing some over the past few hours. Okay, so she'd let him see her in her underwear. Okay, so there had been some innuendos and some not-so-bright moments when she'd felt sparks between them.

But that did *not* make kissing Marc a good idea. Or a forgivable idea. Yeah, it had been a peck on the lips. Nothing more than she'd given many of her friends over the years. But she'd wanted it to be more. And she knew that Marc knew that.

That was the particularly bad part. He didn't like her, he didn't trust her, she had broken his best friend's heart and he loved to rattle her and infuriate her and fight with her. It was not a good idea to give him any more ammunition. Ammunition like knowing that she was attracted to him.

God only knew what he might do with that knowledge.

"Let's go already." He was suddenly beside the table, looking as irritated as when he left.

"I'm ready. Geez." Her exasperation was apparent, she was sure, as she slid out of the booth and stood.

"Do you need to go to the bathroom?"

"I'm not a child. If I need to go to the bathroom I'll let you know."

"I'm extremely aware that you're not a child, Sabrina,

regardless of how you act sometimes."

"What is your problem?" she asked, hands on her hips.

"We need to get on the road. The longer we spend together..."

She raised her eyebrows. "Yes?" She really wanted to hear this.

"The longer we spend together, the more time you have to drive me nuts."

Oh, really? She seemed unable to resist pushing Marc's buttons. It probably was childish, but she took her time pulling one last drink from her straw, wiping her hands on the napkin, reaching for her purse...

"Sabrina," he said warningly.

"Come to think of it, maybe I should go to the bathroom."

"Get in the fucking car."

"I see you didn't find any extra charm while you were gone."

"How's this for charming—get in the car or I'll carry you out there and throw you in."

"Yeah, sure. You'll pick me up in front of all these people—"

He turned back with a large sigh. Then he leaned over and scooped her up into his arms.

"Marc!"

But he didn't even look down at her as he strode toward the door.

He didn't get even as far as the cash register before the woman in the red T-shirt stepped in front of him. She signed "Are you all right?" to Sabrina.

Sabrina grinned. She was surprised about Marc's reaction, aware of the entire diner watching them and a little turned on, but yes, she was alright. Great in fact. Marc wasn't doing it on purpose and she was reading way too much into it, but it felt great to be held, to be taken care of, to be less than in charge.

She would never admit it to him, or anyone, but over the past few days when she'd been totally on her own—miles from any of the homes or friends she knew—all alone, completely independent, like she'd always wanted to be, it had been scary and stressful and *not* fancy free.

That was why she always wanted to have a roommate, whether they could pay or not. She knew what it was like to have nowhere to go and how much it meant to have someone reach out a hand. She also didn't like to be alone. At all. She hated that about herself but it was true. She liked having someone there, caring what time she came home at night, someone to pick up shampoo if she forgot, someone who would leave leftovers in the fridge from time to time, someone who would take a phone message for her.

She hadn't known it about herself until she'd moved to Seattle and broken up with her first band, but being alone pretty much sucked and she'd worked hard to not be that way again after that.

Now, having Marc buy her hydrocortisone cream, force her to eat and carry her to the car all felt pathetically nice.

"I'm good," she signed back. "It's been four years since we saw each other."

The woman's eyes widened. "Don't forget to lock the door." With a smile, she headed back to her table.

"You had a deaf roommate?" Marc asked as he shoved the diner door open with his foot and headed for the car.

"A roommate who grew up with a deaf brother."

"Holy shit, Seattle. You might have learned something useful after all."

When they reached the car, Marc put her on her feet and started to unlock the door. It was such a relief to get off of her tender behind. She rubbed her hands over her posterior. Some hydrocortisone cream would be *so* nice right now.

"What is with you?"

Sabrina jumped and looked over her shoulder to find Marc watching her massage her backside.

"Nothing, why?"

"You were squirming during the entire drive down here and all through dinner. You act like you can't sit still. Now you're standing in public rubbing your ass. What's going on?"

She hoped she wasn't blushing. "First of all, there's no one else here so technically it's not public. And I told you that I needed that cream and what it was for."

His eyes dropped to her rear end. "Oh."

She scowled at him and turned around so that he couldn't see her tender side.

"You're really that sore?"

"Yes. I'm really that sore." She wished he'd quit talking about it.

"How are you going to sit in the car for four hours if you're that miserable after four blocks?"

"Are you enjoying this?"

"No. I'm serious. It's a long drive."

"I need to put some cream on."

He frowned and almost looked concerned. "Would a pillow help?"

Great, now he was going to be nice. "I think the pillow would rub too."

"Are you going to be able to sit at all?"

"I guess I'm going to have to."

He looked toward the car. "You could lie on the back seat on your stomach."

"I couldn't..." She glanced at the car. On second thought... "Yeah. I guess."

It would make talking, and therefore disagreeing and arguing, that much more difficult.

Five minutes later they were on the interstate, headed for Nebraska, Marc in the front seat, Sabrina lying prone on the backseat. She lay with her head on the passenger side so she could see the side of his face.

The silence was nice. They weren't talking, but they weren't arguing and he wasn't making any comments that made her think about kissing him—or worse. Truly, silence between her and Marc seemed the best way to go.

He apparently didn't agree.

"So," Marc said, settling into his seat more comfortably, "Why are you coming back to Justice?"

She jerked her head up. "What?"

"Why are you coming back? It isn't a major holiday. Not that you've ever come home for those anyway. And why doesn't anyone know about it?"

"Kat knows."

That seemed to surprise him. "She hasn't said anything."

"I asked her not to."

"Why not tell anyone else?"

"It doesn't involve anyone else."

"It involves Kat?"

"Kind of."

He didn't say anything to that and she started to relax. It didn't last.

"Do you really think that this doesn't involve Luke?"

"This isn't about Luke."

"Do you think he'll see it that way? Or that he'll stay uninvolved once you're back?"

"Luke had his chance."

"What's that mean?"

"Luke had his chance to be with me. In fact, if he *had* been with me a lot of things would be different now."

"I suppose the same could be said if you had stayed with him in Justice."

Yeah, well damn. There was that.

Not that it hadn't occurred to her before this. If she'd stayed in Justice with Luke there was no doubt that she wouldn't be in the situation she was right now. Luke had always been her safety net. With him she didn't worry much about consequences, because there really weren't any for her. He took care of things.

Unfortunately, some habits were hard to break even after she left and no longer had Luke to back her up. She'd made a series of bad choices in the past four years—the culmination of which took the form of a spontaneous vacation and unprotected sex with a stranger.

Inarguably, her track record showed that she should simply do the opposite of whatever she was inclined to do.

When a Jamaican vacation sounded like a great idea, she should have said no.

When another drink with rum in it sounded harmless, she

should have said no.

When a hot one-night stand with a guy she'd known for an hour sounded tempting, she should have said no.

When going home to Justice—even though Luke was still there and would be sticking his nose into her business immediately—sounded like the last thing she wanted to do, she should definitely do it.

"I don't see any way of avoiding Luke once I'm back in Justice," she finally said.

"Exactly," Marc muttered.

She waited for him to go on, but several minutes passed with nothing more and she let herself relax again.

Marc tipped the rearview mirror down to look into the backseat five minutes later.

She was asleep.

Part of him was relieved. He didn't have any answers but hearing her admit that she knew Luke would be sucked back in when she returned to Justice made him crazy. Luke deserved better. He deserved a chance at happiness and if Sabrina was living within one hundred miles of him he'd never let himself get close to another woman.

Marc yawned widely. He was glad to not be arguing with her or listening to her admit she knew the effect she had on Luke—and not sound apologetic about it—but at least those two things were keeping him awake.

An hour later, she was still sound asleep and his yawns were coming closer together. He signaled and pulled into a brightly lit, twenty-four-hour gas station. A cup of coffee was exactly what he needed.

"Are we there?" Her sleepy voice drifted to him as he pulled up next to one of the gas pumps.

"No. Just a pit stop."

She pushed herself into a sitting position and brushed her hair back from her face. Under the tall lamps of the parking lot he could see her soft, sleepy expression and his heart tripped in spite of himself. She looked so sweet and innocent and that little stretch that pulled her shirt up exposing a strip of skin on her stomach made his blood pump harder.

"I could use something to drink," she said, sliding gingerly across the seat.

"Don't forget to write it down," he muttered, not meaning it.

Sabrina stood next to him taking deep breaths of the fresh night air and gazing at the half moon that glowed softly in the ink black sky as he filled the tank. It was a beautiful night. It was one of those perfect summer nights that Marc loved. The breeze was enough to ruffle his hair, the temperature was warm enough that he didn't need a jacket, but cool enough to be refreshing and the sky was an absolute masterpiece.

"Coffee?"

Sabrina moved her gaze from the view overhead to his face. For a moment, it looked as if she'd forgotten where she was. "Um, I was thinking juice."

"Juice it is."

She followed him into the store and headed for the refrigerated section with the bottles of soda and water, while he pulled the largest Styrofoam cup from the dispenser and filled it with hot, caffeinated coffee.

Marc paid for the drinks and the box of animal crackers that Sabrina set next to her bottle of apple juice. On the way back to the car he asked, "Do you think you could handle sitting in front for awhile?"

She glanced at the car. "I guess."

"I wouldn't ask except that I'm getting sleepy and I could use some conversation."

"Do you want me to drive for a while? Then you could sleep in back."

It was a good suggestion and made a lot of sense if they were driving through to Justice. But he had other plans.

"Nah. Let's just talk."

She shrugged. "Sure. I think if I sit more on the left I'll be okay. Maybe if I put some more cream on it would help too."

Marc glanced around the parking lot. "You want to go back inside to put it on?"

She followed his gaze. "No, I'll do it here." She reached into the backseat and retrieved the tube of cream from her purse. She squeezed a blob out onto her index finger and then raised an eyebrow at him. "You want to watch?"

"Sort of."

She rolled her eyes. "Red, chapped skin does it for you, huh?"

He grinned and turned his back to her as she applied the cream. If it was her skin he wasn't sure red and chapped would be that much of a turn-off. He tried hard not to imagine the area she was spreading the cream over. It didn't work.

"Ready to go."

Everything seemed back in place as he turned back to face her. Still, his imagination was vivid. He tried imagining her skin red and broken out, but his mind refused to see anything but smooth, silky skin, curving into— He almost slammed his fingers in the door.

Marc pulled out onto the highway as Sabrina popped the top on her apple juice. She took a long drink, then began opening the box of animal crackers, making a lot of noise as she did. Three crackers disappeared, with loud crunching, followed by half the bottle of juice before she wiped her mouth.

"What do you want to talk about?"

"Baseball?"

She wrinkled her nose.

"Politics?"

She shook her head and put a cracker in her mouth.

"Why you're coming back to Justice?"

She stopped mid-crunch. "Why do you keep insisting there's a special reason?"

"Because I know you. I've known you for a long time. I know how you feel about your dad and I know that you believe that you can't do what you want to do in Justice. You also believe that what *you* want is the most important thing."

She stared at him, with her mouth partly open. "I can't believe that's what you think of me."

"You sound like I'm giving you an opinion."

"Aren't you?"

"No. I'm telling you the facts. There must be something *you* need in Justice or you wouldn't be coming back. Which means it can't be something Kat asked you to come back for and it can't be something with your dad. Or anyone else."

"You can be a real jerk, you know that?" she asked.

"For telling the truth?"

"For being mean."

"Tell me I'm wrong. Tell me you're coming back for someone else's sake."

"Can't I be coming back to visit?"

"Because *you* felt the need to come home for a visit? Because *you* missed someone or something?"

She tossed her empty juice bottle on the floor of the car and set the box of crackers on the seat between them. "Okay, you're right. I'm coming home because *I* need something. But I had no idea you thought so little of me."

"I haven't thought of you in a long time."

"Thanks," she muttered. She turned slightly and leaned back against the car door. She crossed her arms. "Don't you want to know what I need?"

He took a long drink of his coffee before answering. "Justice is a small town. I'll find out eventually," he said, trying to distance himself from the sudden nearly overwhelming urge to shout *What? What do you need?* Wow, she was something. He'd never understood Luke's pathetic pull toward her. But now, after only a few hours in her company, he was feeling it. Fuck.

In his peripheral vision he could see her gritting her teeth and her fingers digging into the skin of her arms where they crossed. "I am coming back because I need something, but I can tell you truthfully that it's not totally selfish."

"How's that?"

"I am coming home to Justice for someone else's sake too. There is someone else who will benefit from me being home."

He glanced at her. "Who?"

She looked at him for a long moment, worrying her bottom lip. "No one you know," she finally said.

"No one..." he repeated. "Who is it?"

"You'll find out." She turned and looked out the side

window, clearly trying to end the conversation.

"Who is it, Sabrina?"

If she was bringing a man back to Justice...that would kill Luke.

Marc's imagination, overactive as it was, kicked into high gear.

"You'll find out who it is," she repeated.

"*When*?" So much for casual and unaffected.

"Soon."

He took a deep breath. Fine. He didn't need to know. It didn't matter to him if she was bringing some guy home. It didn't matter to him...

"Is it a guy?" he asked, his tone sharp.

She turned to look at him. "A guy?"

"Yes, a guy. A man, a boy, a lov—" he coughed, "—lover."

She looked at him with a mixture of confusion and amusement. "If I was bringing a man home, would I be traveling alone?"

"Maybe he's coming in a few days. Maybe you're coming home first to talk to your dad so it's not a huge shock."

She laughed lightly. "Breaking it to Dad easy would take all the fun out of it." Sabrina seemed to be enjoying some imagined mental picture. "Shocking my father is a hobby I haven't enjoyed for a long time."

Now *that* was believable. "Who is it?"

"I don't want to talk about it."

"Does Kat know this person?"

"I take it you don't care that I don't want to talk about it?"

"We have a long way to go, what else are we going to talk about?"

"Why don't you ask me to tell you about what I've been doing for the past year or so?"

He grimaced, which he hoped she would miss in the dim lights of the dashboard. "No thanks."

She shifted in her seat to face him. "Why not?"

"I don't need more details than I already have." The things Kat had told him and Luke had made Luke crazy and Marc amazed. He hadn't liked Sabrina but he'd always considered her intelligent. Until she left Justice. Then it seemed, from the stories anyway, that she couldn't make a good decision to save her life.

"What details do you have?" She sounded genuinely curious.

"That you lived in dumpy apartments with heating that worked sporadically at best. You had offers to pose for porn films and magazines to help supplement your income. Which you didn't take as far as I know," he added. "And if you did do *not* tell me. You were also the cause of at least two bar fights both of which ended up with a man going to jail. You gave an agent almost two thousand dollars shortly after you left Justice and then never saw him again. Should I go on?"

"No," she muttered. "That's plenty."

"I'm amazed you're actually here in one piece."

He didn't have to look at her to know that her expression was surprised.

"You were worried about me?"

"I was disgusted by your lack of sense," he said. "Does Kat know this mystery person?" he asked again, trying to turn the conversation.

Sabrina hesitated before answering, a fact that Marc carefully took note of. "She knows *of* this person, anyway," she finally answered.

"How about your dad? Does he know this person?"

She shook her head adamantly. "No way."

"Does he know *of* this person?"

"*No.*"

"It's someone he won't approve of?"

Probably. Those were the people Sabrina loved to introduce to her father.

"I guess you could say that he won't approve," Sabrina said, frowning at the dashboard.

"What did he say when you told him you're coming home?" Marc glanced at Sabrina's stubborn expression.

"He doesn't know I am coming home."

"You're kidding."

Of course, that made sense. Bill hadn't said anything about it to Luke and had he known, he would have come to Luke with the news right away. Marc would have known about it shortly after that.

"You're planning to surprise him?"

She didn't smile. "I guess if I see him he'll be surprised."

"*If* you see him?

"I'm staying with Kat."

"Oh?" He tried to make it sound casual, not judgmental. By the scowl on Sabrina's face, however, he assumed he'd failed.

"I'm not running home to daddy. I'm coming back to Justice for...a few reasons, but I don't want to deal with Dad, or anyone else," she said with a pointed look in Marc's direction, "thinking that I'm home because it didn't work out on the road with the music. There are other considerations. It has nothing to do with my music."

She was doing more than informing him, he realized. She was convincing him, or trying to, anyway.

"In fact," she went on, "I never intended to come back to Justice. I'm coming back because I have to, for now. I don't know that I'm even coming back for good. This might just be a layover while I figure things out."

That was a good thing. Which didn't totally explain why he was annoyed.

It was because Sabrina had always looked down on Justice.

He, on the other hand, loved their hometown. Everything about it. And he shared that love with Luke and Bill. They loved the Midwest, loved knowing all of their neighbors and they loved being a true part of the community where they depended on others and knew that those people, in turn, depended on them.

Both Bill and Luke had tried to instill that love and contentment in Sabrina. They'd insisted that she would be happiest in Justice—with them. Because, in spite of their problems, Bill loved his daughter. He wanted her to have a home, caring neighbors, the safety of a small town, the reward of contributing on a real, direct level to a community and, most of all, a family—a loving husband and a bunch of kids.

That was Bill's idea of true happiness. Which, of course, meant that Sabrina was going to rebel against it. Anything Bill wanted, Sabrina automatically rejected.

She wanted her own life. She wanted to do her thing, her way. She'd left town and never looked back. Until now.

"Why are you coming home? You hate Justice, you want something Justice can never give you. You and your father can barely have a civil conversation. And you better not be coming home for Luke. Because that isn't going to happen." He felt—and sounded—surly. He didn't care.

"It's not like Luke's been waiting around, pining away for me," she snapped.

This sounded interesting. "What's that mean?"

"Kat hasn't only been telling *you* stories about *me*, you know. She's told me all about Luke's women." She said *women* with an almost contemptuous tone.

It sounded like Sabrina was bothered by what she'd heard. That made him feel better. "What has she told you?"

"She's told me about how he's been dating steadily ever since I left. But she, and everyone else apparently, are curious about why he strictly dates women from out of town. He also never takes any of them to any functions or shows in Justice. They never come to The Camelot. He never introduces any of them to his friends, or to Karen or Dave."

"Kat's irritated because she doesn't get any dirt on any of the women we date."

He and Luke both made a habit of not dating women from Justice. It made things messy when they broke up if they were running into each other at the grocery store and town events. Or worse, at The Camelot. Either things were tense, which didn't make for a good environment, or the women stopped coming in, which was bad for business. Even worse if the woman's friends and family also stopped coming in too.

"She doesn't know them, but she does have some opinions. Especially on the ones you take out."

"And?"

"She says they're all sluts."

Marc couldn't help but laugh. The blunt way Sabrina said

it indicated that she believed Kat. "Like I said, Kat hasn't gotten to know any of them. They are nice, professional women who have no criminal records, no sexually transmitted diseases and no major addictions."

"Must be the way they dress."

He laughed again. "Kat's seen maybe two of them ever, and I can assure you, they all dress very nicely."

"But your idea of nice and Kat's idea of nice might be different," Sabrina pointed out.

That could be true. He tended to like a more sophisticated look and Kat had a distinct look of her own. Always had. She liked black, wore fitted clothes in interesting combinations and changed her hair color nearly every other month. Of course her various piercings and body paint made her stand out in a town like Justice. She was a native, though, and a fantastic doctor so everyone forgave her fashion statements.

"Marian's has a fairly obvious dress code," he commented.

Sabrina whistled. "Marian's huh? You must like them." It was the nicest restaurant in the area, next to The Camelot, of course.

He shrugged. His choice of restaurant didn't have so much to do with how much he liked the woman as it did with wanting them to like him, or at least think he was a decent guy. He could admit it—he still felt like he was proving to the Hamiltons and the town and everyone that he had been a risk worth taking after he'd been orphaned and taken into their family. He knew they loved him and were proud of him. But he owed them everything and he made sure there was never a reason for them to be upset, embarrassed or disappointed.

"I wouldn't date them if I didn't like them," he said.

"But why keep them so mysterious? Why not date some of the women from Justice?"

"Maybe because I don't want everyone in town discussing my love life," he said, rather than telling her the whole truth. Sabrina was not someone he wanted to be completely open, honest and vulnerable with. Luke had been and look what had happened to him.

"But they *are* discussing your love life."

"But they don't have any facts. Besides, I'm providing some much-needed entertainment. Obviously, Kat doesn't have much else to think or talk about."

Ten minutes later, Marc took Exit 297.

"Marc?"

"Yeah?" He didn't look at her.

"Do we need gas again?" She leaned over to look at the gas gauge.

"Nope."

"Bathroom?"

"Nope."

"Why are we getting off?"

"This is the exit to the airport."

"I noticed. Why does that matter?" Her heart started beating harder. She shouldn't jump to conclusions. There might be reasons Marc was taking her to the airport other than putting her on a flight.

"I'm putting you on a flight."

Except in this case where her conclusions were completely right. "You are not."

"Oh, yes I am."

Sure, where had he been four weeks ago when she'd spent a huge chunk of her measly savings on a spontaneous plane ticket to Jamaica? She could have used someone adamant about her flying that day. "Where do you think I'm going?"

"Anywhere but Justice."

A tingle of temptation zinged through her. Anywhere but Justice sounded really good to her.

"What do you mean anywhere?"

"I mean anywhere you want to go."

That list was actually pretty long. But if she had to pick just one destination, she knew exactly where it would be—

She forced her thoughts from that. She was sticking with her plan to do the *opposite* of everything she was tempted to do.

Even if there was a music competition taking place in

Nashville in a few weeks that she'd really love a shot at singing in.

Besides, in Nashville she'd still be pregnant and broke, without a job, a place to live, health insurance—or a clue about pregnancy and babies. In Justice she'd have a roof over her head, a lower cost of living, and her own personal physician who would only expect pedicures in exchange for her services.

She looked at Marc. He stubbornly kept his eyes on the road. "You were planning this the whole time?"

"Laramie is the closest airport that can get you anywhere in the country. You'll fly to Denver and then anywhere from there. Your pick. My treat."

I can be responsible. I can make good choices. I can do the right thing for my baby.

But damn she wanted a free ticket to Nashville.

And damn Marc seemed sincere about giving it to her.

"Why is my not going back to Justice worth four or five hundred dollars to you?" she asked, already knowing some of it.

"Not four or five. I'll set you up with a few months rent, some money for a new car, give you references for a job, whatever you need."

It was like waving hundred dollars bills at an addicted gambler and saying, "just pick your game."

She clenched her fists and focused. She couldn't go to Nashville, whether it was free or not. It wasn't just about having a place to live and groceries. In Justice she'd have a doctor she trusted, who wouldn't laugh at how clueless she really was. She'd be able to hire a daycare provider that Luke's mom had known for ten years through her church committees. She'd be able to walk to the park without mace in her pocket.

Justice was what was good for the baby. That was what mattered.

"No."

He sighed and she knew he'd been expecting her answer. "Come on, Sabrina. It's the best offer you'll get."

"I don't need a plane ticket or rent to live in Justice."

"I need you to not live in Justice."

"Why is this such a big deal?" But she knew. It was about

Luke and the fact that she was returning to basically create the life he'd wanted to give her.

Marc said nothing as he took the ticket from the machine at the entrance to the airport's parking garage and rolled through two levels before pulling into a space. He shut the car off and turned to face her.

"If you come back to Justice, you'll ruin everything for Luke."

"This isn't about Luke." But her stomach felt queasy as she said it.

"Luke will make it about Luke. If you come home, it will turn things upside down for him. And you know it." He frowned at her.

She frowned back. "I don't have anywhere else to go."

"That's bullshit. You can go anywhere you want. Back to Seattle. If you need money, I'll give you money. Or somewhere new. New York City. Miami. Chicago. Big cities with all the lights and excitement and nightlife that you want."

She looked down at her hands, clasped tightly in her lap. "I don't want those things anymore." She hoped that would be true eventually.

"You have the FBI after you or something?"

She snorted. "I think the FBI might think to look in my hometown if I disappeared, don't you?"

"A crazy ex-boyfriend? A stalker?"

Crazy wasn't the word she'd use to describe Paul. And coming after her was the last thing he was going to do. In fact, he'd high-tailed it in the opposite direction as soon as he'd had what he needed—her bank account number and credit cards.

"No, nothing like that."

"A kidney? I'm willing to see if I'm a match."

She didn't think he was trying to be funny but she laughed anyway. "Thanks. But no."

He let his head fall back against the seat. "Please get on a plane. I'll do anything."

"I..." She meant to say *can't* next but it didn't come out. Instead, she looked at Marc. "Is Luke really still hung up on me?" She needed to know. That fact alone could change the course of her future.

Even as melodramatic as that sounded.

Marc's head came up quickly and he scowled at her. "You like that? You like knowing that you still have him wrapped around your little finger?"

"No, I ..." But dammit—maybe it made her a manipulative bitch in some ways—she kind of did. Luke was the only person in her entire life who'd thought she was absolutely wonderful and okay, so that was a little addictive. That was actually normal, wasn't it? To *like* the person who thought you hung the moon?

"He doesn't cry himself to sleep at night, if that's what you're wondering, and he's moved on. He's dated. A couple women for a few months. He's definitely having sex."

She flinched, not so much from the truth of it, but from the contempt in Marc's voice.

"He doesn't think about you constantly. Probably not even daily. But..." He leaned in, pinning her with a harsh stare. "You have some weird power over us. You can disappear for years and then suddenly appear again and our brains get mushy. You play the sweet and vulnerable part perfectly. You make men want to put on shiny knight armor and find a fucking white horse. You and your hair and your lips and your breasts..." His gaze flickered over each part as he spoke and Sabrina felt tingles start in her scalp and travel down her neck to her nipples.

"You know how to use it all to keep us whipped enough that we can't look at other women without comparing them to you. Do I think that if you come home Luke will drop everything else and follow you around like a puppy? The answer is fuck yeah."

She was staring at him by the end of his tirade, her breathing shallow and choppy. She'd heard every word, but the only one she could focus on for some reason was *us* and *we*.

"I thought we were talking about Luke," she said breathlessly. Did Marc really feel that way? Like she made his brain mushy? Like he didn't want to look at other women when she was around?

When had that happened?

And who cared anyway?

Except that she was afraid she might.

"We *are* talking about Luke. He deserves a life with a woman who wants what he wants, who truly loves him and wants him. Not one who sees him as her backup plan."

Sabrina let Marc ignore the *us* and *we* that were distracting her. "Backup plan?"

She wanted to sound adamant and offended. But crap. He wasn't wrong. Luke was the one she always turned to if she needed anything—money, a ride, advice, something heavy carried, something creepy killed and yes, the occasional ego boost. Didn't everyone need someone who told them they were wonderful once in awhile?

But she'd spent four years without that personal fan club. And she'd survived. She'd had to learn how to face her failures and flaws by herself.

Not that she'd ever made a mistake quite as big as the one she was bringing home now.

Did she like hearing that Luke would forgive her and be there for her, the safety net, the rock? Definitely. If that made her a bad person, then so be it. She was way out of her element here.

"You always kept Luke on a short leash. Anytime you felt like his time and attention had been spent on something or someone else too much you'd have some crisis and reel him back in. Because if he got to close to another girl he might not be there when *you* needed him."

"You make it sound like I didn't want him to be happy."

"I think you were okay with him being happy, as long as you were part of it. But look at what you did the night of The Camelot's grand opening."

"What I did?" She'd realized that Luke was an amazing guy. What was wrong with that?

"He was wrapped up in the restaurant and the business—things that had nothing to do with you. He was completely happy and busy. So you had to do something drastic. You seduced him *that* night Sabrina. You'd known him your whole life but suddenly you had to have him *that* night."

"It wasn't because—" She stopped. Had she been feeling left out and lonely that night? Not really. She knew every one of the hundred plus people who were at the party. That night Luke had finally fully put his roots down in Justice. There was no changing his mind, no going back, no veering off course as of that night. Luke believed she was the missing piece to him having everything he wanted. So, she had to see if she could give him that.

He'd always done whatever she needed him to do, he'd always been there, making her life better, easier, happier. She'd wanted to give that back. For whatever reason, she was special to him, she was what he wanted, the only thing he wanted that he didn't have. It had felt good to know that she could give him something he wanted so much, that no one else could give.

She was, amazingly, the woman of his dreams and if anyone deserved to have his dreams come true, it was Luke. So it made sense to go to him on the night when all the rest of his dreams and desires were being fulfilled.

Marc thought she'd done it for herself. Ironically, if she had been thinking more about how she really felt instead of how Luke felt and how she *wanted* to feel, she would have never asked him to kiss her.

"You think you know everything, don't you?" she asked.

"I've just been paying attention." He tore open the pack of cinnamon gum that lay in the depression between the seats and shoved a piece in his mouth, chomping angrily. The muscles in his jaw tensed and relaxed, tensed and relaxed and she felt her own tension winding up.

She turned to stare out the windshield. She didn't even see the gray SUV parked in front of them. She was seeing Luke's face. And how it would look when he saw her again in Justice.

"You don't even want to come to Justice," Marc said, his voice calmer. "You said earlier that you don't even know if this is permanent. It's probably just a pit stop."

She didn't know. She wanted to get through the next week without feeling like she was losing her mind. Then the next week. Then the next.

Right now, in this moment, going home to Justice seemed the best choice. That was all she could focus on.

Was there a time limit on how long a pit stop could be? Was eighteen years too long to be considered temporary?

"It's probably just a pit stop," she agreed.

"So don't do this."

She turned. It sounded like Marc was actually pleading.

"Don't come back and turn him inside out and then leave again. Leave him alone."

The butterflies that never seemed too far off kicked up a dance party in her stomach again. She didn't want to mess things up for Luke. Or anyone else. She wanted to do the right thing—for a change.

Maybe Marc was right. Maybe she should consider somewhere else. Maybe Nashville wasn't the worst idea.

The moment she stepped foot in Justice her whole life was going to change. Leaving again would be nearly impossible. And staying would mean a total life makeover. No more nights at the clubs, no more band, no more transient roommates to expand her thoughts and experiences. There would be community rummage sales, sensible shoes and seeing her father regularly.

The butterflies turned up the rhythm.

Justice seemed like the reasonable choice. The fact that she didn't want to go home probably meant that was exactly where she should go. But it was a permanent decision. She wasn't very good at permanent.

"Can I think about it?" she finally asked.

"Think about what?"

"Where I want to go?"

Marc glanced at the airport then back at her. "For how long?"

A few months would be good. "At least tonight."

He hesitated, then said, "You want to spend the night here in Laramie?"

She nodded. "Then we can talk about it in the morning."

He considered that. She could feel that he didn't like it but he didn't have a great argument against it. "Fine," he finally said.

"I'll pay you back for the motel room."

"That's not the issue."

"You have to get back to work?"

"Not necessarily."

"You're completely sick of being with me?"

He didn't answer and she turned to look at him.

"Marc?"

"Yeah?" He wouldn't look at her.

"What's the problem? It's a few more hours."

"Yeah. Seems like a simple request."

"But?"

"Not sure that being in another motel room with you is a good idea."

"You think I'm going to smother you in your sleep?"

He looked at her, not amused. "Because Luke, and everyone else, won't like it if they find out we spent the night in a motel together."

"But nothing is going to happen."

"You sure about that?"

The temperature in the car shot up several degrees with his words—and the look on his face.

"I have an idea," she said, wanting to get away from him as quickly as possible and wanting to get as close as she could at the same time.

Ridiculous. She didn't even like him.

"An idea about what?"

"We go out somewhere. Somewhere with lots of other people. And we stay out until it's terribly late and we're exhausted and all we want to do is go to bed. To sleep," she added quickly.

He sat looking at her, his gaze dropping to her mouth, then back to her eyes. "It's worth a try I guess."

Chapter Four

Of course, the best place to stay out late with a bunch of other people was a bar. And he chose a bar with a live band. Not on purpose, but Sabrina's eyes lit up when she saw the sign and some of the tightness he'd felt coiling in his gut since deciding to take her to the airport unwound.

Putting her on a plane to anywhere else was a great idea. He knew that.

But even before she'd figured it out and started fighting him, he'd had a knot in his stomach.

There was a reason she was coming back to Justice and, dammit, he was concerned.

She swore no one was after her, but something didn't feel right. It wasn't a visit. It wasn't a vacation. There was something going on and it was driving him nuts.

Almost as nuts as the idea of being in a motel room with her again.

The twenty minutes they'd spent in Grimy Glitch had nearly done him in between her purple underwear and her tattoos and all.

A whole night? After she'd kissed him in the diner? He'd be a goner.

Staying out all night seemed like an okay option. Getting drunk sounded even better.

He ordered two beers and found Sabrina at a table near the far wall. Her eyes were firmly on the stage and her lips were moving along with the words to the not-too-sucky cover of Bruce Springsteen's "Born to Run".

She knew every word to one of the Boss's best songs ever.

Marc liked her a little more in that moment.

They finished and she put her fingers to her lips and gave a sharp whistle as everyone applauded.

"Let's dance," she said, already on her feet and moving toward the dance floor as the band started the first notes of Bruce's "Fire".

Needing fortification, Marc downed three long pulls of beer, then followed her.

"You know all these words too?" he asked. He did.

She started singing with the band as he pulled her into his arms. Damn. Such a great idea and horrible idea at the same time. She didn't hesitate to get close and her voice was husky as she sang, "'Cause when we kiss, ooh, fire."

God, he loved this song.

They danced close and she sang the rest of the song. Marc fought the urge to cup her butt and pull her up where he wanted her. It was the music, the bar, the beer—so what if he'd only had three mouthfuls. Fatigue. That was it. Fatigue and stress and frustration. And Sabrina. Any guy who had her up against him and had her singing those words in his ear would be thinking at least a few of the things he was thinking.

When the song ended, she pulled back, looking up at him, her eyes bright, breathing hard. Much harder than the exertion dancing would have required.

She smiled up at him. "I do love this."

"Dancing with me?" he teased. He somehow knew what she was talking about.

"Live music. The connection. The *feel* of it." She looked toward the stage. "No matter which end I'm on—the stage or the audience."

She was beautiful like this. He was starting to understand his best friend's obsession. She hadn't moved away from him and her arms were still around his neck. The next song started, but he didn't hear anything but the beat. The slow beat.

They naturally started to sway.

"You'll miss this in Justice," he said. It was why she'd left in the first place. It was what had kept her away for four years.

The music and the freedom.

Now she was coming back. She'd have to give up both. Surely she knew that.

She nodded. "Yeah." No hesitation, no apologies.

He'd seen her perform. He knew she was amazing. He'd never quite understood why Luke had been surprised that she'd left.

Except that he thought they were in love.

Which was exactly what Marc was afraid would happen again. She'd come home, Luke would think that meant a second chance and then she'd go again. Eventually. It was inevitable. She couldn't give it up.

Which gave him an idea.

If he wanted her on a plane in the morning, he should give her all the reasons why it was a good idea, remind her what the world could offer her that Justice couldn't.

And it wouldn't be bad to put some physical space between them. His body was humming from this new need, the need for her. And there wasn't a whole lot to keep him from turning that hum up a few decibels. They were far from home, neither of them tied down.

If he liked her, this would be a no brainer. Which was a possible problem.

"Don't you want something to drink?" he asked.

She pulled back and looked up at him. She must have seen something in his eyes, or felt something below his belt, that made her eyes widen. "Yeah, maybe some water."

"'Kay." He turned her toward the bar and nudged her, not so subtly, to fetch her own drink. She rolled her eyes but headed in that direction.

He looked around the room. There had to be one other woman in a crowd this size who would attract his attention. Someone else he could dance with. Maybe even take the edge off with. Because this building heat between him and Sabrina was going to get them into trouble.

There was no one who caught his eye on the way to the stage. There were plenty of beautiful women, several of whom gave him smiles as he passed, but none who stopped him in his tracks.

He was contemplating the fact that he was being way too damned picky and he should grab the first blonde he saw—no brunettes, no one who might remind him of Sabrina at inconvenient moments—when he got to the stage. There were three guys standing to the side, watching the band, but dressed alike in plain black T-shirts and black jeans who he assumed were part of the crew.

"Hey, I have an offer for you," he said to the closest.

"Yeah?"

"Fifty bucks if the band lets my friend sing with them."

The man chuckled. "Fifty?"

"One hundred. For you if you convince them. And a hundred for the band. Then if they don't like her, another hundred."

He looked less than impressed but he removed his earpiece and leaned in toward another of the crew. He repeated the info and the other guy looked Marc up and down.

"She any good? Seriously?"

"Amazing."

"It's her birthday or something?"

"No occasion. We're passing through."

"You tryin' to get laid?"

He was trying to *not* want to get laid. "No."

The guy shrugged. "I'll run it past Jeff. No promises."

"Got it."

The band finished another song and then announced they were taking a break. Marc saw the two guys approach the lead singer. The guy, a young twenty-something with shaggy blond hair and a goatee, looked over at Marc. He said something to the guys, then approached Marc alone.

"If she sucks, I want two hundred bucks, not one," was all he said.

Marc grinned. "Not a problem at all."

"I'll hunt you down and beat it out of you if you try to stiff me."

Marc nodded and grinned wider. "Got it."

The guy looked suspicious. "Does she play?"

Marc wasn't sure what he was talking about. "What do—"

The guy held up the guitar he'd been carrying by the neck. "Does she play?"

"Yeah. She's great." He was pretty sure she played guitar. She fiddled apparently.

"Is she hot?"

Marc swallowed. That one was easy. "Definitely."

"She can work the crowd?"

He hadn't seen her on stage since college. But he nodded. "You bet."

"She tryin' to get discovered or something? 'Cuz that's not happenin' here."

"Nah, it's for fun," Marc assured him. "To blow off steam, you know?"

The guy looked at him for several seconds, then said, "If she's any good, I'll give you half your money back."

Marc slapped him on the shoulder. "Keep it. But let her do two songs."

They let her do five.

She was amazing. She took the stage without a moment's hesitation, launched into the first song like she'd been singing it nightly to sold-out stadiums, played guitar and keyboard, and flirted and laughed with the entire band and the crowd.

She was a huge hit.

In fact, the band's singer found Marc after her last song, handed him every dollar back and said, "Thanks, man. If you talk her into staying here and singing with us regularly, *I'll* give *you* two hundred bucks."

When she left the stage Marc tried to keep as many people between them as he could.

He was in worse trouble than when he'd started. She was sexy and talented and sexy and...there was something about her voice.

When she sang he felt it to his bones. His gut clenched—in

a good way. And his skin tingled—in a good way. His chest felt tight—in a good way.

It was all really fucking bad.

He didn't remember that from college. Or high school. He'd heard her sing. Dozens of times. She'd been singing to the radio in the car on the way to Laramie.

She was good. Good enough that even to the radio it was obvious.

But on stage—she was dangerous.

He now realized where Luke was coming from and he thought back to the story of Odysseus in high school. The sirens whose voices entranced sailors and lured them closer in their ships.

The ships were dashed on the rocks and everyone drowned.

Great story.

Better lesson.

He needed to stay away from her feeling like he was. He already knew a night in a motel room with her was a bad idea. If he'd had inklings of wanting her before, at this point he wasn't sure he'd survive her smiling at him without taking her up against the wall.

She spotted him and started in his direction, but someone in the crowd stopped her and Marc took the opportunity to move.

He couldn't face her right then. He was completely turned on and there was no way he was going to be able to hide it from her.

She extricated herself from the cowboys who had stopped her and stretched on tiptoe. He ducked behind, not surprisingly, another cowboy. The place was full of them.

She headed in the opposite direction and he let out a breath. He took a step back, keeping the top of her head in sight.

Marc thought his best course of action was to find a corner where his back was protected by a wall, where he wouldn't interact with any other human beings and he could hide in the shadows. He moved in the direction of just such a corner. He skirted around another waitress and twisted away from a group of young guys trying to impress some girls with their dance moves.

He was almost safe when he felt a hand on his shoulder and he nearly jumped out of his skin. He was a mess. A complete and total mess. All because of a tiny brunette.

"Excuse me?"

He turned. It wasn't Sabrina so he took a deep breath. "Yeah?" he choked out.

"Do you want to dance?" the girl asked. She was beautiful. Gorgeous actually. Long blonde hair spilled to her shoulder blades and her tight pink T-shirt encased generous breasts.

"Dance? Um, I..."

"Finally I found you."

He did jump this time. Sabrina had snuck up on him as he was trying to answer the blonde. He'd never felt so wound up and it was all the fault of the females.

"What are you doing?" Sabrina asked, looking from the girl to Marc and back again.

"I wanted to dance with him," the blonde said.

Sabrina looked up at him. "Maybe you should."

She didn't care? Marc frowned. He cared that she didn't care?

Mushy brain. That was what he'd told Sabrina she did to guys. He was no exception.

Marc shrugged. "Maybe I should."

"Go ahead," Sabrina said.

"Maybe I will."

"What's stopping you?"

"Nothing." Not her, that was for sure. Who he danced with had nothing to do with Sabrina. Nothing he did had anything to do with Sabrina. They'd danced together and it had been great. That didn't mean that he shouldn't, or couldn't, dance with someone else. Or that he wouldn't.

But he didn't want to.

And that pissed him off.

He wanted to dance with Sabrina again. If he were honest he would admit that he wanted to get Sabrina up against him again.

That pissed him off more.

Luke was in huge trouble. Because Marc didn't even like Sabrina and she was having an effect on him. Truly being in love with her would be nothing but a disaster.

"Are we dancing then?" the girl asked looking from Marc to Sabrina to Marc again.

"No." He was disgusted with himself. He wanted to be turned on by her. He wanted to want to do the things he wanted to do with Sabrina with her.

But he wanted to kiss Sabrina.

Which meant it was time to get the hell out of the bar, away from the liquor, away from the possibility that she might get up on stage again, and get to sleep.

Unconsciousness was his only hope.

"Come on, Seattle. Time to go."

Sabrina couldn't describe exactly how she was feeling.

She always felt energized after performing, but tonight it was different. The hum in her veins didn't dissipate once she was off stage. In fact, it seemed to grow stronger as she'd searched for and finally found Marc.

Maybe the problem was that she'd felt his eyes on her the entire time she was performing. Maybe it was that she'd seen him ask three different women, who were quite clearly wallflowers, to dance. He hadn't gone for the flashy, flirty ones. He'd asked the ones who were sitting and hadn't been dancing. They'd all said yes. With big smiles. Maybe it was that—how happy he made them, how sweet that was, how he'd smiled and held them and twirled them.

But he'd still kept his eyes on her throughout her performance. And she'd loved it. She almost never noticed specific people in the crowd, but it seemed that she couldn't avoid watching Marc.

They hadn't touched. She resisted the urge to touch his arm or even brush against him. It was like she was wound so tight that one touch would release...something. She was too afraid to find out what it was.

Or was she?

She snuck a glance at him as he drove. He was chomping on a piece of gum and staring, almost angrily, out the windshield.

He was good-looking. That wasn't exactly a revelation. She'd known Marc for years and it was an established fact that he was a good-looking guy. But she'd never been attracted.

Or had she?

These questions were driving her crazy. She'd never felt this chemistry, never thought about kissing him, never *wanted* to kiss him—or anything else.

And now that she was thinking about it, she couldn't *stop* thinking about it.

"Knock it off," he growled, not looking at her.

"What?"

"You're staring at me."

"I was thinking."

He cleared his throat. "About what?"

"Why do you think there's sexual tension between us now when there hasn't been before?"

He looked at her quickly, then back to the road. "Just put that right out there why don't you?"

She'd gotten used to being bold growing up. Being direct and specific about what she wanted and needed and was thinking was necessary to be sure her dad heard her. When she left home, she'd learned that being vague got vague results. Bold and fearless. That's what got ahead in the world.

And he wasn't denying the tension.

"Is there a reason we shouldn't talk about it?"

"It's awkward, don't you think?" he asked, staring resolutely at the road in front of the car.

"It's awkward whether we talk about it or not."

"It's easier to ignore when we don't talk about it."

He had a point. On the other hand, ignoring things rarely made them better. "Why ignore it?"

"How many reasons do you want?"

"Four."

"One, Luke. Two, we don't like each other. Three, you're leaving in the morning never to return. Four, Luke."

That had been pretty easy for him. She frowned. "One, sexual tension between us has nothing to do with Luke. Two, as you said earlier, you don't have to like me to want to see me naked. Three is negotiable. Four, you don't want me to be involved with Luke anyway so I would think my being attracted to someone else would be a good thing."

He scowled at her. "One, sexual tension between us would upset Luke—to say the least. Two, *wanting* to see you naked and *seeing* you naked are different things. Three is not negotiable. Four, why can't you be attracted to someone who lives in Dublin or something? Why me?"

She laughed. She couldn't help it. "Dublin? Ireland? Why there?"

"It's far away."

"Ah. And why you? Hell if I know. I'm as surprised as you are."

He pulled into a motel parking lot. "It's probably hero worship."

She looked at him, waiting for the punch line. He parked the car and turned off the ignition then moved to open the door. "What's probably hero worship?"

"How you're feeling about me."

She snorted. "There are two words wrong with that. Hero and worship. You've been anything but a hero to me for as long as I've known you and I think you need to look up the definition of worship if you think that's how I feel."

He turned in his seat to face her, pinning her with a direct stare. "I haven't been a hero to you? You're in Laramie, Wyoming rather than Soggy Swamp. Who did that?"

"You brought me here to put me on a plane."

"I could have left you alongside the road."

"You came to save Luke, not me."

"I bought you dinner."

"I'm paying you back."

"You know, Seattle, you could be a little grateful."

She sat looking at him. This was Marc Sterling. He thought she was selfish and self-centered. And she'd often wondered if he was right. Like she wondered if Luke and her father were right about the fact that she couldn't make a good decision until she'd tried all the bad ones.

"You're right," she finally said softly. "I should be grateful. You came to get me when there was no one else."

Obviously her acquiescence surprised him.

"That's better."

He started to move to open the door again, but she put her hand on his arm. He froze.

"No, really, Marc. Thank you. You saved me. If you hadn't come I'd... Well, I don't know what I would have done." The reality of that hit her and she had to swallow past a thickness in her throat. "I was out of options."

The muscles in his arm under her hand bunched.

"Luke or Kat would have come eventually if I hadn't."

"But you did."

"I couldn't have just left you there."

"Because you're a good guy. We haven't always been the best of friends, but you still helped me out and I won't forget that. Maybe we can..."

He was watching her closely. "We can what?"

For some reason it felt like the temperature in the car went up a few degrees. "Be friends?" she asked.

He didn't say anything for a long moment. He seemed to be studying her for something. Then he drawled, "Being sweet and agreeable isn't going to keep me from driving you to the airport tomorrow morning, Seattle."

It was strange. He kept calling her Seattle and she liked it. Not because she loved Seattle. She did, but there had been some not so great times there too. But because it felt—intimate. No one else called her that.

Being intimate with Marc was a bad—tempting, but bad—idea.

Then she remembered the rest of his words. "I'm not being agreeable to win you over."

"Talking about having sex with me isn't going to win me

over either."

Sabrina glared at him. "I wasn't talking about having sex with you. But," she said as a thought hit her and adrenaline surged, "if I did have sex with you, it would make you want to do anything I want for the rest of your life."

She wasn't sure where the bravado came from. She knew for a fact that having sex with her didn't exactly make men fall at her feet. Maybe Luke, but he'd been—she could admit it— pretty much at her feet already. And she hadn't hung around for long after to see how it went. Paul had high-tailed it in the other direction, in fact. Maybe not because of the sex, but that certainly hadn't slowed his departure. Still, there was—and always had been—something about Marc that made her want to push him, no matter how dumb that was.

Marc leaned in and his voice dropped low. "Having sex with you would be a diversion while I'm far from home and on edge. Trust me when I say that I'm not worried about the rest of my life."

She leaned in too and narrowed her eyes, in spite of the fact that her stomach flipped simply in response to his husky voice. The sexual chemistry between them was not one-sided and while she doubted there would be worshipping from either of them, she wasn't going to let him be quite that nonchalant.

"I don't think it's sudden hero worship," she said.

He seemed to lean closer. "You been harboring secret desires for me for years? You should have said something."

"Why?"

"I could have helped you out. Then you could have left Luke alone."

"I did leave Luke alone. Like a few thousand miles and four years alone."

"Not soon enough." Marc's jaw tightened, but then he paused and visibly relaxed. "But if you and I were getting it on, Luke would have been pissed off enough to stay away from you."

She'd been a virgin until she was twenty and she'd had no sexual feelings for Marc that she remembered, but now thinking about having sweaty, new, teenage sex with him on a blanket by the river or in the backseat of his car made her thighs clench and rush of heat flow from head to toe.

"You would have risked pissing Luke off that way?"

Marc's gaze flickered to her mouth, then slid lower, over her body, then back up. "As a dumb, horny teenage boy? Very likely."

"And now?"

"I'm not a teenager anymore."

"What about the dumb and horny part?"

"Some times more than others."

He was kind of funny. Which also surprised her. "How about now?"

"Feeling dumber by the second."

That definitely caused a stomach flip. "Funny, I'm feeling one of those things too."

"Yeah?"

"I'm always wound up after I perform."

"Wound up?"

"You know, wound up, energized, stimulated..."

"You get...stimulated...every time you sing?"

"I thank God for D batteries every night," she said without batting an eye. She didn't know how she was keeping her cool exactly but it was fun to see his pupils dilate and his lips part as he sucked in a quick breath.

"Is that right? You're so independent you don't even need someone for orgasms, huh?"

It shouldn't be that easy for him, but just the word orgasms from him and she was nearly panting. Unwilling to let him get away with teasing her like that—because she was going to be wishing for those batteries pretty quick—she said, "You get what you pay for with vibrators and I have a high credit limit on all my cards."

"I'm okay with watching."

She cleared her throat before she could think about it. "Who said you're invited?"

"They only had one room open tonight."

That tripped her up. She hadn't even thought about that as

a possibility. And there were complications far beyond her being able to use or not use her plastic BFF.

"I thought you were concerned about being in a hotel room with me tonight."

"I am." He sounded frustrated. "I thought we were going out so we'd be so tired we wouldn't be thinking of anything but sleep."

Yep. That had been the plan.

Of course, none of her plans had worked out for months so she wasn't sure why she'd thought this one would.

"You're not tired?"

"That's not the first word to register, no," he said.

The desire on his face was clear.

She was wound up from performing and he was clearly turned on by—whatever. There had been underlying currents all day.

Inevitable seemed to be the word registering for her.

"Are you doing this to piss Luke off so he'll stay away from me?" she asked.

Marc thought about that. It would work. No doubt about it. Luke wouldn't stand the idea of Sabrina with another guy but especially his best friend. The problem was, Marc didn't need to fake one ounce of what he was feeling for her at the moment and that was a huge flashing neon sign that read *Big Trouble*.

Clearly dumb and horny went together for males even after their teenage years.

"Are *you* doing this because you feel the need to constantly drive me nuts and you know I think this is a bad idea? Or is it the horny-from-singing thing?"

She looked up at him, searching his eyes. "Which do you think works better?"

He got it. It was easier if there was a reason other than truly wanting each other. It was easier if there was an excuse. But part of him wanted her to be so hot for him she couldn't do anything other than beg him to take her. Which they both knew was a lot closer to the truth.

Probably.

Marc didn't like that twinge of insecurity. She hadn't just gotten off stage when there'd been sparks flying between them in the motel room, or the diner, or the grocery store parking lot. But she had been tired. And stressed out. And hungry. And a million other things that might explain her acting out of character. A million other things besides a wild and crazy chemistry between them that she couldn't deny.

Leave it to Sabrina to put doubts like these in his head. He was going to have performance anxiety if he wasn't careful. It would be typical that he'd get Sabrina naked and then not be able to follow through.

That wasn't going to happen.

"Do you always have sex after you perform?"

She grinned up at him. "Define sex."

He leaned in, almost touching her lips with his. "If you don't know the definition maybe you've been doing it wrong. I can help with that."

There. He hadn't imagined the quick little breath she took or the way her pupils dilated.

"I meant... I mean... I um..."

And he wasn't imaging her having trouble forming words. Determined to affect her, determined to prove she was affected and determined to make sure *she* knew it as well as he did, he threaded his fingers through her hair, cupped the back of her head and urged her forward into a kiss.

The kiss wasn't passionate or hungry like a spontaneous lustful kiss should have been. It was more deliberate than that. It was slow and thorough.

For a fleeting moment he thought maybe this would be enough. Enough to prove that the heat between them was simply a matter of imagination, a myth that could be easily dispelled. Wanting her made no sense, so maybe it wasn't even real.

It took three seconds for him to realize that it was not only real, but he'd made a very serious error.

Wanting to kiss her was bad enough. Actually doing it was the dumbest thing he'd ever done.

Because now he would never want another man to kiss her and he'd never want to kiss anyone else.

No wonder Luke was such a mess.

Luke.

Fuck.

He pulled back, looking down into her dazed expression.

He couldn't do this. He did not want Sabrina with Luke, but he couldn't have her himself. She just needed to be far away from both of them. As soon as possible.

He stared at her for ten full seconds. "Dammit," he muttered. He pulled back swiftly as images of mythological sirens came to mind.

"Dammit?" she repeated. "What's that mean?"

"It means that I shouldn't have done that."

She crossed her arms. "Regretting kissing me isn't very complimentary."

"I didn't mean for it to be," he snapped.

She slumped back in her seat. "Well, *that* isn't going to help me sleep tonight. It's going to be even worse. Thanks a lot."

He almost smiled, but caught himself. He liked that she was affected because he sure as hell was. But he couldn't find her funny, or interesting...or anything else positive. Their bickering was supposed to be irritating, not fun.

"I can run out for more batteries," he said. "But that's it. This is a bad, bad idea." If kissing her was such a big a deal that he was feeling possessive, then sleeping with her might ruin his life.

"I'm not doing *that* with you in the room."

He wanted her to because that was the self-destructive type of idiot that he was, but he said, "Probably a good idea."

"And *you're* not going to do anything like that either."

"Anything like what?" he asked.

"You know."

He didn't miss how she shifted on the seat as if suddenly uncomfortable.

"Make sure."

"You're not going to...relieve yourself...either. We both

get...relief...or neither of us does."

She was entertaining him. She was miffed that he wouldn't *relieve* her as she put it. But he sighed. "You know we can't sleep together."

He thought she was going to argue and didn't know how much convincing he could take before he took her upstairs.

But she said, "I know. It's crazy. Justice is too small. We can't have sex and then try to have a normal life when we'll be running into each other all the time."

"It's not about Justice." She wasn't coming back to live in Justice anyway. "It's about Luke."

She huffed out an exasperated breath. "It's all about Luke. Good Lord, maybe *you're* in love with him."

"I do love him." He said it quietly, not looking at her. But he felt her pivot in her seat to face him.

"I know you do. I do too."

"You left him."

"I had to."

"Because you didn't *love* him."

She was quiet for a moment. Then said, "At that time in my life, what he wanted wasn't what I wanted."

He felt his blood pressure start to rise. "And now?"

"Now I don't know. He's not the reason I'm coming back to Justice, if that's what you're thinking."

"But he won't believe that. He's hurt that he wasn't enough to keep you from leaving, but if you come back, he'll think it's a second chance."

"I just want to go back to being friends. I can't deal with anything else right now."

"Then tell him that, Seattle. Don't make him guess. He'll keep hoping if you don't *tell* him that you don't want him."

"I don't know if I can." She said it softly, almost sad.

Marc blew out a frustrated breath. That was it. She was getting on a plane in the morning. Period.

Chapter Five

She hadn't lied about not being able to sleep. She tossed and turned, closed her eyes, then flopped onto her back and lay staring up at the ceiling.

She was wound up from performing and from Marc's kiss. Her blood hummed, her skin tingled, her thoughts—every one of them deliciously dirty—played like a porn film. He tasted like cinnamon from the gum he used all the time. Hot and spicy and sweet...

She tried to think about something else.

But the only other thing that came to mind was the reason Marc was here with her in Laramie in the first place.

She was on her way home to Justice.

Which meant she was on her way to admitting to Luke, her dad, even herself that the music hadn't worked out, her stardom hadn't happened, she'd messed up big time and they'd been right. Right to think she'd be better off in Justice, with them, safe and sound.

And bored. And restless. And always wanting more.

No matter what had happened in Seattle, she didn't regret any of it. She wished a few things had been different. She wished the band had stayed together and done something big. She wished they could have recorded an album with a major label. She wished that Matt Lauer wanted to interview her on the Today show.

She wished Paul had used a condom.

But there were a lot of things she wouldn't change. The people she'd met, the things she'd learned, the fact that she'd truly been on her own for the first time in her life and survived.

And when she wasn't puking or thinking about all of the things she didn't know and hating the fact that the only responsible thing to do was move back to Justice, she thought that maybe this baby thing could be okay.

She didn't know anything about babies, but the baby wouldn't know anything about her either. She could start completely fresh, clean slate, all of that.

That was definitely appealing.

And she did know a couple of things about being a mom. Things she'd learned the hard way from losing her own— nothing can truly replace the role of a mother in a child's life and she is the center of that child's universe, for better or worse.

Her mom had divorced her dad when she was ten. He'd been awarded custody and her mom, needing a way to support herself, had decided to go back to college. She was accepted into a program out of state so her visits had been few and far between. Then she remarried and had more children and the gap between them widened. That hole had never healed completely.

That was the bottom line. Her mom had failed in a lot of ways as a mother, yet Sabrina had always loved her. Sabrina had never been the best at anything, but she would be everything to her kid for a long time.

She wanted to be deserving of that.

She clenched her fists, then forced herself to relax. She didn't want to go to Justice and she would love to take Marc up on his offer of money and support. She could go anywhere, start over, try again.

But she was having a baby.

Things weren't about her anymore.

She was going to prove to everyone—to herself—that she wasn't entirely selfish and foolish. She was going to do the right thing for this child, no matter what it meant for her. Going home where Kat could help her, where her child would have a grandparent, where the crime rate was zero and the educational system was superb, was the right thing to do. In Justice her son or daughter could ride his or her bike up and down the sidewalks without worrying about traffic, could play at the park without fear of strangers and could trick-or-treat without concern over what was in the candy.

He or she could have Sabrina's childhood.

With one important difference—there would be unconditional parental love, reinforced daily.

She heard Marc shift in the bed closest to the window. There had been one room, but two beds. Which helped. Some.

"Marc?" she whispered, not sure if he was sleeping but hoping he wasn't.

"Hmm?"

"Are there any jobs open in Justice?"

She heard him shift again. She wondered briefly what he was sleeping in. He hadn't exactly packed a bag for this trip. But she quickly stopped those thoughts. She'd been serious earlier when pointing out that sleeping together would complicate living in the same town. To say the least.

"Jobs like what?"

"Anything. I need to find something."

He yawned. Then said, "Nope. Nothing. Everything's completely full."

She rolled her eyes in the dark. He didn't want her back in Justice but that was pathetic.

"Guess I'll have to look into the stripper thing after all."

"There are a couple of good street corners," he said. "You could probably start your own business."

"Lemonade stands pay well in Justice?"

He chuckled softly. "If *lemonade* is the west coast term for hooker, then sure."

She smiled. "Maybe I'll go for mistress. Who's the richest guy in town?"

Marc said nothing for a moment. "Luke and I are doing pretty well."

She turned to her side so she could face his bed. "Wow. Seriously? You guys are the richest? I should have been nicer to you before this."

It wouldn't surprise her if they were doing that well. The Camelot was amazing and they were both hometown boys, well-liked and respected. It was the perfect set up for success.

It also didn't surprise her that her heart kicked up a bit thinking about becoming Marc's mistress. It was ridiculous, but she couldn't help it.

"Don't know if we've passed Mr. Jensen yet," Marc replied.

Carl Jensen, the bank President, was at least sixty. "Mrs. Jensen taught me piano lessons. I can't do that to her."

"That's the disadvantage to trying to set up business in your hometown I guess," he said.

"Another argument for your side."

"Right. You'd be a great mistress, but you better expand the radius."

"Thanks. I guess."

They were quiet for a minute. Then she asked, "You're as crazy about Justice as Luke is aren't you?"

He shifted again in the dark. "I love Justice. It's home. My family and friends are there. The lifestyle in Justice is something I appreciate. But no, I don't love it as much as Luke does."

She didn't think anyone did. Even her father. He loved it, but more because of who he was there. Luke sincerely loved the town and everything about it. "For Luke The Camelot is about being an important part of the town," she said. "Making a place where the town can get together and have fun. And something to draw people in from other places."

"Yeah," Marc said quietly. "He dreamed up the restaurant when we were sophomores in high school. He loves that it's something special in town and something special about the town."

"How about you?" She'd wanted to love Justice—or anyplace—like that. She had never felt that tied or rooted anywhere.

"It's going to sound corny."

She smiled. "I won't tell anyone."

He gave a big sigh and the mattress creaked as he moved again. "For me it's about taking something that's ordinary—

food, eating, a basic meal—something everyone needs and has every day, but making it even more than they expect. Making it special."

She wasn't sure what to say for a moment. This was a side to Marc she'd never seen and hadn't even imagined. "That's why you wanted to be a chef?"

"It fit. I wanted to be in business in Justice with Luke. The restaurant was his idea, but being a chef fit, the business and me."

He was quiet for a few seconds and Sabrina sensed that she didn't want to interrupt or she'd miss something big.

Finally he said, "It's what the Hamiltons did for me."

She had to swallow hard. Still she said nothing, hoping he'd go on.

"They took me in but they did so much more than give me the basics. It wasn't just a roof over my head or food on the table. It was that, plus love and acceptance and laughter and..." He trailed off and cleared his throat. "They gave me everything and they didn't have to give me anything."

She was choked up. By Marc. Oh, boy.

"Hope you can see why I'm not going to let you hurt Luke again. It would hurt everyone else too. And I will do whatever I can to keep that family from having any heartache."

Crap. He really meant it.

Marc cursed under his breath.

"I have a good reason for not being able to tell him I don't want him," she said.

She didn't know why but it was important to her that Marc not think she was a heartless bitch. Which she was quite sure he did. Understandably. She'd started the whole thing. She'd wondered so many times if she hadn't asked Luke to kiss her if that ring would have stayed safely in his pocket—forever.

She didn't think Marc was going to answer and wondered if she should go on.

Finally he asked, "What reason?"

"Do you care?"

He didn't make a sound and she would have thought he was trying to think of a polite way of saying no, but this was

Marc—he'd never hesitated to say negative things to her.

"It's the damnedest thing," he finally said. "But I think I do care."

"Because of Luke?" she couldn't help but ask.

"Sure, let's say it's because of Luke."

She smiled. She liked Marc. Wow.

Of course, she'd never spent this much time with him before and she couldn't help but wonder if they had been stuck alone together before if they would have ended up as friends. Or more.

She stopped that train of thought immediately.

It wouldn't have mattered. She hadn't seriously dated anyone, knowing her plan was to see the country with only her guitar as company. She'd adamantly avoided anyone she thought she could be serious with because that would have made it more difficult to leave.

Marc could have been a serious one. Surprisingly. So she never would have dated him.

"My dad grew up in Justice," she started. "But he was always wild—getting into trouble, causing problems. The high point was in his early twenties when he and a buddy burned down a barn. He was arrested for arson and spent five years in prison."

"I had no idea."

"Nobody talks about it. I didn't know for years. When he got out my mom didn't want to come back to Justice but he convinced her that it was his chance to prove he was a new man. And the town let him start over."

"Yeah," Marc said gruffly. "I know how second chances feel."

Dang. Sabrina's heart tripped. He was funny and even kind of sweet, but if Marc had vulnerabilities it was really going to throw her. He was going to keep reminding her that he wasn't going to let anything bad—including her—happen to Luke and his family but she knew there was absolute truth behind everything he said.

"After that, he was determined to be the perfect guy," she continued. "He wanted to contribute to the town, be an upstanding citizen. And raise the perfect daughter." She took a deep breath. She'd often wondered if she'd known about her dad's past if she would have understood him better and understood the pressure he put on her. "He pushed me into everything he thought Justice would see as a sign that he was doing a good job. But I didn't care about being Homecoming Queen or being on student council. Girl Scouts were boring for me, I sucked at sports, I didn't care about committees and community service."

"You and your dad argued?"

"Outright fought. A lot. Until Luke got involved."

Sabrina heard Marc breathe deep and wished she could see his face.

"How did Luke get involved exactly?"

Luke had become her hero one morning when she was thirteen. "One night Luke found me in his tree house crying. Dad and I had fought about him signing me up for a four-day project rebuilding this tiny country church that had been hit by a tornado. It was a nice project, don't get me wrong, but I had zero interest. Dad was going to force me to go with him and I was way more upset about the fact that he didn't care how I felt or giving me a choice than I was about going."

"What'd Luke do?"

"He told me not to worry about it and helped me sneak back in my window. Then the next morning he came over, told my dad he heard about the project and asked if he could go."

"He took your place?"

"From then on. Everything my dad wanted to do, Luke did. When Dad was mad at me about something, Luke would come over and distract him by asking for help fixing something or for advice. If my dad was getting upset about me not doing something, Luke would do it instead."

"I always wondered why Luke spent so much time at your house before your boobs developed."

She appreciated him lightening the moment. "That's the funny thing. He volunteered for that building project to get Dad to leave me alone, but he had a great time. They camped out at the build site and Dad taught him to build a campfire and all that stuff. Luke ate it up. You know that his dad was gone all the time with business and this was some major male bonding."

"He always really enjoyed the stuff he did with your dad."

"Yeah. In fact, Luke quickly became my dad's biggest fan."

"Meaning he agreed with everything your dad thought?"

"Pretty much. Dad was off my back since he had Luke, but slowly Luke started trying to talk me into things like getting more involved at school, going on trips with them..."

"Giving up your music."

She swallowed hard. "Yeah. That and being content with a life in Justice. As we got older he got more insistent. He was almost worse than my dad."

"And when you moved back with us after college he thought you'd made your choice."

She, Luke, Marc and Kat had rented a U-Haul and moved back to Justice together that summer after college. Kat went on to medical school in September and construction on the restaurant had been completed in October. Sabrina had left town on October twelfth.

Her throat grew tight. "I know." She could feel the tension from Marc. She took a deep breath. "It's the only thing Luke's ever wanted from me."

"You regret not staying? Not saying yes?" He sounded angry.

"I just... He's never asked me for anything. Except to be with him."

"And you think you owe him something?"

"I do owe him."

"Son of a bitch."

She jumped, then heard and saw the shadow of Marc shift to sitting on the edge of the bed.

"You like to keep him hanging on because you like being important to him," he accused. "Not because you feel some debt to him."

"Of course I like being important to him! He's a great guy. Being important to him is a compliment."

It meant she wasn't a total loss. She had redeeming

qualities for a guy like Luke to care. He'd seen her selfish, rebellious moments, the moments when her own father didn't like her and he'd wanted her anyway. That had felt good. It still did.

"After all he did for me, after all he meant to me... If I'd stayed, I wouldn't have been able to say no to him."

"Fuck," Marc muttered.

She heard the mattress squeak and felt more than saw him stand.

"I'm going out."

"Now?" Clothes rustled and she heard what sounded like a knee against a chair followed by an expletive.

"Yes, now. We're done."

Then the door opened and shut and she was alone.

Pregnant and alone. Again.

Oh, and pathetic. She couldn't forget pathetic.

"Okay, Seattle, let's go." He smacked her butt as he walked by the bed. "Time's a-wastin'."

Sabrina rolled to her back and blinked. It was morning already? No way.

She was equally surprised that she'd slept at all.

He rushed her through showering and getting dressed simply by being a damned nuisance and nagging her incessantly. Forty minutes later they were walking through the sliding glass doors of the Laramie airport.

"This is a waste of time," she said for the third time as Marc strode ahead of her a good ten feet, her bag in tow.

"You're getting on a plane."

She glanced at the monitor listing departures. Sixty minutes from now she could be on a plane that would take her to Nashville.

But no. She had to resist. The plane ticket to Nashville was the new umbrella drink in her life. It wasn't the problem in and of itself—the problem was what it would allow her to do. Like make bad decisions, indulge, and forget that she knew better.

No. She was sticking with her plan. The more she wanted something, the harder she was going to resist.

"I'm not getting on a plane." She felt that she'd said it as resolutely as she possibly could.

"You know it's a good idea."

It probably was, from his perspective. But his perspective was minus one important piece of information—the baby.

"Marc, I'm going to Justice. At least for a while."

He glanced down at his BlackBerry, then up at the departures. "Eleven twenty-five. You'll be in Seattle by five twenty-five." He started for the ticket counter.

"I'm not going back to Seattle." That much was for sure.

He stopped, sighed and turned back. "Fine. How about New York?"

"No."

"San Antonio. Gorgeous city."

"No." She crossed her arms and watched him. She could do this all day.

"Kansas City. Still closer to home but..."

"No."

"San Diego."

She studied her nails.

"Vegas."

She put her arms overhead and stretched.

"New Orleans. You'd love it there."

She put her hands on her hips and started humming.

Marc came toward her, his eyes stormy, jaw tight. "Then *I'll* decide." He took her upper arm in a firm grip that was unbreakable and started again toward the counter.

Sabrina tried to dig her heels in, but he was strong and determined. She tried to pull free from his grip, but he held on. So she tried pleading.

"Come on, Marc. You don't know the whole story. I have a good reason. A few months. Let me get back on my feet. I'll stay away from Luke..." But he wasn't listening. They were in line at the counter behind two businessmen, three college-aged girls and a family of six. There were also four security guards.

It was Marc's own fault. He wasn't listening. He wasn't being rational.

He left her with no choice.

"No!" she suddenly shouted. "You can't make me go!"

Heads turned—including Marc's—and conversation stopped.

"I'm pregnant! You can't just put me on a plane and forget about me!"

Marc looked down at her in shock. His lips barely moved as he said, "Not. Funny."

"I'm not joking! I need to stay! This baby deserves a good home!"

"Knock it off, Sabrina," he said tightly.

"No, I won't shut up! You can't do this. Please don't make me go!" She threw herself at him, wrapping her arms tightly around his waist and burying her head in his chest.

Marc dropped her bag and his hands went to her shoulders. He started pushing as she heard, "Sir, we're going to have to ask you to come with us."

She turned her face so that she didn't have to look up at Marc but could see the two security guards standing with their hands on their guns.

She felt Marc take a breath, readying a response, so she jumped in. "I didn't mean to get pregnant. It was an accident. But he can't make me leave. I want to be home. I want to raise my baby in my hometown."

"Ma'am, you need to settle down. We're going to help you, but we need to talk to you both. Quietly and calmly."

She gripped Marc tighter, feeling his anger in the tension through his whole body. "I want him to take me home, where I can be with my friends and family. Then he can pretend to know nothing about this. I just want him to take me home."

"Ma'am, you need to calm down." One of the guards stepped forward and reached out a hand. "I need you to come with me. We'll straighten this out."

She didn't look at Marc as she extricated herself and let the guard take her arm, but she turned back and said to the other guard, "He's going to tell you I'm not even pregnant. You watch.

103

He's going to say he knows nothing about this."

She let the guard lead her away but she could feel Marc's anger stretching across the distance even as it widened.

It was his own damned fault. All he had to do was drive the car east and not give her any opinions and everything would have been good.

Marc had most definitely wanted to strangle Sabrina in the past. But never as much as he did when he saw her sashaying her way toward him down the airport hallway an hour later.

An hour during which he tried to convince the guards about his real relationship with Sabrina, what they were doing in Laramie and that she was lying about being pregnant.

Unfortunately, the story sounded hokey even to him after a while and he finally admitted that Sabrina was his girlfriend, he'd knocked her up and he promised to take her to Justice so she could be with her family.

He didn't—couldn't—say a word to Sabrina as she got in the passenger side of the car and strapped on her seatbelt. He drove out of the parking garage, got onto the road leading to the interstate, merged with the interstate traffic and headed for Justice.

In fact, it was thirty minutes before he said a word.

"Unbelievable."

She didn't seem surprised that he'd finally spoken. "I told you I wasn't getting on a plane. You should have listened."

"They were ready to call the real cops."

"But they didn't."

"I thought your talents were limited to singing. You missed your call as an actress. Of course," he continued. "Actors basically get paid to lie. Shouldn't surprise me that you're good at that."

"I didn't lie."

He snorted.

"You *were* trying to put me on a plane against my will."

"And what about the part about my being the father of your

unborn baby?"

"They jumped to the conclusion that you were the father. I never said that."

"But you did shout out in the middle of the airport that you were pregnant."

"Yes."

"That wasn't a lie?"

"No."

"See, so..." He glanced at her sharply. "What did you say?"

"I said no."

"No what?"

"No that wasn't a lie."

"No *what* wasn't a lie?"

She took a deep breath, then let it out. "I am pregnant."

They drove in silence for nearly half an hour, both lost in thought after Sabrina's confession.

Finally she asked to pull over to apply more cream then offered to drive—demanded actually—and he gratefully took the passenger seat, tipped it back and slept for almost an hour. The unconsciousness was a relief. He was exhausted, but even more there was no talking and he was unaware of scent of her body wash, the smooth expanse of her thigh and the absolute inability to keep his eyes from straying to her stomach every few minutes.

He awoke to her singing along with Faith Hill on the radio. The song transported him back to high school, where things had seemed impossible but were really impossibly simple. He glanced at Sabrina. She seemed comfortable and relaxed. He could have sworn he even saw a small smile on her lips.

He still couldn't believe it. She was pregnant.

And from here on out *everything* would be different.

He felt himself frown as he stared at the yellow dashed line flashing past them on the highway. Sabrina had never taken good care of herself. She was too skinny, too worried, too angry all the time.

How was she going to take care of a baby? She was used to late nights on the road, smoky bars, loud music. She'd always been a night owl. How was she going to get up in the middle of the night with a crying infant? She also couldn't cook worth a damn. In college she'd survived on delivery pizza and microwave dinners, or the things she ate at his and Luke's house. Baby food would get her through for awhile, but eventually the child would be older and would want real food.

She hardly ever spent money on herself. She would wear her shoes right out, a fact that used to drive her father crazy. Luke had once believed that she never bought new clothes to annoy her dad, but Marc couldn't help but wonder if it wasn't because she felt that clothes were too trivial to worry about.

She needed someone to take care of *her* while she took care of the baby.

Someone. Like, oh, maybe the father of the child?

"Who's the father?" He couldn't believe the question hadn't occurred to him before this.

Sabrina looked over at him, seemingly startled. "No one you know."

He waited but she seemed to be content leaving it at that. He wasn't content, however.

"And when will he be joining you in Justice?" he asked with mock nonchalance.

Marc irrationally and vehemently hated the idea that there was a man who would be sharing all of this with Sabrina. It was the most asinine thing he'd probably ever felt, but there it was.

"He won't be." She stared at the road.

"Ever?"

"Ever."

Okay. That was something he couldn't help but be curious about. "Why not?"

"We aren't together, a couple, whatever. He's just a guy I met one weekend and this was totally unplanned. And I don't want him to be involved. End of story."

Marc felt relieved and intensely interested at the same time.

"Is he—"

"It's really none of your business. You don't know him,

you'll never meet him, he's not in the picture. End. Of. Story."

Fine. He could live with that. For now.

"Have you thought about how much work a baby is going to be?" he asked.

Sabrina looked at him then back to the road. "What?"

"The baby. He or she will be a lot of work. Do you know anything about babies?"

"There are lots of books."

Sabrina was smart. She'd aced every class she'd taken in college for her business degree. She picked things up quickly when she set her mind to something. Her music had been like that. She played four instruments well and many others better than most. She read music but she could also play almost anything by ear after hearing it a few times. She had amazing range and tone when singing and she loved nearly every kind of music. It was the one thing that gave her complete joy and the thing that made her proud.

He was sure she would pick up many essentials from parenting books, but that wouldn't necessarily replace years of bad habits.

"You won't always have time to run and look something up. What happens when the baby gets a fever or starts throwing up?"

Her eyes widened. "I'll call the doctor."

"What happens when the baby is crying but isn't sick? What happens when you can't figure out what's wrong?"

She looked a little worried now. "I'd probably—I'll probably call Karen."

Marc smiled at that. Karen would love that. And that was a good answer. Karen would know. She was a great mother.

"What about the first time he gets called into the Principal's office?"

"My child will *not* get called into the Principal's office."

"You don't know that. What about the first time she asks you where babies come from?"

She groaned. "What are you trying to do?"

"Just pointing out that it won't be easy."

107

"Thanks, that's very supportive."

His grin died. Supportive? He was supposed to be supportive? They were friends now?

Then why did he still want to see her naked?

She was *pregnant* and about to turn his best friend's life upside down and he still wanted to know what color her nipples were.

This was not good. It was getting less good by the minute in fact.

"Luke is going to freak out."

"I know." She said it quietly.

"I would recommend not telling him right away."

"I'd prefer to never tell him."

"Actually, I'd prefer that too."

They sat in silence, Luke's pending reaction dominating their thoughts. After a moment she asked, "How far is it anyway?"

"Three and a half hours or so."

She sat up even straighter and swallowed hard.

Three and a half hours until she would be back in her hometown for the first time since leaving without a look back, vowing not to return until she was successful, rich and famous.

So much for that idea.

Sabrina settled back into her seat with the weight of what was happening and what she was doing suddenly overwhelming her. She did, however, fight the urge to curl her knees up to her chest and feel sorry for herself. She would handle this. She had to. She glanced over at the man sitting next to her.

The knot in her gut loosened as she studied Marc's profile.

That was stupid considering that he didn't like her, thought she was a screw up and didn't want her anywhere near Justice. But having him next to her made her feel better.

She was clearly delusional.

They listened to the radio without conversation for a long stretch, then stopped for the bathroom, food and to change drivers. They made small talk about Justice and the people who lived there. Marc told her about the restaurant and some trips he'd taken. She told him about the cities she'd seen and some of the funny stories that being on the road, in clubs every night playing live music, had produced.

Finally, Sabrina got her first look at her hometown in four years. They came over the top of the hill to the west of Justice and she looked down on the scene that she'd seen more times than any other she could think of. When she'd thought of Justice while away this was the picture her mind conjured.

She felt her throat tighten and tears prick the back of her eyes as they passed the city limit sign and started down Main Street. It was ridiculous that the sight of the swimming pool where she'd learned to swim could choke her up, but the nostalgia was crashing over her in waves. She was overwhelmed that the good memories from Justice were outnumbering the bad.

"It doesn't look like Kat's home yet."

They rolled past her best friend's house. A house Sabrina had never seen but that she knew Kat was crazy about.

"How can you tell?"

"The newspapers are still on the porch."

"Ah."

Now what? She couldn't go to her dad's and—

"You should come to my place."

She whipped her head to the side so fast that her neck hurt. "What?"

"Where else are you going to go?" Marc asked, his eyes still on the road. "Hell, we already stayed together last night. What difference does it make?"

It sounded simple enough.

But nothing about this was simple.

This wasn't just a visit. This wasn't just a long holiday weekend. This was going to be her life. For now anyway. For long enough, though, that everyone would know about the baby.

Only Marc and Kat knew she was pregnant. They were both still talking to her. She should cling to them.

"Okay. I'll stay with you until Kat gets home."

Marc carried her bag into the house through the back kitchen door and she had to smile thinking about how different this was than when he'd carried it into the airport.

"Guest room is second at the top of the stairs. I'll take your bag up."

She wasn't going to need the room for at least ten hours or so. "'Kay."

"Towels and stuff are in the bathroom."

Marc seemed uncomfortable for some reason. Good to know. "Great."

"Help yourself to any food in the kitchen."

"Thanks."

"I'd better go to work."

Her heart thumped. Work. At The Camelot. With Luke. "Is Luke there?"

"Probably."

"Are you going to tell him I'm here?"

Marc looked at her, then sighed. "He'll find out eventually. Isn't it better if I break it to him instead of him running into you?"

Yeah, maybe. Probably. Hell, she didn't know. "What do you think?"

"I think I need to tell him."

"That I'm here or..."

Marc shook his head. "Let's start with you being here. That will be enough of a shock."

She breathed again. "Yeah." She wasn't ready to see Luke, talk to Luke, or tell Luke about the baby.

Of course, she'd never be ready and she didn't think it could wait quite that long.

"I'm going to go up and change and then head out."

"I'll be fine."

"We'll...talk later."

She had no idea what that meant. He was the chef in a restaurant. He wouldn't be home until late. And she didn't expect him to entertain her, or cook for her, or play host.

He headed up the stairs two at a time, leaving her alone to study his house. She'd never been here. In college, he and Luke had shared a house with two other guys and she'd been there a number of times, but when they moved back to Justice they were all in transition and both guys moved back in with Dave and Karen until the restaurant got up and going. Kat had told her that they'd each bought a house the following year.

She smiled as she made her way through Marc's house. Photographs of his friends and family hung on the large wall across from the front door. She could see through the arched doorway into the living room. There was a fireplace and a huge, bulky dark gray couch, a big screen TV, an extensive home theater and music system and a coffee table piled high with magazines and newspapers and a coffee cup. There were more photos on the wall and along the mantel as well as some art prints hanging on the walls. Two floor lamps, three table lamps and an old video arcade game—Ms. Pac-Man—completed the cozy, obviously lived-in room.

It was comfortable. A real home. She found herself less surprised by Marc's surroundings than she would have guessed. She didn't think she knew him that well, but his house was somehow what she would have expected.

The house smelled good too—a combination of wood polish and lemon-scented cleaning fluid along with the spices that he used in his cooking.

It made sense that after losing his parents and going to live with the Hamiltons, family and home were important to Marc. She was surprised that she'd noticed that but now that she thought about it cooking, entertaining and collecting mementos were all habits that she associated with Marc, even in college. Comfort, happiness and security were important to him.

"I'm gonna..."

She turned toward his voice. He was dressed for work in gray pants and a black knit polo. He looked really, really good.

Marc stopped short at the bottom of the stairs. "Are you crying?"

She sniffed and smiled at him. "No."

"Yes you are. Are you okay?"

"I'm great. I like your house." She sniffed again.

"You do?"

"It's you."

Surprise lit his eyes. "What does that mean?"

"Sounds dumb, I know, since I didn't think we knew each other that well. But this place feels good."

He came forward and she realized that he'd been keeping a healthy distance between them. Probably a good idea since the minute he came a few inches closer she wanted nothing more than to have him fold her into his arms and complete the feeling of a safe, happy homecoming that was welling up inside of her.

Really weird since he wanted this homecoming less than anyone in the world.

Before she could think of any reasons why it was a bad idea, Sabrina took a large step toward him, wrapped both arms around his waist and hugged him tightly. It took a second, but she felt his arms around her a moment later. She closed her eyes, leaning into him fully. She breathed in the scent of soap and cinnamon—the spice she would forever associate with Marc—and absorbed the comforting warmth and strength of his chest.

"This feels good too," she whispered.

He cleared his throat, the sound rumbling through his chest against her ear. She felt his hand on the back of her head, stroking her hair and she moved her cheek against the softness of his shirt.

"Seattle—"

She pulled back enough to tip her chin up and meet his gaze. That's all it took.

"Ah, hell," he muttered just before his lips met hers.

Everything within her softened and melted into him.

It was a gentle kiss at first, his lips exploring hers, as if asking permission. But once she gave that permission, something else took a hold of them both. Passion, want, need quickly consumed them and their lips and tongues moved wildly, tasting and tempting, asking and answering a whole host of questions all at once. And the answer to the most important question resonated for them both even when Marc pulled back and stood staring down at her: *Yes, I want you.*

He took a deep breath. "That probably shouldn't keep happening. You sure you're okay?"

She nodded and smiled. "I'm absolutely okay. I..."

"You're tired," he said when she trailed off.

She shook her head. "No. I'm overwhelmed. It's been a long time since I've been in a place where I felt comfortable and been able to go to bed knowing that I'll be safe and not alone."

He pulled away, something flashing in his eyes. "How long?"

"How long what?"

"How long since you've felt safe going to bed?"

"A while," she admitted. It was over so she might as well tell him the truth. "There were these guys who lived down the hall who would come home drunk almost every night, make all kinds of noise and sometimes come banging on doors looking for more beer, or drugs, or..."

"Or?" Marc pressed, his jaw tight.

"Money. Whatever they needed."

"Did they ever threaten you?" His eyes were hard and Sabrina was glad they were so far from Seattle. If they'd been in her old apartment, she had no doubt Marc would have gone storming down the hall looking for her obnoxious neighbors.

She wasn't stupid. She knew those were all excellent reasons to choose Justice over Seattle to raise her child. She also knew she was lucky to have the choice. Not every single mom did.

"No, they never threatened me. But they did give my friends across the hall a hard time one night. One of the girls had to pull her gun out before they'd leave her alone."

"You lived across the hall from a woman who kept a gun?" Marc asked incredulously.

"She had a nasty ex-boyfriend."

"Hell," Marc said, pushing a hand through his hair. "Why did you stay there?"

"It was my home," she said with a shrug.

"That wasn't a home. Not if you were scared when you were

there," Marc said firmly.

Sabrina looked around the living room again and she knew she couldn't argue with that.

"Thanks for letting me stay here."

He swallowed and nodded. "No problem. I'll find Kat. Her receptionist likes me. You stay and rest. And eat later. Something good."

"I'm fine."

He gave her a dubious look. "You could pack your whole wardrobe in those bags under your eyes and you were heavier when you were in seventh grade than you are now."

She looked down at her waist. It would begin thickening anytime now, she supposed, though she wasn't exactly sure how this went. She'd probably need to get one of those books soon so she would know what to expect. But, he was right. She had lost a lot of weight.

"That doesn't mean the bags are very big. I don't have much of a wardrobe." She meant it as a joke, but his eyes narrowed.

"Then you'll need to go shopping too."

"I don't have any money."

"I know. I'll take care of it," he said through gritted teeth.

She didn't like that he might assume her lack of money was because of her inability to get or hold a job, or because she was terrible at managing her finances. Things hadn't been a piece of cake, but she'd done fine. And it wasn't her fault— Okay, it wasn't *entirely* her fault that Paul had stolen her credit cards and accessed her bank records online, then drained all her accounts. It wasn't like she'd had millions, but she'd had enough to pay her rent and bills. On time. In full. Every month, thank you.

Marc was assuming the worst of her and that annoyed her. She hadn't been living on the street, wasn't addicted to anything, wasn't in prison. She was pretty sure all of those possibilities had occurred to him and he should at least acknowledge that she'd done better than that.

"I will get my own clothes," she told him.

He raised an eyebrow at her surly tone.

"Right after I get a job."

"I'd recommend the corner at Fifth and Main."

Her eyes narrowed as she remembered their conversation from the night before. "Should I ask how you know where all the good hooker corners are in town?"

He leaned in close. "Women want to pay *me* when it's over. Trust me."

It was good he said things like that. If he stopped being irritating, she might like him all the time. And that would likely be a bigger problem than being penniless, alone and pregnant.

Chapter Six

Captain Crunch. That was all Sabrina could focus on as she made her way down the staircase. She'd seen it on the counter when she'd come through the kitchen. She loved Captain Crunch.

She'd ended up sleeping after all—for over an hour—then showering. She smelled like Marc's shampoo and soap—not necessarily a bad thing but more masculine than she was used to for sure—and was wearing a T-shirt she'd found on the chair in his room. Her clothes were all dirty. She hadn't had the money to stop at a Laundromat on her way to Justice. And she hadn't expected the trip to take her as long as it did. So, she'd thrown a load in the washer before she'd laid down—sleeping in the nude again like she had in Wyoming. She'd fallen asleep before transferring them to the drier.

The clock above the stove read one thirty-four.

Her students at the community center would be arriving for their two o'clock lesson. Summer break meant classes at the community center, the senior center and private lessons at the school. It was amazing to her that in the same day she could have students who were five years old and eighty-five years old, students from the poorest families in the area and students from the most affluent families. She loved it all and was incredibly proud of the programs she'd built. The private lessons were pretty straightforward—every instrument and ability level imaginable—but the programs for the at-risk kids and the seniors were about more than learning to play instruments. They were about music appreciation, composing, styles of music and the role music played in various cultures. It was fun, plain and simple, and she'd quickly learned that teaching others to appreciate and create music could be as fun as doing it herself.

She frowned at the pang of sadness she felt thinking about her students at both locations. Yes, she would miss them and for the first couple of weeks they'd miss her, but someone would take over. Both had become popular programs. Sure it had been her idea. Sure she had been the one carting all the instruments to and from. Sure it was always a thrill to see someone's face light up when she played the right note or when he strung those notes together into a song for the first time. But it could be a thrill for someone else. Nothing wrong with that.

She needed to focus on the things she would *not* miss. Not being able to nap in the middle of the day, for instance.

There was no doubt that she was more of a night person and sleeping through the morning into the afternoon had been commonplace in her life for a long time. The first two years had been spent on the road with the band, as everyone assumed. In clubs until the wee hours of the morning, working odd jobs— bartending, waitressing, cashier—to pay the bills, practice sessions in the evening or hitting the road to the next town. That was more the schedule her internal clock enjoyed. Napping in the afternoon again felt wonderful.

On top of that, the bed in Marc's guestroom was so comfortable, the quilt so cozy and the room so quiet that she'd been unable to resist. She'd probably still be sleeping but her bladder woke her up and then her anxiety about being back in Justice had not allowed her to go back to sleep.

Yep, she was sure napping would take the place of helping her students find the joy and comfort of music. No problem. Ha.

She poured a glass of orange juice and was pouring the Peanut Butter Captain Crunch cereal into a bowel when the back door banged open. She jumped, spilling little cereal balls all over the counter. She swung to find Marc inside the door, looking panicked.

"Go upstairs." He looked back over his shoulder.

"What are you talking about?"

"Get out of sight. Seriously." He came toward her, took her by the shoulders to point her in the direction of the living room and pushed. She dug her heels in.

"Marc, what's going on?" She was concerned now. "Why are—" She tried to face him.

"No!" He gripped her shoulders, preventing her from turning. "Upstairs."

She tripped over her own feet. "Marc!"

Suddenly he stopped pushing and his hands dropped away. "What are you wearing?"

"I'm doing laundry." She pointed to the bras she had hanging over the back of a kitchen chair. She pulled at the neck of the T-shirt. "This is yours."

His eyes widened. "Please tell me you have underwear on."

"I'm. Doing. Laundry," she repeated.

He closed his eyes and groaned. "You have to get out of here—"

"*Sabrina?*"

She turned in the direction of the amazed whisper.

Luke stood at the back door.

Crap. Hell. Damn.

She pasted on a big smile. "Hi, Luke."

"Sabrina?" he repeated, clearly shocked.

"Yeah. It's me." She wasn't ready for this. She knew eventually she would have to see him, but she'd thought she would be in control of when and where. Obviously, she wouldn't have chosen to see him for the first time barely dressed, in Marc's kitchen.

"You're a *terrible* listener," Marc muttered to her.

"What did you expect? You looked like a crazy person. I was *concerned*," she told him, her eyes still on Luke. He looked like he might throw up or something.

"Josie told me that he was on his way over to check the house for me. I drove like a maniac to beat him here."

"Good job," she commented dryly. "You couldn't call me? Would have saved you time and me a heart attack."

"You would have answered my phone?" he asked with a frown. "That's not cool."

"Well, I..." She realized he had a point there.

"My *God*. What are you doing here?" Luke finally interrupted.

"I'm...back."

Suddenly she was enfolded in Luke's arms.

"Holy shit," Luke whispered against her head.

That about summed it up.

"Are you okay? What happened? What are you doing here?" Luke crushed her to his chest. "When did you get here?"

She focused on the one question she felt prepared to answer. "Today. A few hours ago."

Luke was dressed for business with gray pants, a white shirt and a gray and black tie.

He pulled back but kept his grip on her upper arms. "You came to Marc's house when you got here? Why?"

"Marc came to pick me up. My car broke down on the way back." Yeah, that sounded as bizarre as she'd expected.

Luke looked confused. "Why didn't you call me?"

"I called the restaurant and he was the one who answered and when he heard the problem he offered to come. You were busy or something."

"Interviewing," Marc answered.

Sabrina looked at him quickly. He sounded annoyed. He was leaning against the counter, frowning, his arms crossed watching her and Luke.

His eyes dropped to her butt. "Maybe you should put some clothes on."

She blushed. She felt it—and hated it—at the same moment she became aware of the draft against the bare skin of her buttocks, revealed by the shirt pulling up while Luke hugged her. Only Marc could see. But that was more than enough to cause a hot flush.

"Right." She glanced from Marc to Luke and back. "Don't talk about anything interesting until I get back." She narrowed her eyes at Marc in particular.

"Nothing more interesting than the messed up order of drinking straws," Marc replied.

She pulled the hem of the T-shirt down as she turned and

hurried from the room.

Marc turned to face his friend and business partner. "There's a huge mess up with our drinking straw order."

"First I've heard of it," Luke said sarcastically. He crossed his arms and leaned back against the kitchen table, mimicking Marc's posture. He looked like he was waiting for something.

Marc had a pretty good idea what it was, but there was no way he was bringing up the reason Sabrina was back in Justice. No. Way. In. Hell.

He did not want Sabrina to tell Luke she was pregnant. He couldn't explain why but he didn't want Luke to know. Yet.

Because he would have to know eventually. Everyone would.

Just not yet.

He wanted a chance to talk to Sabrina. It felt like things weren't quite worked out. He wasn't sure why things needed to be worked out between them. Or what things even needed to be worked out. Or what worked out meant exactly.

But he wasn't ready for Luke to know.

He wanted to talk to her before she told anyone else.

Not that he knew what he was going to say. Or how he was going to explain to her why he needed to say it.

He was getting used to things having to do with Sabrina being complicated.

"I'm back." Sabrina breezed back into the room. She still wore Marc's T-shirt but now she also had his bathrobe on. Which was huge on her. It hung to her ankles, the shoulders were halfway to her elbows and the sleeves hung several inches past her fingers. At least she was covered.

"That's dressed?" he asked as she walked past.

"What part of doing laundry do you not understand?" She frowned at him.

"I need new machines. This is taking forever." Though he had a feeling that if it was anyone else, or she was wearing anything else, the time wouldn't have felt so torturously long.

"Luke." Sabrina moved toward the table. "I have something I need to tell you."

Marc started sweating as if he was in the middle of a run. *No. Not yet.*

How could he stop it, though?

Luke shifted where he was leaning on the counter but kept his arms crossed. Had he not known him so well, Marc wouldn't have realized he was incredibly uncomfortable, fighting hugging Sabrina again or storming out of the house. "How long are you staying?

"I, um..." Sabrina glanced at Marc. "A while. A few months for sure."

"Oh. I had no idea you were coming home." Luke was clearly trying to sound casual. Marc could hear the tension in his voice though.

"I didn't know until recently myself."

"Your dad doesn't know."

"No. Luke, I have some news."

She said it confidently and Marc felt his gut clench. *Not yet. I have to tell you...*

He had no idea what he had to tell her but he had to tell her *something*.

"Great," Luke replied. His fingers dug into his arms.

Marc could tell Luke was struggling to stay calm. He hated this. For both of them. This was going to be a bad moment. Luke Hamilton didn't yell. Often.

"I'm—"

"Oh, shit!"

Both Luke and Sabrina turned to face him.

"*What?*" Sabrina demanded.

"I forgot to tell you that the straws are backordered," Marc said looking at Luke. And avoiding looking at Sabrina.

"Oookay," Luke said slowly.

"It's going to be like two more weeks." In reality the straws would probably be there the next day. He'd straightened the whole order out that morning.

"Two weeks?" Luke looked confused.

"I was *talking*," Sabrina said through gritted teeth.

"This is important," Marc said. "It is our livelihood." He'd never used the word livelihood in his life.

She swung back to face Luke. "Luke, I'm—"

"Was that the buzzer on the dryer?" Maybe if she went into the laundry room he could find a way to follow her and tell her whatever it was that he needed to tell her so badly.

"*No.*" She glared at him over her shoulder. "I didn't hear anything." She turned back to Luke. "I—"

Marc panicked. He did the only thing he could think of and knocked the glass on the counter to the floor. Orange juice splattered everywhere. Especially down the back of Sabrina. And his bathrobe.

"What the f—" She spun, obviously irate. "What's your problem?"

"I knocked it off the counter. Accidentally. Sorry."

She glared at him for a minute, then her expression changed. Marc realized she'd figured out what he was up to.

She turned back to Luke and said quickly, "I'm pregnant."

Marc felt like she'd punched him in the stomach. Luke looked like he felt the same way.

Sabrina looked surprised that it had come out that way.

A minute ago she'd been planning to say it and now she looked surprised.

He shook his head. The woman drove him nuts.

Then he focused on his friend. The man who looked like he was about to have a heart attack.

"Luke?" He moved forward in case he needed to catch him.

"You're *pregnant*?" Luke asked, staring at Sabrina.

She nodded.

"Wh... How... Who..."

"Doesn't matter," she said, waving all of his partial questions away. "I am. I'm here. I thought you should know."

"Who's the father?" Luke demanded. "Where is he?"

Sabrina faced him and said firmly, "That doesn't matter. He isn't here, he isn't coming here. He's not an issue."

"I want to know who the hell he is," Luke said. "Is he going to be responsible? Is he going to marry you?"

Sabrina was shaking her head before he even finished. "No. To all of that. He's not involved with me or the baby and it's going to stay that way."

Luke's face got redder and Marc grew concerned.

"Buddy, are you—" Marc started.

But Luke turned on his heel and stomped to the door. The kitchen door slammed behind him hard enough to make Sabrina jump. The next thing they heard was Luke's truck roaring out of the driveway.

She blew out a long breath. "Dammit."

"You didn't think that reaction was a possibility?" Marc asked dryly, moving to get a towel to clean up the juice on the floor.

"I didn't know what to expect. I just had to get it over with." She watched him mop up the juice and asked, "What got into you with all the stupid interruptions?"

"I didn't think the timing was right."

"When is the best time to tell my best friend, who almost proposed to me once, who I haven't seen in four years, that I'm pregnant with another man's baby?" she asked.

"Maybe not in the first ten minutes of seeing him again." Marc stood with the dishrag. "Based on experience," he added, looking toward the door that he was surprised still had an intact glass window in it.

She looked at the door too and sighed. "Yeah, maybe."

The Camelot was beautiful. She'd almost forgotten how incredibly warm and welcoming it was. Going to dinner at The Camelot was like a mini-vacation—exactly the way Luke and Marc had intended it to be.

The Camelot's main dining room had a stone fireplace in the center that opened on two sides and was surrounded by heavy round oak tables with padded chairs. Soft music played and the dishes were china and crystal, yet the atmosphere was friendly rather than conservative, and even though families were seated at their own tables, conversation was often exchanged from table to table, with laughter the most prominent noise in the room.

They had extended the comfort to the waiting area as well. It was the largest she'd ever seen in a restaurant, almost one-fourth of the entire building. The room was filled with smaller glass tables surrounded by overstuffed armchairs and even the occasional loveseat. Drinks, specialized coffees, appetizers and desserts were served there and people felt more like they were sitting in a friend's living room than waiting in a restaurant. No one minded waiting out here. The food was certainly worth it, the service was the best and, above all, the atmosphere was relaxing and uplifting. It was *the* social spot in Justice and for nearly a ninety-mile radius. They also did a pretty decent business from people traveling through the area who heard from the locals that they had to stop and people who'd stopped once and then made a point to end up in town around dinnertime when they came through the next time.

Besides the restaurant, there was a large reception hall with a high ceiling, a polished wood floor and one wall made entirely of glass. It was beautiful on clear nights when the moon and stars shone in. Every Saturday there was entertainment of some kind from bands to comedians and once a month they opened the hall for a youth dance.

There was also a lounge with a huge center bar that served every drink imaginable. They had several non-alcoholic specials and the entire establishment was non-smoking. There was a huge jukebox in the corner and three pool tables in back. This area then led out to a patio area complete with tables, three grills and another smaller bar. This was the area that, according to Kat, they wanted to expand with a sand volleyball court and outside activities during the summer.

All in all, Marc and Luke had done exactly what they'd always dreamed of doing. They had created a place where people could go to see friends and family and feel welcome, comfortable and at home. They also, of course, employed all locals, making an important economic contribution to the town.

Both guys felt strongly that they were giving back to the community that had given them so much.

The restaurant was quiet now, between the lunch and

dinner crowds, and even the front hostess podium was vacant at the moment.

She took a seat in one of the chairs by the door. She'd hung out at Marc's for a while, but she'd found herself getting comfortable. Really comfortable. She loved Marc's house. It felt good being there and she knew that she couldn't let that sink in. She was moving in with Kat as soon as her friend got back to town and that would be only temporary too. They hadn't set a timeline of course, but she couldn't live with her friend forever.

The problem was, Sabrina wasn't good with permanence. There was a lot of pressure to it. She had a hard time doing anything with forever in mind. What if she chose wrong?

It was easier to face things knowing that it wouldn't last or that she could change her mind. She lived in apartments with no longer than a six-month lease. She had roommates that never stayed more than two or three months. She had jobs that she could leave if she grew frustrated or bored or something better came along.

Those were the thoughts that brought her back to the fact that she was embarking upon the most permanent thing she'd ever done—being a mom. There weren't re-dos with that. She couldn't change her mind or move on if it didn't work out.

Her mom had done that.

Sabrina was in this for the long haul no matter what.

And it scared her to death.

So she wasn't doing anything else that required a long-term commitment. She wasn't doing anything crazy like buying a house and she had to get out of Marc's before she started thinking about how great it would be to have a home like that.

Now she was sitting in the only other place in town she could really go—The Camelot.

She realized rather quickly that she didn't have any friends other than Kat and Luke here anymore. Not friends who would drop their work day to come and see her anyway. Which was her fault. She hadn't kept in touch with anyone. Leaving had been hard enough without keeping relationships going. She knew she'd missed weddings and birthdays and holidays. But it was easier to ignore it when she wasn't getting invitations, announcements and cards.

Which all meant that she was pretty lonely and bored right now.

If this was what her days were going to be like, she needed something to do.

With that thought, she headed for the bar.

He should have known.

The strange woman behind the bar who told Josie, the hostess, that she was "just fine, thank you", was Sabrina.

"Miss being surrounded by liquor bottles and the smell of beer?"

"I'm auditioning." She didn't look surprised to see him. She didn't even look up from measuring a clear liquid into a blender.

"For what?"

"You need a bartender. I saw the sign up front and heard you say Luke was interviewing someone the other day."

"Maybe we hired that person and don't need any more help."

"That's why I'm auditioning. I'm going to show you I'm better than that person."

"You don't even know who it is."

"Doesn't matter."

He shook his head, fighting a smile. "You could re-think the stripper thing, though. That's something we haven't tried here."

"How about in about three months? That should be attractive." She looked up and smiled at him as she patted her stomach.

His own stomach clenched. Shouldn't being pregnant make her less appealing to him? It wasn't working that way. At all.

Great.

"You know how to do more than pour beer?" he asked, looking at the blender she was adding ice and some green liquid to.

"Well, gee, if I could just find the directions to how to use the bottle opener, I'd be okay."

He caught himself before he smiled.

"You're trial period starts today. You have three days to prove that you know what you're doing. You'll start at thirteen dollars an hour. Here's a book you might find helpful." He tossed a paperback book toward her. She caught it easily and turned it over to look at the cover. It was a recipe book—page after page of drink recipes.

"Trial period?" She propped a hand on her hip. "What if I don't do well?"

"Then I guess you'll have to find another job."

She gaped at him. "You would seriously not hire me?"

He sighed instead of smiling. "I have a business to run, Sabrina. People come here expecting something and I make sure they get it. If you can't handle the job, I can't hire you. It's up to you."

"Be back here in thirty minutes," she said, putting the top on the blender. "You'll be sorry you ever doubted me."

Then she hit the on button, drowning out anything he would have said in reply.

Twenty minutes later, Marc headed back for the bar. He wouldn't admit it to anyone—even the CIA under threat of imprisonment—but he'd been unable to concentrate on anything else since leaving her.

Which in and of itself was a problem.

He couldn't give her a job here if it was going to distract him this badly. He had a kitchen to oversee, a business to run. They were known for their food—specifically his own concoctions and their desserts. He couldn't get sloppy.

But maybe it was that he was afraid Luke might find her.

He had been in his office with the door shut most of the morning. Then he'd headed out to meet with a new glassware supplier. But he'd be back eventually. And she'd be here. In Justice.

Luke would spend time with her again at some point.

That reality shouldn't make Marc antsy.

He rounded the corner and saw she was alone at the bar. She was pouring something pink into a glass.

Almost every glass from the bar was full, each with something different. Jars and bottles and cans littered the counters behind the bar, empty of their ingredients now. Sabrina herself was covered with streaks and drops of all kinds of liquor, fruit juice and a few unidentifiable ingredients.

"How's it going?" he asked, carefully keeping his expression neutral. If he laughed, she'd be furious.

"Fine." She glanced around her, then down at her clothes. "I guess."

"What are you doing?" he asked.

She spread her arms wide, encompassing the whole bar and all of its many containers. "Using the book you gave me."

"You made every single thing in there?" Marc took a seat on one of the barstools.

"The complicated ones. You're going to sample each. Then you're going to decide if I get the job or not."

"You have three days."

"I don't want three days. I want you to decide today."

It wasn't exactly his terms, but he should have expected that. And he liked her grit. "That's risky. I can't base the decision solely on mixing drinks."

She pushed her hair back from her face with the back of one sticky hand. "What else?"

"You'll have to wait on some customers while I watch and assess your style."

She frowned at him. "They'll be people I know."

"Yes. Were you hoping to only wait on strangers? Because in that case this is not the right job for you."

"No, of course not. I was hoping to avoid facing the whole town so soon. But I can't really say why." Her brow wrinkled into a confused little frown. "Might as well get it over with, I guess."

He hated her look of insecurity. He much preferred her looking irritated. "So, you're doing all of this—" he swept his hands over the top of the bar indicating all of the drinks she'd made, "—to impress me."

She frowned. "I..." she said slowly. "I'm doing it to show you that you should give me the job."

"Because I'll be your boss. You basically need to impress me."

It was obvious she didn't like his choice of words. One eyebrow up, she crossed her arms. "I suppose."

"I think I'll like being in charge of you." He picked up one of the drinks closest to him and peered at it as if he was extremely intrigued by it. He sniffed it, swirled it around and then sipped from it. It was very good. But he was mostly interested in getting Sabrina riled up.

He had no reason other than that it was fun.

"In charge of me?" Sabrina repeated. "I think I might need some examples."

He picked up another drink and tasted it, licked his lips—it was also quite good—and then replaced it on the bar before answering. "The most obvious that comes to mind is your attitude. I have a strict policy about insubordination."

He chose an orange frothy drink a few inches away, pretending rapt interest, as if the drinks were much more interesting than the conversation they were having.

When Sabrina didn't reply, he risked a glance at her face. She looked more suspicious than annoyed. "Basically you're saying that I have to do everything you tell me to."

That sounded appealing and, unfortunately, sexual. He was sure she didn't mean it that way, but that was how his mind took it. "Basically."

She propped one hand on her hip. "And what happens if I don't?"

He dipped his finger into a glass on the end of the bar and tasted the concoction before glancing up. "Punishment, of course."

When he glanced at her, her cheeks were pink. "How do you punish your current employees? Because I'm pretty sure a lot of them don't like you."

He grinned. "They don't have to like me. They have to do what I tell them to."

"What kinds of things are you going to tell me to do?"

Oh, this was too fun. And easy. If he wanted to shock her, or tease her—or seduce her, he could come up with all kinds of things.

Of course he didn't want to do any of those things.

Sure and he planned to walk on the moon next month.

"Get me coffee, for instance."

Her eyes narrowed. "Uh, huh. I hear arsenic dissolves nicely in hot liquid."

He would not smile. But it was tough. "Wash my apron."

Her eyes narrowed. "You should know that I have a condition that manifests by spontaneously sewing pink ruffles on things."

"Alphabetize my recipes."

"The only letters I know are F and U."

He moved around the end of the bar, smiling in spite of himself. "How about inventory? I need someone to count my mushrooms."

"Yeah, once you run out of fingers it gets tough doesn't it?" She didn't move away from him as he came to stand directly in front of her.

"You have to handle them just right. Not everyone can do it the way I like."

"Are we still talking about mushrooms?" she asked.

Not exactly. He smiled. Sexual innuendos with food were easy. There were a million.

As important as food was in his life, it was surprising that he'd never been that into using it during sex. Not even chocolate syrup or whipped cream.

But he wanted to lick whatever that blue streak was off her cheek. And if there were any that had dipped under the neckline of her white T-shirt...

"Do you like mushrooms?" he asked.

"I like...mushrooms...*so* much," she purred.

It occurred to him to worry, but he loved the way she was tiptoeing her fingers up his chest.

"But I'm thinking I'd be good with a mallet."

She was such a smart ass.

He lifted a finger and ran it through the blue streak. Then he sucked it clean. Sweet, tart and delicious.

"Mmm."

She didn't move away from him. "Raspberry."

"What do you put it in?"

"This one. It's a Magic Pixie."

He sipped. It was great. But— "That's not in the recipe."

"I know. My invention. Or addition at least."

He couldn't help but admire that. He was a chef. Combining flavors to make them even better was his passion.

"But that's not the recipe."

Her eyebrows went up. "So? It's better."

"You have to follow the rules. No insubordination, remember?"

She narrowed her eyes. "Rules don't always make things better."

"They generally make things safer."

"Raspberry syrup is dangerous?" She smiled.

"On you it is."

"I—"

But her response was cut off as he dipped his head bringing his lips to the corner of her mouth, then flicked his tongue out and licked up the little bit of syrup there.

With a small sigh—resignation or surrender, he wasn't sure—she turned her head, just ten degrees to the left, and their lips met.

Then she opened her mouth and Marc's groan was absolutely in surrender. He slid his tongue deep along hers.

Fire exploded in his chest, lust shot straight to his groin, and he cupped the back of her head at the same time she opened her mouth wider, accepting him deeper.

Her hands went to his chest, gripping his shirt in both hands and he felt her go up on tiptoe. He slanted his mouth, tasting her, relishing that she returned every stroke. His hand lifted to cup her breast and she moaned. The hard tip of her nipple seemed to brand the center of his palm.

"Tell him I'll call him back."

Luke.

Marc's head came up quickly. Luke was coming down the hall toward the bar.

"About three," Luke called to whoever he was talking to—likely Josie.

Marc managed to let go of Sabrina, step back and straighten his shirt before Luke strode into the room.

Sabrina looked dazed. And well-kissed.

Her lips were swollen, her cheeks flushed and she was breathing hard. She was also staring up at him and looking like she was more than ready to drive right back in. Which would be great, if not for—

"I'm glad you're both here."

Luke.

Marc turned to face his friend. He moved a few inches away from Sabrina, aware that they were standing way too close to look casual.

Luke didn't seem to notice. Hell, he probably couldn't see around the huge bouquet of roses—easily three dozen—that he carried.

"I bought you a car," he announced.

Sabrina looked from Luke to Marc and back. "You bought *me* a car?"

"And I've been thinking." He looked serious and determined.

"Wait," Sabrina interrupted. "You bought me a *car?*"

"Yes." Luke looked impatient. "It's nothing fancy, but will get you around." He handed her the keys.

She didn't even glance down at them. "Luke, you didn't have to—"

He cut her off. "You need things. Like the car. And that got me thinking."

"About what?" Sabrina seemed to be ignoring the overwhelming bunch of flowers that were so obviously for her Marc felt like laughing.

Except that his best friend giving an obscene arrangement of flowers to the women he'd been making out with was *not* funny.

"The weather, I'm sure," Marc muttered sarcastically. What else could Luke have possibly been thinking about all day other than *her?*

"This whole thing. There's only one solution," Luke said.

For a moment Marc worried that Luke meant him kissing Sabrina. But her sigh and "What solution?" somehow bounced him back to reality, where Sabrina was home and pregnant. Marc supposed he was simply more used to the idea.

"You said the baby's father isn't in the picture. And never will be."

"That's right," she said. "Never."

"Then the only thing left to do," Luke said, "is claim the baby is mine. We'll get married."

Silence stretched.

Marc wasn't sure what to do. His instincts shouted *No!* and he wanted to shove Luke back away from Sabrina. He stood ten feet away, separated by a bazillion roses, and it seemed too close. Which should have concerned him. Instead, the expression on Sabrina's face concerned him.

She looked like she might cry.

"Are you sure?" she finally asked.

Luke simply nodded. Marc's stomach knotted.

"I'm sure. We'll get married, you'll be financially stable, you'll have a home, the baby will have a father."

"Luke, come on," Marc said. "You're overreacting."

Except that he understood. This was a way for Luke to bind Sabrina to him. Really bind her. Forever.

Marc's heart rate kicked up.

"She needs to be married." Luke finally looked at Marc. His gaze flickered down over the front of Marc's shirt then back to his face. "I'm the best choice for her."

Marc looked down. Splotches and streaks of color—liquor and juice—painted the front of his shirt. Much as they did Sabrina's. Damn. That was going to be hard to explain. Luke wasn't an idiot.

But why did he have to explain?

She certainly hadn't pushed him away.

And she wasn't Luke's.

Not yet.

"She doesn't *need* to be married, that's ridiculous."

"She's pregnant."

"I know. And there are thousands of single moms in the world."

"Sabrina doesn't need to be a single mom."

"She doesn't *need* to be a married mom either."

Luke turned his attention back on Sabrina. "You came home for a reason. You could have stayed in Seattle. They have everything you need there."

"I know, but—"

She looked to Marc for help but he had none. Luke was right on this one.

She closed her eyes and breathed in deeply through her nose.

"Okay. I got robbed. Someone stole my credit cards, maxed them out, drained my savings and ruined my credit."

"You got *robbed*?" Luke demanded.

She frowned at him. "Not on purpose."

"Jesus, Sabrina," Luke snapped. "On the street? In your apartment?"

Marc instinctively stepped between them. Luke's eyes narrowed, noticing the protective action.

"Take it down a notch," Marc told him. "It doesn't matter how it happened. She's here now. And you're yelling at the woman you bought roses for."

That seemed to make an impact. Luke looked at the flowers, then thrust them at Sabrina.

She took them, still scowling.

"Will you marry me?" His tone was short and cross.

Marc rolled his eyes. "Nice."

"Um..."

"Um?" Marc turned to Sabrina. "Um?"

She looked at him. "Well—"

"*Um*?" He repeated. Where was the firm resounding no?

"I guess—"

Marc moved in to block her view of Luke. "Say no."

"Say yes," Luke said from behind him. Marc grit his teeth and stared hard at her.

She hadn't wanted to marry Luke four years ago. But now she was broke and pregnant and she'd always, *always*, leaned on Luke.

Looking at her now he saw something startling. Insecurity.

The feisty women who'd packed up and left home without a look back four years ago, looked unsure.

Marc shook his head. This was a bad idea no matter what was going on in either head.

Besides, five minutes ago she'd been kissing him like she wouldn't mind having raspberry syrup poured all over her.

"Sabrina?" Luke asked.

"Sabrina—" Marc said at the same time.

She took a deep breath and looked back and forth between them. She let the breath out and finally said, "Maybe."

They both stared at her.

"What?" Marc demanded.

Luke simply nodded.

"I said maybe." She turned and walked out through the kitchen.

Kat was finally back in Justice. Thank God. Sabrina didn't think she could handle being at Marc's for another minute. Not after that kiss behind the bar at The Camelot. Damn that guy could kiss.

She slammed the top dresser drawer in Kat's guest room.

She hadn't seen her best friend yet and if she'd ever needed girl talk it was now. But Kat had returned from her conference and had been immediately called to the hospital. But Luke had a spare key to Kat's house and seemed more than willing to help move Sabrina out of Marc's.

She thought about that as she hung her clothes. Luke seemed to sense something between her and Marc.

Not that it had kept him from proposing.

But how was she going to explain the fact that she and Marc didn't hate each other anymore? She didn't think he'd seen them kissing but Luke knew them both. She'd never been able to hide her emotions from Luke. He would be able to tell if something was going on. And she'd never be able to lie if he asked.

But what would she say? That she felt like ripping Marc's clothes off when he looked at her a certain way? That she felt like ripping her own off when he touched her? That she had *never* felt like she did when he kissed her—not even singing on stage. That had always been the ultimate rush. Until now.

That was where she got tripped up.

There had never been anything like performing for her. It had been like a drug, giving her a high she craved over and over again.

Alcohol had never done it.

Danger—motorcycle racing, skydiving and the like—had never done it.

Sex had never done it. Falling in love had never done it.

But kissing Marc Sterling did it.

Thank goodness she wasn't stupid.

Marc might make her feel amazing physically. But what Luke was offering was *more*. In a lot of ways.

Security, help, support, a father for her baby—that was all more important, more responsible, less selfish than going for the rush. The rush Marc provided. And the rush her music provided.

The only thing her music had ever consistently given her was a thrill. Sure, she'd made a few bucks now and then but she'd always had to work other jobs to actually pay the bills. Sure, she'd met some great people, but they were good for some laughs, not people she could really depend on or open up to. The music hadn't provided *enough* of anything.

Marc was giving her a thrill too. No question. The things he could make her feel—the tingles, the goose bumps, the heat— were great at the moment, but they wouldn't be enough either.

She didn't need tingles and goose bumps and heat. She

needed a good car seat and a crib and hell, a whole bunch of stuff she didn't even know she needed.

Marc was just a guy responding to the chemistry between them. They'd been flirting, he'd leaned in, she'd turned her head, and he went with it. And why not? They were both single and obviously in the mood. But he wasn't interested in car seats and he wasn't making any promises.

She wouldn't have believed them if he had. They'd just discovered they didn't despise one another. There was no way she could consider him a part of her plans of any kind.

So if Luke asked about her and Marc she'd say it was nothing, a moment of stupidity, a surprise attraction that didn't mean anything.

And it didn't matter that she kind of wished it could mean something.

It was just a temporary thrill and thrills always wore off, leaving her wanting more. Always.

Chapter Seven

Maybe.

She'd said *maybe* to Luke's proposal.

When Marc repeated those thoughts in his head for the twenty-sixth time, he finally tossed down his spoon and whipped off his apron.

That crazy chick.

They'd talked about this. She was supposed to tell Luke how she honestly felt about him once and for all so he could get over her and move on.

And what did she do with the perfect opportunity? She said *maybe.*

Luke was probably out reserving the church and ordering flowers right now.

Flowers. Marc scoffed at that too. Luke had brought Sabrina roses? She wasn't a roses kind of girl. She wasn't a sweet romance kind of girl. She was sexy, fun, up-all-night, stay-in-bed-all-day kind of girl.

Luke was a roses, sweet romance kind of guy.

This was never going to work.

But she'd said *maybe.*

Holy hell. Luke was giving everything up for her. *She* was giving everything up for him.

Did she realize that? Luke was a Justice birth-to-death guy. If she married him she would never leave, she'd never sing again, she'd never travel. And Luke. He thought he loved her. He'd have the white picket fence and the kids and the dog. But he wouldn't have a woman who worshipped the ground he walked on.

And he deserved that.

What were they thinking?

Marc grabbed his car keys off his desk and headed for the parking lot, barking orders to his staff over his shoulder as he went. He decided to ask Sabrina what was going on first. And not analyze why he wanted to see her so much more than he wanted to see Luke.

He pounded on Kat's front door seven minutes later.

Sabrina came to the door, her hair up in a ponytail, a pair of short shorts that rode low on her hips and a tight white tank top that bared her stomach. And no bra.

She didn't even say hello.

Neither did he.

His gaze slid from head to toe and back up. "That's what you're wearing around?"

She didn't look surprised to see him. She spread her arms wide and asked, "Like what you see?"

To anyone else in the world she would look like a woman who'd been moving and unpacking.

To him she looked sexy as sin.

He stepped across the threshold, crowding close to her when she didn't back up to let him in. "The only thing about your body that I have issue with is your mouth."

"Really?" She blinked up at him with fake innocence. "But there are so many great things about mouths."

And he wanted her to demonstrate every single one of them. On him. Twice.

But that was beside the point. "Yeah, maybe when they're shut," he said.

"What are you pissed about now?" She finally stepped back and let him in.

"You said *maybe*. What the fuck is that?"

"It's an answer." She scowled at him. "He asked me a question and I answered."

"I thought we talked about what a bad idea you being with Luke is."

"We did."

"I thought I said that you needed to tell him you didn't want him."

"I thought I told you that I wouldn't be able to do that."

"He deserves more than gratitude. He deserves love. Do you want him, Seattle?" Mark moved in close, backing her up against the wall by the stairs. "Because there's no maybe there. It's a yes or no. You do or you don't." He kicked the door shut behind him.

She looked up at him. He, unfortunately, looked down. And saw that her nipples were beaded, clearly outlined against the soft cotton of her tank top. She was turned on. By him.

He finally admitted that *this* was why he'd come over. They'd been interrupted before and his palm still tingled with the memory of the shape and weight of her breast. And her reaction to him.

Marc lifted a hand, making sure Sabrina knew exactly what he was doing. She sucked in a breath but didn't stop him.

He cupped her breast, brushing the tip with his thumb and she moaned, her eyes slipping shut. Marc watched her face as he brushed it again, then took her nipple between his thumb and finger and rolled it, squeezing gently.

"Feel that?" he asked gruffly. "*That's* want."

She opened her eyes, met his gaze and licked her lips. "I know."

He bent his head and she came up on tiptoe at the same time, their mouths meeting hungrily. Her breast pressed more fully into his hand and her hand went behind his head, keeping him close.

"Marc," she gasped as he pressed in pelvis to pelvis.

"I want to see you," he rasped. This was insane, but he was done thinking.

Without hesitation she reached down between them and pulled her tank top off and over her head.

Her bare breasts begged for him to touch. They were small and round and firm, the nipples his favorite color of pink. He ran the tip of his finger from the base of her throat, where her skin was flushed, to the tip of her right breast, where he played for a minute.

"You look good in pink," he said, lifting his eyes to hers.

"Thanks," she breathed with a little smile.

"Show me more."

"You still think I have more piercings, don't you?" she asked. Her teasing was breathless but he loved that she was teasing. This wasn't mindless lust. She knew exactly what she was doing.

And so did he.

"I want to take inventory of a lot more than piercings. I want to know every single freckle on your body." He kissed her again, his hand moving to cup her mound.

She ground against his hand, moaning. "Yes."

She was hot, even through her shorts and he needed to feel that heat on his skin. He slipped his hand into the front of her loose shorts. Her stomach tensed, but her back arched, bringing her closer to his searching fingers. He felt a silky strip, leading straight to her clit. As the pad of his middle finger skimmed over it, she moaned his name. Loving that sound he returned to the sweet spot, pressing and circling.

She gripped his biceps in her hands and her head bumped back against the wall. He bent to kiss her neck, his finger sliding lower and finally into the wet heat that he craved. She was panting as he pumped first one finger then two into her, returning to her clit, then plunging deep again and again.

"Marc," she groaned.

He lifted his head, looked at her with her eyes shut, her breasts bouncing softly, her one leg wrapped around his so that her heel was at the back of his knee.

He wanted nothing more in that moment than for her to come and come hard. He didn't care about the intense pressure behind his fly. He didn't care that his heart was pounding so hard he could barely hear her moans. He wanted her to come. For him. "Seattle, look at me," he said huskily.

Her eyes fluttered open, but they were unfocused.

"Let go," he urged. He continued to fill her again and again with one hand as he reached to cup her breast with the other. He ran his palm over the hard center, then tugged the nipple gently. "Give it up for me."

Her eyes met his and she pulled herself forward to kiss him. He ate at her mouth as he found her clit again with his thumb, his middle two fingers deep.

Then he felt her inner muscles begin to tremble. Her tongue stroked his greedily and he pressed and stroked and circled until finally she broke, the orgasm tightening her muscles around his fingers, pressing her pelvis into his hand, his name gasping from her lips.

They both heard the car pull into the driveway at the same time.

She dropped her head to his shoulder and pulled in a deep breath. "Thank God that whoever that is wasn't five minutes earlier."

"Or even two." He couldn't help the smug smile he felt on his lips. He'd done that to her. He'd made her feel *that*.

She pulled away from him and he reluctantly removed his hand from her pants. She grabbed her tank top and started to pull it on.

"Why don't you go put some clothes on?" he suggested. "I'll answer the door."

"I have clothes on." She glanced down at herself as she said it.

He stopped for a moment and looked at her. She was mussed, her lips swollen, her cheeks were pink from the rub of his whiskers and her nipples were still prominent through the soft cotton.

"*More* clothes on. You need to wear more clothes period."

"It's probably Kat."

"It might be Luke."

She froze and her eyes flew to his.

His words seemed to echo off the walls.

It might be Luke. Marc wanted her more dressed in case it was the man who had proposed to her—who she had said maybe to. The man who, if she said yes, would have the right to see her dressed in anything—or nothing at all.

Marc felt his gut tighten at the thought and gritted his teeth. Stupid, stupid, stupid.

"You might want to untuck your shirt too," she finally said, glancing at his crotch—and the still very present erection—before she turned and took the steps two at a time.

He took a deep breath as the doorbell rang.

So it wasn't Kat.

Marc strode across the foyer to the door and yanked it open. If it was Luke he was going to tell him to back off. Sabrina needed some time to think about things.

It wasn't Luke.

"Marc? Hi, son. What are you doing here?" Bill Cassidy pushed in past him. "I'm here to see Sabrina."

"I'm here helping her get settled," Marc said, shutting the door behind Sabrina's father. "She just moved over here."

"Yeah, I heard." Bill turned a huge grin on Marc. "'Course she'll be moving again soon. Hope you didn't unpack everything."

"Moving again?" Marc asked, glancing at the steps, hoping Sabrina would stay up there. "How about coffee?" Maybe if they were in the kitchen she wouldn't hear her dad's voice and come down.

Bill needed to not know about the baby and the proposal. He would be thrilled with Luke and Sabrina being together and if he knew there was a baby he'd likely insist on the wedding being tomorrow.

"She won't move in until after the wedding," Bill said. "But we'll do that ASAP. So no sense in her getting too settled here."

Marc scowled. Apparently he'd been right on with the thrilled and the wedding-tomorrow stuff. "I take it you've talked to Luke?"

"I just left The Camelot. He told me all of it."

"Did he tell you she didn't give him an answer?" Marc was surprised by how much he hated that Luke was talking, by how much Bill loved the idea and by how sharp his own words sounded.

Bill frowned. "What do you mean? He said he proposed."

"He did. But she didn't answer."

"Why not?" Bill shook his head and sighed. "That girl has *never* had any sense."

Marc clenched and unclenched his fist. He knew from Sabrina's story that Bill had pushed his daughter out of a sense of not being quite good enough himself. Marc understood that. But Bill had always wanted more than whatever she gave. She was more than good enough—she was amazing. And that was true with or without Bill pushing her. In fact, it seemed true in spite of Bill.

"She's thinking it over. That's smart, don't you think? It's a big decision."

"It shouldn't be. This is Luke. She should say yes and drag him to a church before he changes his mind."

Marc shook his head. "Sir, I don't think you have any idea who your daughter really is."

Sabrina stood at the top of the stairs listening to Marc and her father.

Her father.

Of course he'd talked to Luke. They talked every day and Luke would never think of keeping her arrival in town a secret. Or his proposal. Dammit. Her father would think this was fantastic. Just like he'd said to Marc.

What was keeping her rooted to the spot instead of stomping down the steps was Marc. He sounded angry and was defending her.

She'd never had anyone defend her to her father. Luke had kept him calm. Luke had distracted him. But he'd never outright told Bill that he was wrong.

In fact, she wasn't sure Luke had ever thought Bill was wrong.

"What's that supposed to mean?" Bill asked Marc.

"If you think any man, could change his mind about being with your daughter, then you don't know her very well."

"I know that Luke is successful, well-liked, smart, secure and an upstanding member of this community. Exactly the kind of man Sabrina should be with."

Her dad sounded mad. Which she was sure Marc knew he would be. But he'd said it anyway. And what he'd said was amazing.

He kissed like a god, had made her come within five minutes of touching her—a definite record—and was now telling her father that any guy would be lucky to have her.

She'd just fallen a little bit in love with Marc Sterling.

"And you're here to..." Marc trailed off.

"Talk to my daughter about her upcoming wedding," Bill said firmly.

"She's sleeping and not feeling well. You should wait until later."

"I haven't seen her in four years," Bill protested.

"Part of that's on you, Bill," Marc said, his voice firm but calm.

"She was in California."

She could hear Marc's sigh from the second floor.

"Seattle, actually."

Her stomach flipped hearing him say Seattle, even when it wasn't as the nickname he'd given her. She loved that he called her that. She wanted to hear it every day.

Luke wouldn't like that.

Her chest felt tight at that thought.

"Wherever," Bill said.

"Wherever?"

She could hear the tension in Marc's voice.

"Like it doesn't matter?" Marc asked.

"It doesn't matter now. She's back."

"It shouldn't matter where she is and what she's doing only when she's where you think she should be and doing what you want." Marc's voice was low and clearly angry.

Sabrina put a hand to her mouth. She couldn't believe Marc had said that. He couldn't know that she'd tried calling Bill once and had been hung up on. He didn't know that she'd sent postcards to Bill like she did to Luke.

"I don't know what this is, but you're overstepping," Bill said tightly.

"Maybe," Marc agreed. "But I guess I'm not done. She'll be coming in to work tonight at the restaurant. You can see her then."

Sabrina barely muffled another gasp. Marc was throwing her dad out.

And he'd decided to give her the bartending job, apparently.

Seeing her dad in public like that the first time would be so much easier. How did Marc know that? Or did he?

She couldn't hear Bill's answer but could hear the displeasure in his voice and she would put twenty bucks on the fact that he was going to go straight to Luke and tattle on how Marc had treated him.

And Luke would likely side with Bill.

Luke had always seen things Bill's way. She believed that he truly cared about her dad. In fact, she'd often believed that he cared more about Bill than he did Sabrina. Taking care of Sabrina had pleased her father. Luke had taken some of Bill's burden, truth be told.

She heard the front door shut and held her breath, waiting. Would Marc come upstairs?

If he did, would she be able to keep her clothes on?

And if she didn't, was that a bad thing?

But a minute later Marc was not climbing the stairs. In fact, she heard no noise on the lower level at all.

She heard her dad's car start up. Then another engine start as well.

She ran to into the bedroom that overlooked the driveway and saw her father back out, then Marc.

He was *leaving*? He gave her a hard and fast orgasm up against the wall in the hallway, stood toe to toe with her father for her, then left without a word?

Sabrina backed up and sat down on the edge of Kat's bed.

He'd given her a hard and fast orgasm up against the wall in the hallway.

She'd never been that hot, that turned on, ever. She'd wanted him, all of him, more than she'd ever wanted anything. She would have given him anything he wanted in those moments.

She dropped her head to her hands.

No one had ever had that effect on her before.

Certainly not Luke.

The man she'd said *maybe* to earlier that day.

Marrying Luke was a smart thing to do. It was. It made sense. He was everything she should want. Everything any woman should want. He was all of the things her father said, along with good-looking, sweet and willing to marry her in spite of the baby that wasn't his.

He'd be a fantastic father. A wife and family to raise in Justice was as much a part of Luke's dreams as The Camelot.

She'd had a chance at her dream and it hadn't worked out.

Maybe it was time to focus on a dream she could make come true—even if it was someone else's.

She put her hand against her stomach.

She could make everything turn out right for *two* people.

Luke and the baby who she was completely responsible for. The baby she wanted to do the right things for. The baby who needed her to make a series of very important, very right decisions.

It was all on her shoulders.

Another life.

A child.

Her child.

Marrying Luke was the logical, sensible, smart, reasonable thing to do.

It was time for her to be logical, sensible, smart and reasonable.

Rather than go back to The Camelot, Marc found himself headed for the Hamiltons'. Karen would be there and he suddenly had the urge to see her.

As he let himself in through the front door he passed the wall display of family photographs and he stopped, as he always did, to look at his favorites. He was in many of them but his favorite by far was the family portrait they'd had taken for Christmas when he was twelve.

His parents had been killed in late April that year. He'd been a part of the Hamiltons' family since early May. They'd been loving, accepting, supportive from day one, but when they'd all gathered for the family picture that would be on the front of their Christmas card that year, he'd been amazed. They'd put him right in front with Luke, Karen and David around him—literally surrounding him with their love and bringing him firmly into the center of their family in the same way they'd done figuratively all along.

He'd never felt like an extra. He'd been a Hamilton as of May third even if the adoption papers said August. He'd felt it.

That meant everything to him. It still did.

Without the Hamiltons he would have been alone in the world. He wouldn't have been in the photographs that he kept and preserved almost obsessively. He wouldn't have treasured mementos like the rocks he and Luke had collected on a family vacation to the Black Hills, or the ticket stubs he'd kept from the major league baseball games David had taken them to, or the watch Karen and David had given him on his sixteenth birthday. He had memories and keepsakes and gifts because he'd had a family. Because of the Hamiltons.

He'd never do anything to hurt them.

Being with Sabrina would hurt Luke, which would hurt Karen and David. Sabrina was probably the most amazing woman he'd ever met, but he couldn't risk it. Not just because he loved them, but because he needed the family dinners and holidays, the phone calls checking on him when he had a cold, the fishing trips with David and helping Karen redo the linoleum in the kitchen. He needed to be needed, to belong, to have people who cared where and how he was. Not wanting to hurt them wasn't purely selfless.

"Mom?" he called as he headed for the kitchen. "You here?"

"Of course," she called back.

The smell of cinnamon led him. The house always smelled like cinnamon. Karen baked three times a week and her specialties were apple pie and snickerdoodle cookies.

It was no secret to Marc why cinnamon was his favorite flavor and scent. It reminded him of home.

"How are you, honey?" Karen paused in her mixing to kiss his cheek as he hugged her.

"I'm okay. Been a long couple of days. Thought I'd come by for some TLC."

"I've got plenty of that," she said with a laugh, motioning for him to sit at the table. "Anything I can help with?"

Marc knew she meant it. If there was something she could do to make things better for him she would. "Nah. Just need to sort through some things."

Like wanting the pregnant woman who might be marrying his brother.

Just for instance.

Karen put cookies and milk in front of him and Marc didn't even pretend to be too old or mature. He dug in.

"I have a strange question for you," he said after the first cookie was gone.

"Okay, I'm intrigued," Karen answered, sliding another full cookie sheet into the oven.

"What do you like best about being a mom?"

She turned with a funny look on her face. "That's a great question. Just a little out of the blue. Any special reason why you want to know? Are you okay?"

Dunking a cookie, he tried not to make eye contact. He had a hard time lying, or even bending the truth, with Karen.

Karen was going to say that being a mom was wonderful, but he wanted to hear specifics. He wanted to know that the baby was going to be good for Sabrina and that it would give her some of the things she hadn't had before. Some of the things she needed. Love, trust, acceptance, someone who thought she was wonderful.

He couldn't put his finger on the moment when he'd started caring so much about how she felt, but he did. Talking with her father earlier had only reinforced that. Her dad had always wanted more from her than what she gave. Luke had always wanted something different from her than what she gave. Her mom hadn't even been around. But Marc knew from personal experience that a child would look at her with stars in their eyes. He or she would believe that Sabrina had super powers

149

and could do no wrong.

And in many ways they would be right. Moms had special powers, for sure. And he was glad that Sabrina was going to have someone who believed that of her.

"I just found out a friend is pregnant," he said, stretching the truth only slightly. He and Sabrina hadn't been friends for long, that was certain, but he could honestly say that he no longer disliked her. "So it's been on my mind."

Karen seemed to sense that this was more than a casual conversation. She took her apron off and joined him at the table with a cup of coffee.

"Okay, what did I like best about being a mom?" She sipped her coffee, thinking. "Well, first of all the question sounds a little past-tense. What I liked about being a mom in the past is the same thing I like about being a mom now. I like seeing my children happy."

Marc met her eyes. The woman across from him had become his mother at a time when he'd never believed he could be happy again, and she'd made sure he remembered the happy times with his family before they died as well as ensuring he had hundreds of happy memories since.

He cleared his throat. "That's not very specific," he teased. "I think you're trying to get out of answering."

She smiled and shook her head. "No, it's true. But I can be more specific. I love seeing one of you succeed at something that means a lot to you. The night you opened the restaurant was as thrilling for me as it was for you guys because I could see the pride and happiness in your faces. I love seeing you laugh, I love giving you gifts, I especially love seeing you and Luke together. Your friendship is so important to both of you. That might be what I like the best."

Marc had a hard time swallowing the bite of cookie he'd just taken. She wanted to see them both happy. She loved seeing him and Luke together.

Terrific.

He wasn't surprised. He'd always known that he and Luke were the most important things in Karen's life. He had never felt that Luke ranked higher or meant more just because he was hers biologically. Marc had been equally important and loved without question.

Coming over here, asking these questions, had only served to confirm what he already knew—a relationship with the woman he wanted so much he could barely think straight would effectively end the friendship that meant the world to him. Not to mention hurt his mother, the woman who had given him everything good in his life.

Maybe that's why he'd come. He'd needed that confirmation. He had to keep Sabrina away from Luke but he could *not* fall for her himself.

In fact, it was even more obvious now that he had to get her out of Justice. If she stayed, it wasn't just Luke's heart he was worried about.

"Hey, Mom." Luke came in through the back door. "I have to—" He stopped when he saw Marc. "Didn't know you were here."

"It's cookie day," Marc said, lifting a snickerdoodle. He had to make light here. He couldn't look at Luke and see the man who had proposed to the woman he'd just seriously made out with. He couldn't look at Luke and think about Luke putting his hands on her the way he had. He couldn't look at Luke and think about punching him in the face.

Luke was his brother.

And punching him would upset their mom.

"My favorite." Luke took the chair next to Marc and reached for the last cookie on Marc's plate.

He let him take it without argument. They'd always shared everything. In spite of growing up under the same roof, they'd very rarely disagreed. In fact, Sabrina and Luke's constant need to say *how high?* when she said *jump* was the only thing they'd ever really fought about.

"So who's running the restaurant if you're both here?" Karen asked as the oven timer went off and she rose to take care of the cookies.

"It's a well-oiled machine," Luke said. "Though the kitchen would fall apart without Marc." He gave him a pointed look.

Marc shrugged. "I'm a fantastic teacher. The kitchen staff

can make it through pre-dinner prep without me."

When Karen's back was turned Luke narrowed his eyes. "I need to talk to Mom," he said in a low whisper.

"I know." Marc knew exactly what Luke was here to tell Karen. The same thing he'd told Bill. Prematurely.

"Get lost."

"Why? I already know the happy news. And by the way, are you insane?"

"Insane to want to take care of the woman I love? The woman who needs me? The woman who I haven't been able to take care of for four years?"

"You've missed that then?" Marc hissed back. "You've missed having her call you every time she broke a frickin' nail?"

Luke leaned closer, scowling. "This is a little more than a damned broken nail. She's been living in shit holes, barely making it, now she's been robbed, some asshole knocked her up—" He stopped and lowered his voice again. "Now I can do something about all of that."

Marc glanced at Karen but she was taking her time moving the hot cookies to a cooling rack and then dropping new dough onto the cookie sheet.

He made sure his voice was no more than a whisper. "You think it's your fault? Because you weren't there when all this bad stuff happened to her? That the past four years have been nothing but misery and it's all because you weren't there?"

Marc wondered what Luke would think of Sabrina's multiple roommates and the things she'd learned, the cities she'd traveled to, the odd jobs she'd had. He'd probably hate them all. There was no way he'd see how interesting that made her.

"I know that she's made some pretty stupid decisions without me and I now have the chance to manage the consequences," Luke said.

Marc glanced at Karen again but she was either oblivious to the conversation or was ignoring them on purpose. "How exactly are you going to *manage* the fact there's a baby coming? That's a done deal."

"I can make sure everything goes well from here on out."

"That's why she's here," Marc said exasperated. He had to consciously lower his voice again. "She came back to Justice to make sure everything goes well from here on out. She's here so Kat can give her the advice she needs, so she can live somewhere she can afford to support the baby." As he spoke, he was surprised to find he understood Sabrina's motivations. She'd made some good decisions in coming here. But she was underestimating herself. And she wasn't the only one. "You really don't think she could do this on her own?"

"She doesn't need to. *I* can help her do this."

Marc thought about that as he watched Luke break his cookie into smaller pieces. Luke had things good. Things went his way. He'd dreamed of having a restaurant and he had one. He'd planned to buy a house and live his life in Justice, and he was. He'd intended to stay close to his family and he saw them almost every day.

The only part of his plan that hadn't fallen into place was Sabrina.

She could do this alone. Luke might even know that. But if she did, it would be coloring outside of the lines of Luke's picture-perfect vision.

Everyone knew that Luke was focused. He always had been. When he made a plan he stuck to it. Even with the restaurant he had a hard time thinking outside of the original plans. Now that the business was a reality, and was exactly as he wanted it, he didn't want to change anything. Marc had thought about and proposed at least a dozen ideas for expansion or additions or changes. Luke said no every time.

He didn't like change. Marc knew it came from having so many foster kids in and out of his life early on. But that was also where he got his need to take care of others. It was why he'd wanted Marc in their family permanently. It was why he reveled in being able to run a business that took care of the town. It was why he so despised the idea of how Sabrina had been living—where he couldn't fix everything.

Sabrina was a part of his plan that had taken a detour. Now that she was back, Luke wouldn't be able to think about anything but the fact that she was supposed to be his wife. It didn't matter if she was pregnant with another man's baby or that she hadn't come back for Luke or that she'd only said *maybe* to his proposal. In Luke's mind it was going to happen. For better or worse.

Even if she'd made out with his best friend.

Luke wasn't stupid. He had to have sensed something was going on behind the bar when he'd walked in earlier. But it wouldn't matter. Nothing would derail his plan to marry Sabrina.

Except Sabrina.

She could say no. Yes, Luke would try to talk her into it, even manipulate her a little. But she was the final decision maker.

Marc was going to have to make sure she made the right decision. She had to say no to Luke. For good.

"Will you be my best man?" Luke asked quietly.

Marc looked from his plate to his best friend. He'd always been Luke's best man. And vice versa. He nodded and said honestly, "If Sabrina walks down the aisle with you, I'll be there."

There was no way in hell Sabrina was walking down the aisle with Luke.

"You know," Luke said. "Sabrina is the only thing we've ever fought about."

Marc sighed. "Yes. I'm aware."

"Hey, Mom," Luke said.

Karen turned from her cookies, an innocent look on her face. Marc rolled his eyes. Even if she hadn't heard every word, she'd known he and Luke were talking about something big in those low, tense voices. But she wouldn't pry.

"Sabrina Cassidy is back in town."

Karen's eyes and smile widened. "Oh, that's wonderful. Why didn't you bring her over?"

"She's over at Kat's getting settled. Unpacking," Marc said.

He glanced at Luke thinking maybe he shouldn't make it so obvious that he knew exactly where Sabrina was and what she was doing. Luke frowned at him but said nothing.

"So she's staying for a while?" Karen asked. "That's great."

"Mom, you should know that I proposed to her this afternoon."

Marc swung his head to stare at Luke. What the fuck was with telling everyone about that?

"She hasn't said yes," Marc said.

"She hasn't said no," Luke replied.

Karen's gaze went from one son to the other. "What's going on?"

"She's moving back to Justice and I want to be with her. So I asked her to marry me."

Luke made it sound simple and Marc supposed that it was if he disregarded the fact that the reason she was here was a baby—not because she loved and missed Justice, or even Luke for that matter. Or if he ignored the fact that Justice would hold her only as long as she was afraid of doing more and being on her own. Did Luke intend to just keep her insecure her whole life so she'd stay with him?

That thought made every protective instinct in Marc surge forward.

She didn't need anyone. She'd left home with nothing but a guitar and suitcase. She'd been on her own for four years, without even a steady roommate to rely on. She got up on stage again and again, not letting the previous failure keep her from trying.

She had allowed herself to dream, to experience things no matter what anyone else thought or felt.

He admired that.

He'd never allowed himself do any of that. He'd gone to college in Lincoln because Luke was there. He'd studied restaurant management and culinary arts because it fit in with Luke's plans. He'd moved back to Justice and settled in because to dare to think about something else or something more would mean being ungrateful for the home and family that they'd given him.

He had this life because of them. So he would live that life—happy, grateful, and content. But Sabrina didn't have to wonder *what if?* She'd gone out and looked to see what else there was.

155

"But she hasn't given you an answer?" Karen asked, pulling Marc from his thoughts.

"No. She's thinking about it. It was a little sudden," Luke admitted. "But I didn't see any reason to wait."

"I thought you hadn't been in contact with her over the years," Karen said.

"I haven't."

"But you expected that she would just say yes?"

"She will say yes," Luke said.

Karen looked concerned but Luke was concentrating on his glass of milk. "Well, your plans do seem to have a way of working out."

That was exactly what Marc was afraid of. He needed to find Sabrina and show her that she wanted more—more than Justice, more than Luke could give her. Eventually she would make the right decision and say no to all of this. Then she would find the life she really wanted and deserved. No settling, no fear.

To do that, he'd need a lot of time and contact with her.

He knew he shouldn't feel excited about that.

Luke was going to use her insecurity and her need to do the right thing to convince her to be with him. Marc was going to use her dreams and desires to convince her Luke wasn't her answer.

They would all see soon enough which was stronger.

Sabrina stood in front of the shelves in aisle six of the pharmacy, not at all pleased with what she saw.

There was oil for stretch marks, a back brace specifically made for pregnant women and cream for cracked nipples. *Cracked nipples.* What the *hell* had she gotten herself into?

There was also a bottle that claimed to be the magic cure for morning sickness. Where had that been a couple weeks ago when she'd been kneeling next to her toilet often enough to notice the three tiles missing in the corner of her bathroom?

Interestingly, she hadn't been sick for the past couple of days. It was past the normal time for her stomach to begin that queasy, don't-you-dare-put-anything-in-me feeling.

It was surely a coincidence that she felt better since being in Justice. But she was going to count her blessings where she could find them.

Of course, aisle six was making her feel a different kind of sick.

There were products that talked about natural cures for constipation, arch supports for flat feet, stockings for swollen ankles—all kinds of fun things to look forward to.

Then she moved three feet to the right and she was confronted with another plethora of items that made her anxiety rise and her stomach knot.

Diaper rash cream, No Tears shampoo, baby powder with and without cornstarch, a bulb aspirator—which she wasn't sure she understood the use of—and a rectal thermometer—which she was pretty sure she understood too well.

"Kat?" Thankfully her friend picked up on the first ring. "Are the vitamins I'm taking good enough?"

"Bree, what are you talking about?"

"I'm at the pharmacy and I'm looking at the vitamins and wondering if I need more."

"You don't need more than one-hundred percent of the daily allowance. Which is what you're taking."

"So, I'm good."

"Yes."

Sabrina could hear the amusement in Kat's voice. "Yuck it up, babe. You get to go shopping with me for fat pants."

Kat chuckled. "*Maternity* pants, Bree. Not fat pants. You're not getting fat, the baby is growing."

Sabrina rubbed a hand over her right buttock. "That explains the growth...in *front*."

Kat outright laughed then. "Honey, enjoy it. There are women who can't get pregnant who would give everything they have to be in your position."

"I know." Sabrina was grateful that the baby was healthy. She was even excited every once in awhile. But there were as many moments when she was scared to death.

"So, I heard a rumor today," Kat said conversationally.

"Yes, it's true. I'm pregnant."

"And engaged."

"Eng— How did you hear that?"

"So he really did ask you."

"Can you believe it?"

Kat's voice was soft when she said, "Yes. I can."

"For the record, I didn't panic and beg him to marry me or anything. I'm trying to consider this like a responsible adult. This needs to be a carefully thought out decision..." Sabrina frowned as she noticed the three boxes on the bottom shelf. Breast pumps. Oh, boy.

"No, you wouldn't have to beg."

"What do you mean?"

"Come on Sabrina. It's like Christmas morning and Luke's birthday all rolled in to one."

"It is? Because I'm coming home?" Wow that was—

"Coming home pregnant and pathetic."

Crappy.

"Excuse me?" Sabrina forgot all about breast pumps, cracked nipples, prenatal vitamins and everything else.

"You know what I mean," Kat said with that no-nonsense tone Sabrina usually appreciated. "You're giving him not just one person to take care of but two. An automatic family. A reason to put up a frickin' white picket fence, buy a swing set and get a dog."

Sabrina swallowed, trying not to feel itchy. It was weird how Justice made her itch sometimes. Like she couldn't sit still, couldn't get comfortable.

"He's great. I wouldn't ever have to worry about anything. He wants to do this and I'd be crazy to say no," she told Kat.

"Yeah, you probably would." Kat sounded resigned.

But Sabrina was sure it was that she was concerned. Luke was her friend too and she didn't want anyone getting hurt.

Sabrina would be crazy to not jump on all he was offering, to not appreciate everything that was available to her here, to not realize that there were thousands of women who would trade places with her in a heartbeat. A comfortable small town with good friends and neighbors, a secure and fairly significant financial situation, a home, in-laws she adored and a man who would take care of her as long as they both would live.

If she wanted to leave this, daydreamed about anything else, considered that there was anything more, she'd be crazy. And undeserving. And irresponsible. And selfish.

All of the things she'd always feared were true.

Chapter Eight

Sabrina wished she could get drunk.

She'd been back in Justice for two weeks and she knew that everyone was whispering behind her back.

She knew they were wondering what had happened in the past four years. She knew that they'd heard rumors about something going on between her and Luke. She was pretty sure they were noticing that she was putting on weight. And eating everything in sight.

And it was stressing her out.

Then there was the letter she'd received three days ago.

The roommate who had remained in Sabrina's apartment in Seattle had finally forwarded her mail.

Right on top had been a letter from the singing competition, Next Stop Nashville.

Sabrina had read it two hundred times a day since she'd first torn it open and seen *Congratulations.*

She'd won one of the twenty spots in the competition based on the demo tape she'd sent in before she'd known she was pregnant. Or broke. She had to get there on her own, which obviously wasn't going to happen, baby or not. Her first paycheck from The Camelot had been nice, but would hardly pay for groceries, maternity pants *and* a plane ticket and motel room in Nashville.

She wondered if Marc's offer still stood. Would he still pay to send her to Nashville? Maybe, but it would be a one-way ticket, which was definitely a tempting, but really bad idea.

Much like Marc himself.

She saw him every day. Repeatedly. She saw him more than Luke. Almost like he was intentionally seeking her out. And it was making her crazy.

She liked him. She looked forward to seeing *him*. She wanted to have dinner with *him*.

And she *really* wanted to kiss him some more. Nothing had happened since the day in Kat's foyer but it seemed like every time she saw him she wanted him more.

She was so screwed.

And not in a good way.

"How about a Long Slow One?"

Sabrina snapped out of her thoughts as someone ordered a final drink before they closed. It was one of her own concoctions. She was having fun with that at least. She shoved the letter under the edge of the blender and reached for a glass.

"A Long Slow One?" The deep voice tumbled down her spine like a staircase, goose bumps rippling out and down her limbs. Marc had come behind the bar when she wasn't looking.

"Want one?" she asked, turning to face him.

She loved—loved, loved, loved—the sexual innuendos and teasing between them. It seemed constant. There was a current between them whenever they were in close proximity and neither of them shied away from it.

Which was stupid, but apparently unavoidable.

"I'd be crazy to say no to that wouldn't I?"

He gave her the grin that always made her think *Take me now.*

"Definitely," she said with a smile. "But you should know that the Hard and Fast is another option."

"Now we're talking'." He moved in as if to simply pass behind her but his chest brushed her upper back and his hand slid across her hip and right butt cheek as he did. "What's in it?"

"The most important ingredient is cinnamon schnapps."

The next millisecond she realized what she'd admitted. Marc chewed cinnamon gum. All the time. His kisses were always cinnamon flavored and yes, that had come to mind as she invented the drink. And its name.

"I love cinnamon," he said gruffly. "The Hard and Fast sounds good to me."

She turned to face him, wanting to see his eyes as she said, "I personally like it better than the Long Slow One."

"Should I say that doesn't surprise me or act like I haven't thought about how you like...your drinks?"

Breathing. That was what she was forgetting.

She sucked in a long breath. "I'm not sure what you should say."

"Doesn't matter what I say," he said, his voice low. "I still wonder about it."

"Now you know."

"I won't forget, either."

God, what was she doing? She wasn't even flirting with the man who'd proposed, but she was basically telling his best friend exactly how she'd like him to take her.

The urge to kiss him was nearly overpowering. "You have to stop."

"Stop what?"

"Being so...all of this."

"Sexy?" he suggested with a grin. "Hot? Hard to resist?"

She rolled her eyes, but couldn't stop her smile. "Yes. All of it."

"You think I'm hard to resist?" He sounded surprised.

"Isn't that obvious?"

His smile changed from cocky to something much warmer. Her entire body felt it.

"It's really, really fun, isn't it?" he asked.

It really, really was. But she couldn't shake the weirdness of it. This was Marc after all. Marc who had come to Wyoming to keep her away from Luke...

And that was what was bugging her.

"You're very attentive for a guy who doesn't like me much."

"Until a couple of weeks ago, I didn't like you at all."

"Thanks for clarifying. And for making my point."

"You're wondering why I'm suddenly so..."

"Attentive is the word I'm most comfortable with."

He chuckled. "Okay, you're wondering why I'm suddenly so attentive."

She wasn't sure she wanted the answer to her next question. "Because you don't want me with Luke?"

He crossed his arms and leaned his hip against the back counter. "I *don't* want you with Luke."

"Are you trying to make him look bad?" She regretted it as soon as she'd said it.

He looked very interested in that. "What does that mean?"

She shook her head. "Never mind. Forget it."

She started to move past him, but he caught her arm and pulled her around to face him.

"I'm making him look bad?"

"You're not trying?"

"Dammit, Seattle." He hadn't let go of her yet and he pulled her closer. He sounded intent rather than annoyed. "Tell me how I'm making him look bad."

"You're making me want you more than I want him."

He looked pleased and turned-on in equal parts. Then he frowned. "You want him?"

"I'd be stupid not to."

Something flared in Marc's eyes. Jealousy? Possessiveness? That was wishful thinking. She shook it off.

He stroked his hand up and down her arm, watching the movement. Then he looked into her eyes.

"Has he asked you again?"

"To marry him?"

Marc clenched his jaw before saying tightly, "Yeah."

"No. He's just been sweet. And attentive. He's always bringing me stuff—flowers and muffins and tea—and asking how I am. He bought me a rocking chair."

Marc rolled his eyes. "Of course he did."

"What do you mean?"

"He doesn't get it."

"Get what?"

"What he should be doing to win you over."

"What should he be doing?" She was *very* interested in

Marc's opinion on this.

He moved in a little closer. "He should be telling you that you are the sexiest thing he's ever seen. That he passes by as close to you as possible whenever he can just to smell your hair. That when you laugh it makes him want to French kiss you up against the wall. He should buy you something you'd really appreciate—like cinnamon massage lotion. That he could lick off, slowly and thoroughly, after rubbing it all over your body."

She swallowed hard. "I don't think you're supposed to eat lotion."

"Edible massage lotion is made to be eaten."

At the word *eaten* she had to press her inner thighs together. *Damn.*

He gave her a lazy, sexy smile and continued to hold her arm, but his eyes went to something over her shoulder.

She glanced back and saw Luke heading for them from across the room.

Luke. The guy who'd given her the rocking chair. The rocking chair she was going to use for *the baby.* Should pregnant women really be getting edible massages anyway?

"Maybe the best way to keep you away from him is to marry you myself," Marc muttered.

She swung to face him, shock vibrating through her bones. Uh, oh. That shouldn't be so scary. Or tempting. It should be funny. Because the idea of Marc proposing to her was ridiculous.

"Yeah, right." She tried, *really* tried, to sound flippant.

"Why not?" He was studying her. "What does he have that I don't? I have my own business—the same one, incidentally. I live in a great little town—the same one, incidentally. I have a wonderful family who loves you—the same one, incidentally." He shrugged. "Seems like the only thing that makes me different from Luke is that you want me."

She closed her eyes and shook her head. This was beyond ridiculous. This was...torture.

"People have affairs all the time," she said.

"You'd rather have an affair with me after you marry Luke?"

Her eyes flew open. She couldn't believe how wound up she felt. Like she'd taken a shot of caffeine straight to her heart. "I meant marrying you doesn't ensure I'll leave Luke alone."

Marc moved in, filling the space around her completely. She couldn't look away from his dark green eyes, hot and swirling with emotion. "I promise you that if you were in my bed every night, there's absolutely no way you would want to—or have the energy to—mess around with anyone else."

Oh, God, she believed him.

She swallowed, closed her eyes to tear them from his gaze, took a deep breath. "It would kill Luke if we were together."

She felt Marc's hand fall away from her. She opened her eyes and saw the pained look on his face.

"Yeah, I know," he said quietly.

Before she could say anything—though she had no idea what it would have been anyway—she felt Luke behind her.

"Sabrina."

Marc didn't move away from her and she had to step back as she turned to face Luke. He was the one she should be concentrating on. He was the one she should be flirting with. He was the one she should be trading sexual innuendos with.

Making a guy like Luke happy wasn't exactly difficult. Or shouldn't be, anyway. He found pleasure in fairly simple things. He was the type of guy who would rather sit on the couch and watch a rented DVD on a Saturday night than sit in the most expensive seats for a sold out Broadway show. He was the type of guy who would have more fun pulling his kids through the zoo in a wagon than he would traveling across Europe in first-class accommodations.

He loved that everyone knew everything about him. He loved that he was never truly alone. He believed that having his actions and decisions affect those around him made him part of something. Something he wanted.

"Finish cleaning the bar for her," he said to Marc, staring right at her.

It was closing time. The final patrons were on their way to the front doors and the wait staff was clearing the rest of the tables.

"Seattle—" Marc started.

But Luke grabbed her hand and pulled her away from him quickly.

She probably needed to do a lot more of that, moving away from Marc. The feelings he stirred up in her were not conducive to feeling things for Luke.

She followed Luke down the hall. She wasn't sure what to say to him. He'd seen how close she and Marc had been standing if nothing else. Finally they stepped into his office and she turned to face him bravely. "Luke, we need to talk." She should tell him about Marc. She should tell him they'd kissed. She probably wouldn't tell him the rest—that wouldn't serve much purpose—but he needed to know about the kiss.

Probably.

"I agree."

"You do?" Her heart thudded in her chest.

Did he already know that she and Marc were messing around? She didn't want to hurt him. This was Luke. She cared about him, loved him even.

But it had to be obvious, to Luke and everyone else, that she and Marc were getting along better than they ever had. They weren't making out in public by any stretch. In fact, Marc hadn't done more than touch her—every chance he got—in ways that would seem totally casual to any onlookers. But surely Luke was curious about why they seemed to be spending a lot of time talking. And standing closer to one another than they needed to.

"I asked you a question two weeks ago and you owe me an answer."

That wasn't at all what she'd been mentally preparing for. Of course, she didn't think that Luke was going to let her go without making a decision forever. But for some reason she'd thought he would let her come to him. That was usually how it worked between them.

She swallowed. "Tonight?"

"Right now."

Her thoughts flickered to Marc. Which was probably not a good thing when Luke was essentially asking her if she would marry him. Again.

She really didn't know what to say. She should say yes. That was the smart, responsible thing to do. But she wanted to say no.

Instead of saying anything, she went with another approach.

"Kiss me, Luke."

It was like déjà vu and she saw it in his eyes as he hesitated. Then he made his decision, cupped her chin with one hand, tipped her head up and kissed her. Slow and sweet. Just like before.

She leaned into him, walking him backward until the backs of his legs hit the edge of the chair in front of his desk. She pushed him down and climbed onto his lap, straddling his thighs.

His hands gripped her hips and she ran her hands over his chest and encircled his neck. She wanted this to be good. Better than with Marc, because that would be so much easier. Better than anything, because that would make sense. It should be better. It shouldn't be Marc who—

She shouldn't be thinking about Marc while Luke was kissing her.

She definitely didn't think about Luke when Marc was kissing her.

What the hell was she doing kissing two guys anyway?

Pulling back she took a deep breath. "Dammit. This is so complicated."

"It doesn't have to be."

No, she supposed he was right. If she just stayed far away from Marc... But her heart actually twinged painfully at that thought.

"Let's have hot, crazy sex right here in your office," she blurted out.

Maybe he could make everything else disappear. Maybe he could make her forget about Marc. Maybe she was exactly where she was supposed to be and just needed something to validate it. Like the best sex of her life.

She started to loosen his tie.

"Sabrina, let's just—"

"Stop talking."

His hands stopped her. "Not like this."

"Why?"

"This happened once before if you remember. We made love and I thought it meant something different than what you thought it meant."

She sat back and brushed her hair away from her cheek. She wasn't going to get hot, crazy sex from Luke.

And she should be more disappointed about that than she was.

"So you don't want to do this?"

He sighed. "Of course I do. But I don't want just one night. I want it all. I want to take care of you, protect you, give you everything you and the baby will ever need. Say yes, put my ring on your finger and I'll take you to bed right now. And never let you leave."

Push had just come to shove.

Dammit. She pushed herself off his lap and wiped her palms on the front of her skirt. This was impossible.

Luke was sweet. He was sincere. He wanted to give her a life that any *sane* person would do anything to have.

Marc wanted her—hard and fast. And temporary. He wasn't showing up with any diamonds. Or diapers.

Two of the things she needed, that Luke wanted to give her.

Maybe Nashville wasn't such a bad idea after all. Sure she wouldn't know anyone, would have to work three jobs to afford baby food and she'd have to depend on Kat calling friends of friends of friends from med school to find a good doctor. But her heart wouldn't be in knots. And she'd *know* if she was making poor decisions. That was what she was used to. Here in Justice there was simply too much gray area.

But one thing was pretty black and white—she wanted someone more than she wanted her fiancé.

She'd had sex with Luke and had still left town. For four years.

She hadn't even seen Marc naked and she felt torn up just thinking about not seeing him for twelve consecutive hours.

Marc was right—Luke deserved someone who loved him more than she did.

She took a deep breath and looked at the best friend she'd ever had. "Luke, I can't..." *Hurt you, tell you the truth, marry you, lie to you—give you what you really want.*

"You're taking prenatal vitamins?"

Sabrina swung toward her father as he stepped into Luke's office.

"Dad. What are you doing here?"

"Trying to find you."

Well, that was a first. She'd seen her father almost every night at The Camelot since coming home, but their conversations had been in public, at the bar, with either Marc or Luke—not a coincidence she was sure—present. They'd been civil, friendly even. He had asked exactly zero questions about Seattle and the past four years. They'd talked only about the present, as if the past four years hadn't happened.

He hadn't sought her out anywhere but at The Camelot, hadn't called, hadn't stopped by Kat's.

And it was a relief. She simply didn't have the energy to deal with Bill along with the other men who were making her nuts.

"You found me," she said with a forced smile. She hadn't missed the prenatal vitamin comment, but she was really going to try to ignore it.

"Sheila Thompson wished me congratulations when I stopped in for my blood pressure pills today. Of course I assumed that she'd heard we're having a wedding. Imagine my surprise when she called me 'grandpa'."

It wasn't the perfect way for him to find out, but there wasn't a perfect way so Sabrina just sighed. "Surprise."

"So it's true?" Bill demanded. "You got yourself knocked up?"

Luke moved in closer to her, as was customary when Bill got riled up. "Take it easy, Bill. Everything's going to be okay."

"Of course it is. The baby's yours."

"The baby is *not* Luke's." Sabrina corrected quickly.

"As far as I'm concerned it is," Bill said with a deep scowl.

"And as far as anyone else in this town is concerned. Is that clear?"

Sabrina frowned right back at him. "Of course that's not clear. That's ridiculous. The baby isn't Luke's. Period."

"As soon as you're married it won't matter."

"That isn't—hasn't—" She glanced at Luke. She had to say no and end this, but not like this, not in front of her father. She had to try to help Luke understand that she was saying no for his own good.

"Are you trying to tell me that you moved back here, to Justice, to my town, knocked up, unwed, to have and raise this baby by yourself?" Bill asked. "You don't think I should get a say in this?"

Sabrina wanted to roll her eyes. This was all so typical. It was about his image, about what people would think, about it somehow reflecting badly on him that she really liked rum and was attracted to con artists with good sperm motility.

"I'm here to—"

"How could you let this happen?"

It took Sabrina a moment to realize that Bill was talking to Luke, not her. She looked at Luke. He looked pissed off and frustrated.

"I can't force her, Bill."

"You still haven't said yes?"

Sabrina blinked, realized Bill was addressing her again and said, "No. This is a big decision. I can't just—"

"I thought you were going to fix it this time," he said to Luke. "I thought you'd—"

"Just tell her, Bill," Luke said quietly but firmly. "Before you say something you'll regret, just tell her the truth."

Sabrina didn't want to hear it. Whatever it was. She could tell by Luke's tone of voice and the strained lines around his eyes that it was something intense. And she just couldn't do any more intense.

"Forget it. All of it. I'm having this baby and I'm—"

"Do you remember when you were in fourth grade and I had to come pick you up from school because you were so upset you couldn't stop crying?"

Sabrina froze, half turned toward the door, as her father spoke. She did remember. But she didn't have to say anything. He knew she knew exactly what he was talking about.

Bill went on. "The rest of your class was painting glass vases for their moms for Mother's Day. And you didn't have a mom to give yours to. You threw yours on the floor and ran out of the room."

Sabrina closed her eyes. Of course her teacher thought it was an accident and her tears were because of the broken vase, but she could still remember how satisfying smashing that glass had been.

It wasn't like she was the only kid without a mom in the entire history of Justice. But in her class of twenty-five students, she was the only one with no one to give a vase to. One boy lived with his grandmother, two others had step-moms and another at least had his dad's girlfriend to give something to.

In retrospect she could have mailed the vase. Or waited until she saw her mom for the next visit. But she never knew when that would be, and at the moment, when everyone else was painting hearts and flowers and writing *I love you* it had hit Sabrina that she didn't have the mom she wanted. And needed.

"You want your son or daughter to be able to make Father's Day presents and have a date to Father-Daughter dances and a dad to go on Boy Scout camping trips with, don't you?"

It was a low blow.

It was classic Bill Cassidy.

And he had a point. Not that her child would truly be without. Luke would go to dances whether they were married or not. Bill could fill his mantel with Father's Day gifts from his grandchild. Sabrina herself could go camping.

But it wouldn't be the same. No matter how good it was, it wouldn't be the same thing as having a dad.

Lots of kids didn't have dads. Dads died, dads left, moms made mistakes. And kids could turn out okay anyway.

But most, if not all of them would change it if they could.

Crap.

She swiped the tear from her cheek before turning to face

her father.

"Dammit, Bill." Luke pushed past the older man and came to stand beside her again. "You don't have to be such an ass about it."

Bill didn't look offended. He just watched her.

"Tell her what you're really worried about," Luke said. "And stop making her cry."

Luke never had handled her tears well. She straightened her spine. "I'm fine. I need to get home."

Luke grabbed her arm and made her face her dad. "Tell her."

Bill wouldn't make eye contact with either of them.

"Tell her," Luke said with a low growl. "Tell her that you never went after her in Seattle, never called, never returned her postcards, because it was a good excuse."

Sabrina looked up at him, confused. "Excuse?"

"Tell her that you want her married to me because you think that's the only way you'll ever see her or spend time with her. Tell her that now there's a baby too, you *really* want her with me or you might never see your only grandchild."

She turned wide eyes on her dad. What the hell was Luke talking about? Her dad had written her off when she left. He couldn't care less if he saw her—or her baby—now that she was back. In fact, she'd put money on the fact that he'd be just fine if she left again.

"Excuse?" she heard herself repeat.

Luke looked down at her. "When you left it was the perfect excuse. He could pretend that the reason you didn't talk to him, the reason you didn't share things with him, the reason you didn't spend time with him was because you were so far away. He didn't have to think about the fact that it might be because you didn't want to."

Bill scowled at him. "We were talking about her latest screw up. And how she could keep it from being a disaster."

"Now that you're back," Luke went on. "He'll have to face that not spending time with him is a choice you're making."

"He hasn't tried to spend time with me," she said, her voice rough.

"After Marc kicked him out of Kat's he realized that seeing you at the restaurant would be easier. You wouldn't be able to tell him to get lost here."

Sabrina frowned at her father, but asked Luke, "He told you all of that?"

"I know him pretty well by now," Luke said, affection obviously mixed with his frustration.

"We were talking about *you* and the latest problem you've caused."

Which was exactly the kind of thing she was used to her father saying, but it suddenly didn't stab at her like it usually did. There had been a reason her father hadn't contacted her in four years other than not wanting to?

"I don't know what to say," Sabrina finally answered.

"Say you'll marry Luke," Bill said.

"Stop it," Luke told him. "Just stop." Then he looked down at her. "Sabrina—"

She frowned up at him. She had so many emotions whirling around and mixing with her hormones that she knew she couldn't do this—or any *more* of this anyway—right now.

"I'm leaving. I have to process all of this. But Luke David Hamilton—" she nearly poked him in the eye with the finger she pointed at him, "—if I find out that you proposed to me because my father wanted you to or because it would make him happy or whatever, I'm never speaking to you again."

Luke caught her finger and pulled her up close to him. He looked her directly in the eye when he said, "I proposed to you because this is what *I* want. Always have."

He meant it. She'd known him long enough, well enough, to know that he was telling the truth.

She took a deep breath and gently pulled her finger away. Not able to deal with Luke at the moment, she turned to her father. "And if you want to talk to me or spend time with me you just have to ask. But," she added as he started to speak. "If the conversation turns to anything I don't like or you start giving me opinions I haven't asked for, I'll ask you to leave. And we'll have to try again another time."

Sabrina wasn't sure she'd ever had the last word with her

father, but he simply nodded and watched her with what she'd almost describe as hope.

This coming home thing was just one surprise after another.

She did not, however, get the last word with Luke. Just as she was pulling the door shut behind her he called, "Two weeks, Sabrina. I'm asking you again in two weeks. And you'll give me an answer this time once and for all."

With the heavy office door firmly shut between them, Sabrina paused and took a full, deep breath.

Two weeks.

In two weeks she would have to make the biggest decision of her life.

She knew the exact date too. Because in two weeks was opening night of the Next Stop Nashville competition.

Not that it mattered to her. She was going to call them tomorrow and tell them she couldn't make it.

Of course there weren't any directions in the letter about how to do that. Probably because someone would have to be insane to say no. But there was a phone number on the letter. And an e-mail address. She'd make sure the message was clear and professional. Something like, *I regret to inform you that I will be unable to join you*— No, that was too formal. Maybe, *Thank you for the honor of selecting me*— No, she should just get straight to the point. *Sorry, but I'm completely broke and can't make the trip.*

Sabrina rubbed her forehead. She couldn't go running off to Nashville for reasons other than money. It was a long shot, for one thing. It would upset Luke if she just took off. Her dad too.

Marc would be happy, of course.

And just like that she was back to thinking of Marc.

She headed to get her purse from the locked cabinet behind the bar and wondered if Marc was still in the building.

Not that that mattered either.

Really, the two things she spent the most time thinking about were the two things that had nothing to do with anything *real* in her life. Nashville was just a dream and Marc was just...also a dream.

He was flirting, messing with her, trying to keep her from spending time flirting and messing with Luke. It wasn't anything serious. Just like Nashville wasn't anything serious.

It was a singing competition. There were nineteen other contestants. Her chances of winning were one in a million.

Okay, one in twenty.

Still, even if she won—big *if*—then what? There were no guarantees. If nothing came of it, then what was the point? If something did come of it—well, she couldn't do anything about it anyway. She was going to be a mom. She needed stability, security, a cost of living she could afford.

So, Nashville was a moot point.

Like her attraction to Marc.

Nothing could come of that either. She hadn't been kidding when she said it would kill Luke if she and Marc were together. And Marc wasn't asking to be *with* her anyway.

She grabbed her purse and dug to find the letter. She had to find that phone number so she could tell them she wasn't coming. At least that would take Nashville officially off her list of options. She should have done it right away when she got the letter, but she hadn't been able to. A few days of enjoying the congratulations wasn't a crime.

But now it was taunting her, tempting her, teasing her.

Also like Marc.

She frowned and pulled her wallet, two packs of gum and a granola bar out of her purse trying to find the letter. What had she done with it? She glanced around, then remembered—she'd been reading it when someone ordered a drink.

Turning, she found the letter on the counter. With a tube of cinnamon-flavored edible body lotion on top of it.

She held her breath as she picked up the lotion and immediately saw the *Congratulations* scrawled across the back of the letter. In Marc's handwriting.

"You really should mind your own business." She slammed Marc's back door behind her.

Marc didn't look particularly surprised to see her when he turned away from the oven and set a pie on the counter top. "That is excellent advice. Wish I'd followed it when you called from Wyoming. Or when you needed a job. Or when your dad stopped at Kat's." He wasn't looking at her and the muscle in his jaw twitched as he threw the oven mitts down next to the pie.

She didn't think he really meant it, but there was still a noticeable jab of pain in her chest thinking he might be regretting everything. She crossed her arms. "You really have been butting in a lot haven't you?" It hadn't seemed like he was butting in. It had felt good having him there with her, on her side. Presumably anyway.

"Well, you won't have to worry about that when you're in Nashville, will you?" he asked, stomping to the fridge, withdrawing more butter and slamming the door.

"So you did read it."

"Of course."

"What made you think it was okay for you to do that?"

"I assumed you left it lying there intentionally so I would see it."

"Why would I want you to see it?"

"To prove to me that you've got what it takes. Though I don't need proof of that."

"I didn't— You think I have what it takes?" She'd been told that a few times over the years but there was something about having Marc say it that made her pulse skip.

It occurred to her that she might care what Marc thought of her.

Wanting to sleep with him was problematic. Liking him, wanting to see him and spend time with him was confusing her. But valuing his opinions, especially about her, was a whole new level of complication. He wasn't supposed to have influence in her life. He barely liked her and he had no intention of being involved with her beyond this crazy flirtation—or whatever it was.

"Of course. That should be obvious. You made it into the top twenty. And there are only six other women. And you're the first contestant they've ever had from Nebraska," he said.

She stared at him. "How do you know that?"

"Website." He gestured to his laptop set up on the counter by the fridge.

"You checked the website?" He'd been interested enough to look up the competition's site? Why?

"To see what you'd gotten yourself into."

She tipped her head to one side, watching him. "You were worried?"

"Curious. Had to know when I was going to need a replacement bartender."

She didn't believe him. She wasn't sure why, but she knew that Marc logging into NextStopNashville.com had nothing to do with her bartending schedule.

"Well, you don't have to worry. I'm not going."

"Yes you are." He didn't look up at her, just kept mixing whatever was in the bowl in front of him.

She looked around, realizing for the first time that he was wearing an apron and the center island of his kitchen was completely covered with baking items.

"I'm not going. I already called and told them no."

"No you didn't."

"I did."

"Your name is still on the website."

She looked over at the computer before she could help herself. She wanted to see her name there as a finalist, she couldn't deny it. But she folded her arms instead and said, "So?"

"Go ahead and look. There's a bio of you, a photo, everything. I like that picture by the way."

One of her roommates had been an amateur photographer and had taken her only publicity photos. Paying professionals was far too expensive.

"That's okay. I don't care." But she did. She really wanted to see her name and photo on a website. Still, she resisted.

"You should be happy about it. Proud of yourself. It's a huge thing to make it into that competition. It's the third annual you know. The last two winners both have recording contracts."

She did know that. Of course she knew that. She'd been aware of—and interested in—Next Stop Nashville since she read about the first competition in a music magazine two years ago. "What are you doing?" she asked him instead, wanting to distract both of them from this conversation.

Nashville was not an option and hearing Marc talk about it as if it were a sure thing wasn't helping.

"Making pie."

"At this time of night?"

"Yes."

"For the entire town?" There were at least twelve piecrusts and bowls and bowls of fruit, sacks of sugar and seemingly a thousand other ingredients.

"Yes." He turned back to the oven where he pulled two more finished pies out and set them on top of the stove.

"What are you talking about?"

"Every year The Camelot supplies pies for the town picnic."

She'd never seen so many piecrusts in one place. "How many?"

"Sixteen."

"What kind?"

"All kinds."

"I love cherry."

He turned with a frown. "Why are you here?"

"Oh." She pulled herself up straight. "To yell at you."

"Can you get it over with so I can finish here?"

"Love to. Leave my stuff alone and mind your own business."

"You don't mean that." Marc bent and put another pie in the oven.

It annoyed her that she got distracted by how great his butt looked in the faded jeans. "What?"

"I think you really, really want me messing with your *stuff* and minding your *business*. In fact, I think you've realized that I'm the *only* one you want messing with your stuff and that's why you're here."

"What are you talking about?"

"You don't know?" He looked up and made lasting eye contact for the first time. "You're going to pretend that you don't know? And act surprised that I know exactly what you're doing?"

"What *I'm* doing? I'm not reading your mail and messing with your stuff and confusing everything."

"Is that right? *I'm* the only one messing around and confusing everything?"

"You're the one touching me all the time and flirting and smiling at me—" She stopped, realizing that she was on the verge of admitting things she shouldn't say out loud even to herself.

"And every frickin' time you—" He stopped and visibly gritted his teeth.

She stared at him when he failed to go on. "I *what?*"

He scowled at her. "You respond."

"I respond," she repeated. "What does that mean?" But she knew exactly what he meant. She responded to him in ways she never had to anyone, or anything, before.

"It means that all I can think about is getting you naked and making you *respond* over and over again."

Her body definitely responded to that and she had to concentrate on breathing normally. Still, she tried for flippant. "I think that's maybe more your problem, than mine."

"Maybe it is." He didn't look up and was stirring the ingredients in the bowl like he had a personal vendetta against them. "After all, you have another guy hanging on, don't you? When you get all worked up you can just go off to his office and have *him* scratch the itch. The itch *I* created."

He really seemed upset and she knew he wanted her to believe it was because she was driving him crazy. But she thought just maybe it was her and Luke together that was driving him crazy. Which meant he was jealous. Which made her want to smile. She resisted, but she definitely wanted to. "He's the guy I'm going to be living with. He should be scratching my itches."

"The guy you *might* be living with." Marc threw—not tossed—the spoon into the sink. He thumped the ball of dough he'd created onto the wooden counter top and began flattening it.

The man drove her crazy. "And you're pissed because you think he can do better."

"That's probably why I should be pissed." He hit the dough with the rolling pin.

"But?"

He didn't answer, just kept rolling.

"Why are you pissed then?"

Nothing. His jaw was tight and the dough was getting a beating, but he wouldn't even look up.

"Oh now you're going to shut up? You open this up and now you won't follow through?" She wanted emotion from him, a reaction, even if he was mad about something. She wanted to know that this was more than casual to him. "Let's talk about these itches I need help with." He still didn't look up.

"Come on, Marc. If we're gonna fight, then fight with me!"

"I don't want to *fight* with you," he muttered.

The muttering drove her crazier than any yelling might have done. "Well, I want to fight with you!" And she did. She had so many pent up emotions, so many frustrations and it seemed that many, if not all, stemmed from this man. She wanted to let loose with...something. And Marc was the closest target.

Marc, who was simply rolling out piecrusts and muttering at her.

That wasn't going to fly. If he didn't want to fight with her now, he soon would.

She reached out and grabbed the closest thing, a can of apple pie filling. She scooped out a handful and flung it at him, hitting him directly in the center of the chest.

He froze, the rolling pin gripped in his hands.

When he didn't react further than that, she took another handful and threw it. It hit him on the front of his right shoulder.

He put the rolling pin down and finally looked up her.

There was a dangerous glint in his eyes as he began unbuttoning his shirt. "That's how you want to do this?"

Her heart was pounding and she was sure it was from anger. It had to be anger.

But as more and more of his chest was revealed she knew that lie wasn't going to make it much further. He shrugged out of the shirt entirely a moment later and her heart rate kicked into high gear.

Wow. He was muscled and broad, skin tanned with light hair gracing his pecs and stomach. She wanted to touch it. All of it. With her tongue.

This was bad.

He started toward her. She backed up. "How I want to do what?"

"Get me naked."

"I...don't..." But she couldn't quite get the lie out. She did want him naked. Bad.

"All you had to do was ask, Seattle. And take your own clothes off." He removed the apron and tossed it on the counter.

"I am not taking my clothes off." But she wasn't about to dissuade him from removing his.

"I'm okay with taking them off for you."

She backed up further as he reached out and scooped up a handful of cherry pie filling. She was aware that she was running out of space to retreat. And it ticked her off that she was retreating anyway.

She switched direction and moved around the edge of the kitchen island, pie ingredients once more between them. She scooped up a handful of peach pie filling and threw it at him, attempting to keep him from stalking her.

It landed on his stomach and quickly slid down over the fly of his jeans.

The *prominent* fly of his jeans.

Well, *that* was going to make all of this especially hard to ignore. She winced at even thinking the word *hard*.

Marc was turned on. It wasn't just her heart racing, her skin tingling, her clothes feeling restrictive.

He stopped moving, but his eyes stayed on her as his

181

hands went to his belt buckle. Her eyes widened as he undid his belt, unbuttoned his fly and unzipped.

"Wh-what are you doing?"

"You're messing up my clothes."

"I'll mess up more than that." She picked up an egg and chucked it at him.

He ducked in time to send the egg into the wall behind him. He didn't even glance at it as he started toward her again.

She grabbed another egg, this one hitting him on the thigh.

He rounded the corner of the island and she had to catch herself as she slipped in pie filling that had dripped from his shirt. She grabbed the edge of the island, her eyes landing on the rolling pin.

"I've been throwing soft stuff until now but I swear—" She raised the rolling pin and turned toward him.

Marc caught her wrist, the rolling pin above his head. "My turn."

He walked her backward until her back was against the wall. He pressed her arm over her head against the wall and took the rolling pin from her now slack grip. His whole body crowded against her, his thighs pressing into hers, his chest centimeters from the rapid rise and fall of her breasts as she struggled to breathe. He smelled like cinnamon and nutmeg, laundry detergent and Marc.

"Your turn?" she asked, her voice raspy.

"You said you liked cherry best."

Marc smeared the cherry pie filling across the skin above the scooped neckline of Sabrina's tank top, watching as a cherry rolled down in the valley between her breasts. He wanted to follow that cherry, suck all the sugary goo from her skin, lick it clean...

Then he dragged his hand down the front of her shirt, his palm skimming over her right breast.

She sucked in a sharp breath as he let out a long whoosh of air.

God she felt good. She looked good. Her cheeks were pink,

her eyes bright, her lips parted as she breathed. He could feel her pulse pounding in her wrist that he still held against the wall.

And he was doing it to her. She might have been in Luke's office for far too long and Marc might be reacting to that far too seriously, but here and now she was with *him* and was responding to *him.*

He held his hand still over the mound of her breast, willing himself to go slow. But when she moaned and her head fell back against the wall, her eyes closed, he couldn't.

He moved his palm against the stiff point of her nipple. Her free hand went to his waist and she pulled him closer.

What was he supposed to do now?

"I thought we were fighting," he said, his voice hoarse. Hell, he'd gladly fight with Sabrina daily. She was gorgeous when she was riled up and she made him feel energized like nothing else did.

"We are."

"Are you surrendering?"

Her eyes flew open. "Never."

"How are we gonna know who wins?"

"The first one to beg for mercy of course." The smile she gave him was almost enough to make him fall at her feet right then and there.

Her free hand went to his fly and pulled the zipper the rest of the way down. Her fingers slid through apple and peach pie filling, spreading the sticky mess across his stomach, up to his chest and down again, lower this time.

Marc felt every cell in his body tighten and knew that he had to keep up or begging was a definite possibility.

He pulled one strap from her shoulder down her arm, revealing the soft pink bra underneath. Without hesitation, he tugged the bra cup down to bare her breast and nipple, which he immediately took into his mouth.

Her hand stopped moving as she arched into him. "*Marc.*"

He loved that. Loved hearing his name from her lips, loved making her gasp and groan and press against him. Loved making her as hot as she made him.

He sucked once, hard, then trailed his lips to the streak of cherry between her breasts. He licked the syrup, lapped up the cherry and continued to the other nipple. He swirled his tongue there, tasting the tang of the cherry and the sweetness of Sabrina mingled in a flavor he would never forget.

Her hand started moving again, this time up and down the steel shaft of his erection.

"God, Seattle." He pressed into her hand.

"More," she panted, pulling against his hold on her arm over her head.

She no longer held the rolling pin so he let her go. She quickly skimmed his jeans from his hips and freed him from his boxers.

Her hold on him, skin to skin, was enough for him to think *Mercy, baby, mercy*, but he said nothing, resting his forehead against hers and struggling for control.

As she stroked up and down, he had to mimic the same action and slid his hands up under the short skirt that had been messing with him all night.

He found the edge of her panties and slipped a finger under the elastic band against her inner thigh.

She was nearly bare there as he'd felt the other day. No soft curls, no thatch of hair—one single silky strip and hot, wet folds.

"Yes, please, Marc, please."

That sounded like begging to him, but he wasn't about to break the spell. He circled her clit with just enough pressure to have her pressing against him. Then he slid his finger into her. She was hot, tight, perfect.

He pulled back so he could look down at her. Her nipples were hard, rosy from his mouth, the feel of her stroking him was almost enough to make him lose it but the sight of her small hand on him had him struggling for willpower. Her skirt fell over his hand so he couldn't see what he was doing. But he felt it. All of it.

"More?" he asked, moving to position a second finger at her entrance.

Her eyes slid open and she focused on him. The eye contact

hit him in the gut and his cock pulsed in her hand.

"Everything you've got," she said.

"You know what I've got."

She looked down where she held him and squeezed slightly. "Everything," she repeated.

He slipped the second finger into her sweet tightness but it wasn't enough for either of them. He slid in and out, but she was ready and he didn't want her to come without him.

His hand went to her thigh and he drew her leg up to his hip.

"Do we need protection?"

She gave him a smile. "A little late for that."

"I'm clean," he told her. Pregnancy wasn't the only consideration.

"Me too."

"Let me in."

She didn't let go of him, but her other hand dipped under her skirt and she moved her panties to the side, baring herself. Then she guided the tip of his cock to her entrance.

"Everything you've got," she repeated.

He dipped his knees, his other hand cupped her ass and he surged upward, sliding into her.

Her head fell back again and she wrapped her legs around his waist.

Marc had to take a second to breathe, sheathed deep inside of her, to keep from pumping twice and coming. When he felt a glimmer of control, he moved, pulling out, then sliding home again.

That lasted for two more strokes.

"More, harder," she whispered, her eyes shut. Sabrina was gripping his shoulders, her pretty breasts bouncing softly as he flexed, her inner muscles holding on tight. And he wanted to hear her shouting his name and lots of *oh yeses* and see her looking straight at him.

"Look at me. I want you to know who's making you come harder than you've ever come," he said, squeezing her ass, grinding her against him.

"I know it's you," she breathed as she opened her eyes. She wet her lips. "Of course it's you."

Maybe it was the *of course* or the way she was looking at him—like she'd never felt like she did right now—or maybe it was that she always drove him crazier than any woman ever had no matter what they were doing, but Marc felt his release immediately start building.

No. He wanted her to come first. She *had to* come first.

He reached between them, found her clit with his thumb and finger, stroking the sweet spot as he pumped into her.

She gasped, then her breath hissed out between her teeth and he felt her muscles begin to contract around his length.

"Come on, Seattle."

"I'm... Marc... *Yes.*" The final word was more or less a shout.

He couldn't hold out any longer. He thrust into her, pressing her into the wall, stroking deep until the climax roared from the depths of his gut through him and into her.

He held her up against the wall for several long moments before she wiggled and he let her feet slide to the floor.

"Dammit," she breathed as she pulled her bra and shirt back into place.

He blinked down at her. "Excuse me?"

She frowned up at him and then shoved him back with her hands on his chest. "It just had to be you."

"What had to be me?"

"The best sex I've ever had."

He wasn't sure if grinning was okay, since she was looking more ticked off than satisfied.

"If it's any consolation, you're the best I've ever had too." It was the complete truth and he was less surprised than he would have guessed. There was a chemistry, a passion between them he'd never felt before.

"No, that's not any consolation." She brushed the font of her skirt smooth, looking annoyed.

"You wish it had been bad?" He too pulled his pants back into place.

"Kind of."

He knew what she meant. They were in a mess. Speaking of which—

"You can't leave like that." He gestured at her pie filling covered shirt. "We'll have to do laundry."

The timer on the counter went off and he headed for the sink, washed his hands, then grabbed an oven mitt on his way past the center island.

He heard a snicker behind him and by the time he'd pulled the second pie out and had it on a cooling rack Sabrina was full-out laughing.

With a smile he turned. "What?"

She waved her hand. "Is there anything you can't do? You even timed the sex perfectly so the pies wouldn't burn. And I'm guessing those pies are as good as the sex."

He tossed the mitt on the counter and leaned back against the counter with a smile. "Thanks. And I didn't time the sex. I didn't plan on that at all. Up until you picked up the rolling pin I wasn't even thinking about it."

Sabrina raised an eyebrow. "Liar. You've been thinking about it since you took your shirt off."

"Is that when you started thinking about it?"

She hesitated and Marc found himself irrationally interested in the answer.

"Honestly?" she finally asked.

"Let's try it."

She looked down at her toes. "Honestly, I've been thinking about it since Wyoming."

He loved that answer. And hated it.

All at once it hit him—this wasn't one-sided. This wasn't just in their heads. They weren't avoiding it. What they'd just done against the wall was very anti-avoiding, in fact.

Which meant it wasn't ignorable.

He ran a hand through his hair. "You are a pain in the ass," he told her.

"What?"

He lifted his head and gave her a rueful smile. "Sorry. But

187

it's true. Before you called the other day, everything was good and easy and fine."

"And now?"

"Well." He gestured toward the wall where he'd taken her minutes before and where he'd definitely like to have her again. "Technically, I just did my best friend's fiancée. That's not fine." It had, however, been easy. Far easier than it probably should have been. And it had been very, very good.

She frowned at him. "But that's what you want, right? To mess everything up, to complicate it and confuse everyone so we don't know what the hell to do."

He raised an eyebrow. "Everyone?"

"Okay, me. If I'm confused by you I can't be confident that I'm doing the right thing with Luke..."

"What are you doing with Luke?" He forced himself to relax as tension seemed to grip every muscle in his body.

"Getting married."

"*Maybe.*" There was no way in hell she was marrying Luke.

"It's what I *should be* doing."

"What you should be doing is packing for your trip to Nashville."

She crossed her arms and narrowed her eyes. "Ah, yes. Nashville. You think I'm leaving."

"You are."

"That makes taking your clothes off with me a little easier doesn't it?"

He frowned at her. Nothing about any of this was *easy*.

An hour ago, the thought of her leaving had made him feel sick. Now...well, it was anything but easy.

He was making pies in the middle of the night because he couldn't even sit still, not to mention sleep, since he'd read the letter about the singing contest in Nashville. Between imagining not seeing her every day and wondering what was happening in Luke's office he was so wound up that all he could do was cook. The pies had to be done so he was taking comfort in at least being productive while he went crazy thinking about her getting on a plane. Ironic considering he'd tried to force her to get on one not even a month ago.

He knew it was best if she left. He wouldn't have to hide his feelings from Luke and walk around in a constant state of need when she was in the restaurant. It was best for her, for sure. This was her shot. And it was best for Luke. No way was Sabrina the right woman for Luke. Especially after what had just happened against Marc's kitchen wall.

Not that he blamed her. There was no stopping whatever this was between them. But if she had *that* with him she couldn't have it with Luke. This kind of connection didn't just happen with every other person.

She definitely needed to leave. She needed to sing and he needed to not throw away his relationship with Luke and the Hamiltons—which he was more and more afraid he was going to do if she stayed.

"You came over here tonight, Seattle," he finally said. He'd been trying his damnedest for days now to not do what they'd just done. He found lots of excuses to be in whatever part of the restaurant she was in, he flirted with her and teased her, he touched her more than he should—he was only human after all. But he'd avoided getting her alone, because he'd known exactly where too much alone time with Sabrina would lead.

Then she'd come to him tonight.

He could only be expected to resist so much.

"To yell at you."

"Bullshit. You knew exactly what was going to happen when you showed up here. Just like I knew the minute you walked in that door."

She opened her mouth, then shut it again. She crossed her arms tighter. She swallowed.

"That probably shouldn't happen again."

"It won't. You'll be in Nashville."

She frowned. "What if I'm not?"

"Then it will happen again." Hell, he wanted it to happen again right now. "And again. And again. Until Luke finds out and I ruin my relationship with my best friend. Who is also my business partner. And my brother. After I have no way of making a living and my family is no longer speaking to me, I'll be the one leaving town, and it will stop happening then." The knot in his stomach tightened painfully.

She had to go. Not just so Luke didn't find out how Marc felt about her but because he was absolutely certain that he could not watch her make a life with Luke now. And she couldn't be his. There was no good solution in Justice. At least in Nashville, *her* dreams could come true.

Fuck. Being with her had become something he would dream of now.

"I can't go," she said. "I need—"

"The hell you do," Marc interrupted. "You don't need anyone. You might *want* someone to help you, you might *appreciate* some help, you might *like* some help. But you don't *need* it. You're fine. More than fine. Knock that shit off."

She stood gaping at him, her eyes wide, her mouth in a little *O*.

"What?" he snapped. This was more familiar. Lust and fighting. That he was used to with Sabrina. The softer stuff he was feeling was the problem.

"I was going to say that I need some time to think."

Oh.

"Thinking's your problem," he argued. "You think, you analyze and worry and second-guess yourself. Just do the right thing. Your gut—your heart—will tell you what that is."

"You really think that? That I can do this on my own?"

And just like that the softer stuff was back. "Don't, Seattle."

"Don't what?"

He paused, trying to put his mix of feelings into words. "Don't stop doing what you do best."

"Singing?"

"Trying."

"I'm a dreamer." She said it with an eye roll that said she'd heard that many times before.

"No." He shook his head. Then shrugged. "Yeah, you're a dreamer. But you're not just a dreamer. You're a doer. Dreamers dream and wish and plan and think *what if*. You went out and did it. By yourself. With the people you cared about most telling you it was a bad idea. And you made it work."

190

She laughed. "I did not make it work."

"Yes, you did." He wanted to grab her, hold her, make her listen. She had done so many things he never had. She'd tried new things, she'd made mistakes, she'd learned that messing up just meant trying again and maybe getting something even better. He admired it all and he tried to tell her. "A roommate moves out and instead of worrying, you just find someone new to move in. A song doesn't turn out just right, you rewrite it, or write another one. You hate a job, you get a new one. You need more money, you get another job. You don't get stuck, you don't see limits."

She was staring at him and he knew he sounded crazy. But he saw so many things in her that she didn't. Things that he didn't have.

"I've never done that," he said. "I went to college at the University because Luke went and I didn't want to give up the weekend visits home. If I'd gone further, I would have missed a lot of family stuff. That was more important. I studied something that would work with the restaurant because moving back to Justice meant I could be around family and friends all the time. No starting over, no meeting anyone new, no being on my own."

"I thought you loved it here."

"I do," he said. "I absolutely do. But I don't know what else there is. I've never let myself think there might be something more. I was on my own for a very short period after my family was killed and I never wanted to be there again. Besides, to think about something else or something more would be like being ungrateful for what I do have."

"But—"

It was obvious she didn't know what to say and Marc didn't blame her. He'd never told anyone, or even let on, about these feelings.

"I'm not unhappy," he said. "But I do wonder *what if?* You don't have to. You've tried your what ifs. I think that's amazing."

Her eyes widened and she laughed softly. "You make it sound like I've done all these heroic things. Most of it's just the way it turned out."

He shook his head. "You were up on stage, singing for an audience on a regular basis, right? You saw lots of places, met a lot of people, tried a lot of jobs."

She shrugged. "Right."

"Those are all choices you made."

She took a deep breath, then let it out. "Okay, you have a point."

"So you need to go to Nashville. It's another *what if.* And a mom who goes after her dreams is a great role model for your child to have. You'll make it work. You're smart and brave and resourceful."

She stared at him as if she couldn't believe what she was hearing. "I'm going to need you to write all of that down. Word for word. I have a feeling I'm going to want to refer back to it in the months—and years—ahead."

He looked at her as the words *years ahead* seemed to echo in his head. And his chest. He realized that he wanted to be there with her in the years ahead. He wanted to tell her these things over and over—in person.

Because somewhere between Muddy Gap, Wyoming and this moment he'd done something really stupid. He'd started falling for her.

He had to clear his throat before saying, "Well, you should also know that when it comes to parenting, love has a way of making up for a lot of shortcomings."

She smiled and said softly, "I hope so. That's about all I've got."

He started mixing ingredients for another crust without thinking about it. He needed to keep his hands busy and there was only one other option. She was going to be sore if he kept going with that option. It occurred to him that their conversation shouldn't be lust-inducing, yet he wanted her all over again.

"Love is all that matters in the end. Doesn't matter how you start out, what you make for dinner, if you're at every ball game. If you have love and you're sure to show it, the rest works out."

"You're talking from personal experience?"

"Yes." He focused on the crust.

"Your parents or the Hamiltons?" she asked.

He shouldn't have expected her to tread lightly with his feelings, but he wasn't upset that she was prying.

"Both," he answered. "I was lucky."

"You know more about being a great parent than I do," she said. "You have a double set of good role models for how to do it."

Marc looked up at her in surprise. He knew nothing about babies. More than nothing. He wasn't sure he'd ever held one in his life. Now he stared at Sabrina. The woman he'd just made love to. The woman he couldn't seem to keep his hands, or mind, off of. The woman he liked more every minute he spent with her. The woman he did *not* want to marry another man.

The woman who was pregnant. Which meant she was going to have a baby. A baby he would know nothing about.

He frowned at the crust and started rolling it out. "Are you depending on a having a gut instinct about all the baby stuff?"

Sabrina laughed. "Hell no. I don't even have a gut instinct about which shoes go with which outfit."

"How are you learning everything?"

"Everything?"

He looked at her and couldn't help but smile at her covered in pie filling, looking adorably confused.

"Colic."

"Colic?"

"Do you know what it is?"

She narrowed her eyes and propped her hands on her hips. "Do you?"

"I do. Kind of."

"Me too. Kind of."

"I know I said love is most important. But having a clue is a good idea."

"I have a *clue*. Change it, feed it, burp it."

He chuckled. "How about a bookstore?"

"How about Google?"

"How about we Google a bookstore?"

They grinned at each other. The heat in the room started to edge up.

Over bookstore talk.

Ridiculous.

Sabrina took a deep breath. "I should go."

Marc looked her up and down. He couldn't finish the pie because all of the fillings were all over them.

"You're a mess."

"Yeah. And my clothes have stuff all over them too," she quipped.

He sensed some truth behind her joking. "You're not a mess, Seattle. You're a fighter, an adventurer. Who better to do something like this?"

"You mean accidentally create a life completely dependent on me doing something I've never done before?"

"You have to be a mom for the first time some time."

"I meant make a good decision."

Marc frowned. "Why are you so hard on yourself?"

"Because I keep proving myself right."

"For instance?"

"Having sex with my sort-of fiancé's best friend."

He should have seen that coming. Still, it was a direct hit. "I thought it would take at least twenty-four hours for you to regret that."

She stepped close, something warm in her eyes—not hot, but warm. Weird.

"I don't regret it, Marc. Not one second. And I want to do it again. But you have to admit that it's a great example of me making not-so-wonderful decisions."

He came around the corner of the kitchen island. "The same could be said of marrying a man you don't really love."

"The same could be said for *not* marrying a man who could make the perfect life for my child."

That's what she wanted. To do the right thing—for the first time, in her opinion—for the baby. To give her child the perfect life. That made sense. It was even admirable. In fact, it hit Marc right in the gut. The Hamiltons had done that for him. In the midst of the chaos they had not just given him a room, not just given him meals, not just clothed him—they'd given him a family, love, life, a future.

It was what Sabrina wanted to do and he could only support her in that. He should be leading the do-whatever-it-takes-to-take-care-of-your-kid parade for her.

The question was, did supporting her mean being okay with her marrying his best friend?

No. She was absolutely not marrying Luke. As for Luke giving her kid the perfect life, Marc couldn't help but remember how he'd run through all the ways he was just as good as Luke for her at The Camelot earlier tonight. If Luke was the perfect choice, Marc was too—plus giving her the best sex of her life.

"Time for you to go." He had to get her out of there before he actually proposed to her himself.

"Right."

She looked disappointed, which made him feel better.

"I'll see you." Because, of course, he would.

"Me too."

"Don't marry anyone before your shift tomorrow, okay?" He gave her a teasing smile. She wasn't going to marry anyone tomorrow morning, he knew that. But the less rational part of him really wanted to keep her right here with him—where he could kiss her some more, of course—and where he could keep her to himself.

"I promise," she said.

He missed her before she was even down the driveway.

Chapter Nine

It wasn't right.

Sabrina stared at the page in front of her. The lyrics were perfect, the notes seemed right, but there was something missing. It was driving her nuts.

She hadn't been able to write since getting home from Jamaica. But this morning she'd awakened with a melody in her head and the words had flowed effortlessly.

Until now. She couldn't end it. It needed...something.

She played it again on her guitar. And got stuck in the same spot.

She got up and made a sandwich.

When she came back and played it again she got stuck in the same spot.

She hummed the melody, tried singing it out loud.

And got stuck in the same frickin' spot.

The piano. That's what it needed, she decided. It should be on the piano instead of the guitar. Then maybe she'd hear what was missing.

Unfortunately, Kat didn't have a piano.

The Camelot, however, did.

Her heart sped up as she changed her clothes, pulled her hair into a ponytail and headed for the restaurant. She should just avoid Marc. It would really make everything so much easier on all of them.

But that wasn't realistic.

So the sooner she saw him again the better. Get it over

with. Get past any weirdness.

Eight minutes later she walked into the kitchen at The Camelot. She had to ask permission to use the piano after all— well, not really but it was a great reason to find Marc. And she couldn't ask Luke, she reasoned. All the music stuff made him cranky. Always had.

As if he felt her, Marc looked up immediately when she stepped through the doors.

He smiled and she felt heat swirl through her stomach. Then he shook his head like he didn't know what to do with her.

She had a few ideas.

It wasn't like she expected her attraction to him to be gone, or even lessened, but she hadn't expected to feel it spike because of the night before. But it had. Because now she knew what it would be like. She knew that he knew exactly what he was doing, how to touch her, how to kiss her, how to make her come.

Lord, her whole body heated with that one brief thought.

Several of the staff greeted her and she smiled at them as she casually crossed the room to where Marc was standing. To ask him about using the piano. That was it.

She felt jumpy as she got closer, like her skin was hypersensitive, like it was craving his touch. Watching his hands as he measured and poured wine into the saucepan he was using made her flush and she felt her nipples tighten. She glanced up at his face. He appeared to be concentrating on his task, but she knew he was aware of her and every breath she took. It was weird to be in tune with him being in tune with her. She looked at his lips and felt tingly in places his lips hadn't even been.

The sex had been *so* good. *So* good.

"What's so good?" he asked, slicing mushrooms on the cutting board next to the stove.

She'd apparently said it out loud. Maybe he thought she was talking about the aroma from the saucepan. "The sex," she answered honestly.

He glanced at her sharply. "What sex?"

"Our sex."

He looked around the kitchen but no one was close enough to hear. "Geez, Seattle. This isn't the time or place."

"Why not? I'm giving you a compliment." She grinned. "Well, giving myself one too. I participated."

He swallowed hard even as he rolled his eyes. "Nice day out, huh?"

"It's a little *hot*." Her only excuse for the flirting was that she wanted to punish him a little. Because it was his fault she felt like she was going crazy just standing next to him. "But then, you obviously like heat. And kitchens."

He closed his eyes briefly. "We're going to be busy tonight. We have a big welcome home party for a soldier coming home from Iraq."

"That's awesome. Why are you changing the subject?"

"You remember Jason Gilbert? This is Justin, his younger brother."

They'd graduated with Jason. With eighty other kids. Less than ten years ago. Of course she remembered him. "What's the deal? You don't want to talk about us having sex last night?"

"I'm trying a new sauce for the chicken." He dipped a spoon in the pan and lifted it toward her. "Taste it."

She gave him a knowing smile—he wanted to change the subject because she was getting to him—but opened her mouth and leaned in rather than taking the spoon from him. Heat flared in his eyes and he touched the tip of the spoon against her tongue. Keeping her eyes locked on his she closed her lips around it.

The taste was amazing.

The way he watched her was more so.

She slid her tongue along her bottom lip and moaned softly. "That's so good, Marc."

He stared at her for several seconds. Then he frowned and turned back to the stove. "Stop it," he muttered, sliding sliced mushrooms into the sauce.

"What?"

"You're breathing hard and looking at me like you want to jump me." His voice was low so no one else in the room could hear.

"I was actually looking at you like I'd like *you* to jump *me*."

He rolled his eyes—again—but one corner of his mouth tipped up. "I'm trying to work."

"You're the boss. You can take a break."

He looked at her. His eyes found her mouth, then met hers again. "Should we just do it right here? Or we could go in and clear Luke's desk off. Just to be sure he didn't miss the show."

She knew his sarcasm came from guilt and the fact that he'd very much like to do both those things—well, probably minus Luke's observation. "We're good in kitchens."

Marc pulled in a quick breath through his nose. "I thought we talked about bad decisions and choices."

"We did." She shrugged. "Doesn't mean my body's listening."

His eyes slid over her body, then he returned to his cooking. "You really are a pain in the ass."

She loved flirting with him, loved knowing that she turned him on. But maybe it wasn't fair. If she truly thought it was a bad choice—and she was truly trying to not make bad choices anymore—she shouldn't tease him.

She straightened. "Sorry. You're right. I shouldn't mess around."

The look he gave her was hard to define.

He kept measuring and stirring for a few minutes as she watched. "You know, we have something else in common."

"Something else?"

"Besides being downright amazing together sexually, I mean." She grinned up at him, unable to keep from teasing.

"Seattle," he said warningly.

"No, seriously. Creating recipes is a lot like songwriting."

He looked at her with an eyebrow up.

"Come on," she said, stealing a slice of tomato from the cutting board. "You take some plain old ingredients that are like notes—by themselves they're nothing special. But you put them together into something new, something that wasn't there before. Like magic."

He stared at her for several heartbeats. His voice was rough when he asked, "You like the sauce?"

She dipped her finger into the pan and tasted it again, trying not to lick her finger provocatively or sigh in pleasure. "Yes, it's great." When she looked up at him, she stepped back, recognizing what was in his eyes. He looked like he wanted to kiss her. "Hey, sorry. I wasn't trying to be seductive."

"You don't have to try. That's a bigger problem. Believe me."

It probably made her a sadistic witch, she still liked knowing he felt that way. Because she did too. Even his hands turned her on. So, yeah, she got it. And liked it.

"I know how you feel. If it's any comfort."

He leaned in close. "You're not the one who has to walk around the restaurant with a hard-on. Don't try to comfort me."

She couldn't help it. She grinned. "Try to think pure thoughts."

"You first."

"That will take some work."

"Tell me about it."

"It's probably the kitchen. Bringing back memories," she said, feeling close to giggling.

"Probably," he agreed sarcastically. "I'm sure when I see you behind the bar tonight I won't be thinking about how your nipples taste."

She sucked in a sharp breath as lust twisted her. "Right," she choked.

"And when I see you in the lobby I'm sure I won't remember how you sound when you come," he said in a gravely whisper.

"Exactly," she breathed.

"So, why don't you get out of my *kitchen* while I still have blood circulating in places other than my cock?"

"Got it," she squeaked. She turned and walked quickly toward the door, aware of his eyes on her ass the whole time.

Lord almighty, when he turned it on, he turned it on. She felt like she'd been burned in that kitchen. And liked it.

She should call in sick tonight.

But where would be the fun in that?

Besides, she clearly *was* a sadistic witch so it wasn't in her nature to take pity on someone.

She headed for the dance hall where she knew she'd find the stage and the piano. She hadn't actually asked Marc for permission but she wasn't going back in that kitchen. She knew she didn't really need permission anyway.

She was still thinking about Marc and how they shouldn't have a repeat of the night before but how much she wanted to and didn't register her surroundings until she was halfway across the room. Then she found herself craning her neck around as far as she could make it go in both directions, taking in the details of the room.

It looked exactly like it had the night of the Grand Opening—the night she'd left Justice.

Ringing the dance floor were round tables with chairs, lush green plants and trees and tall wooden posts with lanterns suspended from them. Above her, wires were draped with white lights that would make the ceiling look like a star-studded sky tonight when it was dark. The entire west wall was floor to ceiling windows with French doors that opened out onto the stone paved patio.

It was a gorgeous room. She was sure many happy occasions had occurred here. She knew the room was used for wedding receptions, anniversary parties, church youth group functions, even school dances. The prom was always held at The Camelot now, since the students considered it much nicer for such a big event than the school gymnasium.

At the far end of the room was the stage with a grand piano. But right now there was also a drum set and a keyboard along with amplifiers and two equipment trunks. Looked like they were having a live band for the party tonight.

She went straight for the stage like an alcoholic went for the bottle.

The first note from the keyboard rang out in the huge room. The acoustics were fabulous. The note resonated through her and she was soothed and stimulated at the same time. Much as she felt with Marc.

The thought of Marc was like a shot of adrenaline to her fingers and they began flying over the keyboard, finding the

201

notes and creating the melody with little conscious effort on her part. She smiled as she began to sing, the words and melody coming easily.

Even the ending. Finally. The last note faded away and she smiled. It was a good song.

She loved writing, about whatever was in her heart, what was going on in her life. It was like keeping a journal. Or going to therapy.

She'd always been a songwriter. She hadn't always been good, but she'd always done it, learning and growing and getting better over the years. She'd written in high school and college, but then when she'd left Justice, it had changed. She'd started writing for the bands she was with instead of for herself. First for the girl band, Expectations, she'd left home with and then for Willy Nilly, the band she'd joined when Expectations broke up.

The idea was to be heard and liked. Period. If no one liked the music then playing it didn't matter a whole lot. Her music was written with the idea of selling in mind. It had to be enough like the stuff that was popular at the time that it would be well-received but it had to be different enough that they would be remembered and sought out.

After she was done with the bands, though, she could write whatever she wanted. Mrs. Carlson, the little lady who lived in the apartment directly under Sabrina's apartment, had owned a piano and she let Sabrina use it to play and write in exchange for Sabrina running her errands to the dry cleaners, grocery store and so on. It was a great trade and Sabrina had done some of her best writing there in that cramped apartment that smelled like chocolate chip cookies.

"That was great."

The male voice behind her startled her and she turned quickly.

"Sorry." The man was tall and wide, with a beard that was graying a bit, friendly eyes and a big grin. "Didn't mean to scare you. But I didn't sneak up. You were pretty absorbed in what you were doing."

She felt herself blush. Chase and the other guys in the band had always teased her that the building could fall down around her while she was writing and playing and she wouldn't notice unless it affected the acoustics.

"That was really great though," the man continued, rounding the piano and then leaning his forearms on the top. "What do you call it?"

"'Falling Hard'," Sabrina answered.

He nodded. "You should try a key change there on that last bridge."

She blinked at him. "I should?"

He grinned again. "Hey, it sounds terrific the way it is, but something like this."

Before she could react, he came around the side of the keyboard and positioned his hands over the keys, bumping against her shoulder as he played the melody of the song perfectly, except for a key change on the last bridge.

When he finished, he grinned down at her. "But it's your call. Either way it's great."

"How did you know I wrote it?" she finally asked.

He shrugged. "I've seen that look before."

"What look?"

"The look on your face while you played. It reminds me of how a father looks at his newborn baby for the first time."

She swallowed hard. "You're a musician." It wasn't a question. It was quite obvious.

"Yep. In fact, that's my keyboard you're making sound so good."

She stepped back. "Oh, wow, sorry. I saw it here and didn't even think—"

He laughed. "Don't worry about it. It's not like you ruined it or anything. Besides, that's what its for. Sitting here it's not worth much, but if someone touches it, it can make magic."

He said it matter-of-factly as he moved toward the back of the stage and checked the drum set.

"You're playing tonight, I take it?" she asked. It had been awhile since she'd had a conversation with a fellow musician— other than Chase, of course—and she was drawn to the man by their common bond.

"Every other Saturday. Marc and Luke have been great to work with."

The man bent to unpack a guitar case she hadn't noticed until then. "They let us play here regularly."

"Let you? They pay you don't they?"

"Of course." The man laughed again. "We'd do it for free, but don't tell them that."

Sabrina moved toward a second guitar case and knelt beside it. "What's the name of the band?"

"The Locals," the man answered. "Appropriately. Two of us are from Carson City, one is from Jackson and I'm from Waterton."

Sabrina lifted the guitar from the case and set it beside her. "Are you any good?"

He grinned. "Yeah, we are."

She liked his confidence and easy-going attitude. She helped him arrange the rest of the stage as they chatted. When they finished, he stepped back. "I take it you've done this before?"

"More times than I can count."

"What are you doing tonight?"

Surprised, she shrugged. "Nothing. Hanging out here."

"You wanna play with us tonight?"

"Play with you? The band?" She couldn't believe the way her heart sped up. "Like a rehearsal?"

"No, for the party. We do mostly cover songs—you'd know almost everything. We have a few of our own, but I'm sure you could catch on. It'd be fun to have a female voice. We could do some new stuff."

"I suppose I could. Maybe for a few numbers."

"Why not all night?"

She knew her face was giving her excitement away "What time do we go on?"

"How long is she going to be up there anyway?" Luke asked with a frown as Marc moved behind the bar.

Luke was covering the bar while Sabrina was on stage, but Marc was finding plenty of reason to be out of the kitchen while she was performing.

The Locals had already been booked for tonight, but he'd realized—like he had in Laramie—that the perfect way to remind her how much she loved it, was to get her up on stage again. After she'd left the kitchen and he knew she was in the dance hall at the piano, he'd asked Steve Myers, the lead singer and general go-to guy for the band, if he'd come by and meet her. Marc offered him a hundred extra bucks to let her do a few numbers. Much like in Wyoming, the band had decided to keep her with them all night.

Thinking of Laramie led to him remembering how wound up she was afterward.

And wondering if she would be tonight.

She looked fantastic—sexy, happy, having the time of her life. As was the crowd.

"Those guys aren't dumb," Marc told Luke. "They'll keep her up there all night."

"You enjoying being a smart ass?"

"What are you talking about?" Marc turned to face Luke. "I'm giving her a compliment."

"Don't. Don't remind me that she's never happier than she is when she's up there doing her thing. Don't remind me that at this moment she can barely remember *my* name but she can come up with every word to a song that's twenty years old."

Luke was quite clearly perturbed, which disturbed Marc. "What's your deal?"

"This is why she left." Luke gestured at the stage where Sabrina was playing guitar and singing back up to a Toby Keith song with Steve on lead. "This is what was more important than I was."

Luke had almost proposed to her four years ago. He'd proposed again two weeks ago. Marc knew Luke had some pretty strong feelings for Sabrina, yet for some reason, he was stunned by Luke's obvious disdain toward her performing.

Marc swallowed his own emotions. What was he going to say? *You can't have feelings for her because I do?* He wasn't ready for that.

"You're jealous of her music?"

"Yeah." Luke refilled a soda for someone and passed another a beer.

Luke claimed to have loved her, to have wanted to spend his life with her, but he hadn't gone after her. He hadn't tried to find her. Just like Marc had pointed out to her father. Being without her for four years had been partly their fault too. They claimed to have missed her, to have been worried about her, but they hadn't done a thing after she left but be upset.

If she'd left *him* he would have gone after her.

Marc froze with his hand around a margarita glass.

He would have gone after her?

He thought about that. Was he thinking in general terms? As in, if the woman he loved like Luke claimed to love Sabrina had left him he would've gone after her? Or was he talking about *Sabrina* specifically?

He looked at the stage. She caught his eye and pointed at the fiddle propped next to her.

He gave her a thumbs up and she rewarded him with a bright grin.

"What's that all about?" Luke demanded, having witnessed their silent exchange.

"She fiddles," Marc said with a shrug.

"Why?"

"Because she wants to." He loved that about her. He loved that she went after what she wanted, that she didn't see rules and expectations as a deterrent.

He paused. He loved a lot of things about her.

With a big smile to the crowd, she started to play. Marc felt his heart thump hard and knew that if he'd kissed her even once, made her laugh even once, had her tell him even one secret, he wouldn't have been able to help going after her.

What the hell had Luke been thinking?

"You know," he said to Luke, finally filling the margarita glass from the blender. "I've never understood your contempt for her music. Shouldn't you be happy for her? I mean, of all the people in the world, I would have expected you to be her biggest fan."

"I am," Luke replied. "I'm her best friend. I've heard her perform more times that anyone on earth."

"And you've hated every time."

"I have not." But it wasn't said with much conviction.

Marc looked at him with one eyebrow cocked. "Come on, Luke. You say that you loved her, but... Are you sure?"

Luke frowned. "What are you talking about?"

Marc shrugged. "She's the girl next door. You were best friends. She's beautiful. You love her dad, your parents love her. It made sense. But it never really fit, did it?"

"Of course it fit," Luke said. "It was the perfect fit."

Marc stared at Luke. It seemed without the frustration Marc had harbored for Sabrina he was suddenly seeing things more clearly. Like the fact that Luke wasn't just a victim of her manipulations. He'd had some expectations of Sabrina that weren't at all realistic if he knew and cared about her as he claimed. Like making a life in Justice without her music. "If you really loved her, why wouldn't you want her to do what she's so good at and what she loves?"

"You don't think I really loved her?"

Marc straightened. He had to say it. Yes, they would have to deal with how Luke felt about her now too. But what if he thought he loved her now because he was convinced he *still* loved her? He couldn't be in love with her *again*. He barely knew her. It had been four years since they'd been together. They hadn't spent enough time since her return to fall madly in love yet.

Marc felt his blood begin to race. "You were in love with a very specific idea of who you wanted. And you thought you could turn Sabrina into that. But that's what she wanted to be." He pointed at the stage. "She wanted to travel and live in the big city and let virtual strangers sleep on her pull-out couch so she could learn French and Zumba and other miscellaneous interesting things." He took a deep breath. "If you love *her*, you would want her to be happy and be herself. Instead, you get jealous and pissed because she isn't what you want. That's not love, Luke."

Luke was staring at him as he finished what had turned into a rant.

"You done?" he finally asked.

"I think so. For now."

"You're a love expert now?"

Marc tried not to react. Luke knew him well, could read his expressions and body language extremely easily. He didn't want to be in love and refused to admit that he might be. There was a baby to think about, and that was still enough to freak him out more than he wanted to admit.

"I don't have to be an expert. It's obvious." He looked at his friend. "Isn't it? How can you resent something that makes her look like that?" He gestured at the stage again. They'd finished the song and Sabrina was flushed and breathing harder. She took a bow and smiled a smile of pure happiness. She was gorgeous. "How can you not want her to look and feel like that every day for the rest of her life?"

"I hated that something could make her look like that when I was pretty sure I never would," Luke said quietly. Marc turned to stare at him.

"But you still want to marry her? Knowing that you can't do that for her and knowing that you can't let her be herself?"

"I was hoping she'd gotten all of that out of her system." Luke sounded pissed.

Marc looked at the stage. "Does it look like she's gotten it out of her system?"

"No. But it's time for her to settle down."

Marc swallowed hard. Maybe what he was about to say was overkill but... "She shouldn't have to settle for less than everything she wants."

"And neither should I."

Oh, yeah. That was supposed to be what Marc was preaching—that *Luke* shouldn't have to settle for less than a woman who loved him completely. One who wouldn't cheat on him with his best friend, for instance. "Right. Neither should you."

Luke gave a humorless laugh. "Thanks for the conviction." He poured two more glasses of scotch and pushed them across the bar. "You know," he said, sounding decidedly irritated. "Nothing else will ever make her look like that."

Marc looked at her again. He wanted to argue, but he couldn't push Luke anymore. Luke was his brother, in all the ways that mattered, and he had to try to protect their relationship.

The thing was something else *did* make her look like that.

Marc thought back to how she'd looked in his kitchen the night before. Not just after the amazing-against-the-wall-sex, but when they'd been arguing and talking about babies too. And then today in the kitchen when they'd been teasing. And when they'd been in the motel in Muddy Gap and dancing in Laramie and arguing in the airport.

She'd been wide-eyed and energized and full of life, her mind working fast, her humor full-blown, her feistiness simply spilling over.

Something else could make her look like that all right.

Marc was pretty sure Luke didn't want to hear about that though.

"I'll be up front." Luke headed for the lobby.

How he could pull himself away from the sight on stage was beyond Marc. He crossed his arms and leaned back against the back counter of the bar, settling in. Because God knew nothing could tear him away.

"Sounds like Seattle beat the street dances and little gigs that we've asked you to do with us."

Sabrina smiled at Steve. She'd been thrilled with the invitation to entertain with the band throughout the summer. "It was different," she admitted. But not always in a good way. The people in Justice seemed to truly appreciate the music and their performance. "It's too bad that more people can't hear your music, though. You guys write your own stuff, you all play two or more instruments. That's pretty special."

"But it's not too bad," Steve said. "*We* get to hear it. The people that we care about—our friends and family and neighbors—get to hear it. If my wife says she likes one of my songs, that means a lot more to me than some stranger in New York saying it because he thinks he can sell a million copies."

He had a point, Sabrina thought. That was something she'd never gotten used to when she was with bands in the past. It was a constant pressure, a constant worry about who would like the music, the song, their sound. Or not like it. When she was writing—writing because she *had* to write or her heart would burst with the bottled up words and notes—she felt so much freer and the songs always turned about better than when she was writing something specific for a particular band or a certain gig.

"I know what you mean," she finally said.

"Hey," Todd said. "We're not trying to bring you down. We're talking about us. We've got the musical life that we want. That doesn't mean that it's not okay to want more."

"Have you ever wanted more?" she asked.

Steve nodded. "When we first got together."

"It didn't work out?"

They guys exchanged a look before Steve answered. "Actually, it did work out. We got a record deal."

Sabrina sat up straighter in her chair and stared at him. "You guys had a record deal?"

"We even flew to California and recorded two songs," Todd said.

"And?" Sabrina demanded when he stopped.

"And we realized that it wasn't what we wanted to do," Todd answered. "We were sitting around in the hotel bar complaining about how the label was messing with everything. They kept wanting us to change the lyrics here and there or change the tempo or add some keyboard—"

"Or get a haircut," Jake inserted.

Sabrina smiled. Jake had shoulder length hair that he wore in a ponytail. "A haircut?"

"For our press photos and different possible album covers," Jake said, sounding disgusted.

"But lots of musicians have long hair," she said.

"Of course. If that's part of their image," Steve agreed. "But this label had a specific idea of how they wanted to present us.

It was an entire marketing thing. They matched our sound with what they thought we should look like."

"I think it was the haircut more than anything that changed our minds," Todd laughed. "We were sitting there drinking beer and complaining and then we looked at each other and said, 'What are we doing?' At home people loved us and we had steady gigs. We were having fun. So, we went in the next morning and tore up the contract."

Sabrina's eyes widened. "Wow. Have you ever regretted it?"

"Only when I think that I'd like to buy a cabin on the lake so we could fish more," Steve said with a huge grin. "The money would have been nice. But it's not necessary. Loving the music and enjoying ourselves *is* necessary."

"This way, *our* way, we can have the music and the life we want at the same time," Jake said.

Sabrina thought about that. The music and the life they wanted. It sounded perfect. She'd searched a long time for the contentment and satisfaction that these three men had found. It did not escape her notice, either, that they had found that happiness practically in her own backyard.

But they'd also had the chance to be sure of what they wanted, they'd gotten to make the choice. That was big. Singing on stage in Justice, Nebraska because they wanted to was great. Choosing to do it, knowing they could have had more if they'd really wanted it, was huge.

Maybe she wouldn't like the big time either. But it sure would be nice to be sure. Taking the stage in Justice was fun, but it was also sort of a consolation prize. And she was afraid she'd always feel that way. If she went to Nashville, if she had the chance, if she tried for the big time—

But she couldn't do it.

Could she?

Marc's words from the night before echoed in her head. She'd gone after her *what ifs*. He even admired that about her.

That was enough to make her heart flip.

Marc Sterling not only wanted her—which was surprising enough when thinking back on their past relationship—but he liked her, admired her, enjoyed being around her.

He thought she could do it all. Sure he wanted her gone, out of Justice, out of Luke's life, but she'd seen a sincerity in his eyes last night that said he truly believed she could, and should, go to Nashville.

Marc believed in her.

That was enough to make her let herself think about it.

Interestingly, Marc was becoming a reason that Justice was more attractive than Nashville.

"I haven't been with a band for almost two years," she told them. "I've been working various jobs and running a music program for kids and adults who can't afford formal lessons."

"Wow, no kidding. That's cool," Steve said.

"It is," she said with a smile. "It really is. I do miss performing, though."

"You going to do anything like that here?"

She hadn't thought about that, but Steve's question made her wonder "Why not?"

"You're a *teacher*?"

She swung to find that Marc had snuck up on her. "Um, hi."

"You're a *teacher*?"

She heard scuffling behind her and knew the guys were getting lost. As Steve moved past Marc he handed him a one hundred dollar bill. "I should be paying you, man," he said, clapping Marc on the shoulder. "'Night."

"'Night," Marc answered, pocketing the money without breaking eye contact with Sabrina.

"You paid them like you paid the band in Laramie?"

"They told you?"

"Yeah."

He shrugged. "I have yet to lose anything betting on you."

She wanted to hug him. Instead, she narrowed her eyes. "Thanks."

"So, you're a teacher?"

"Sort of. I don't have a degree, I just teach what I know. I got involved helping some kids as a volunteer with a pro bono music program and got hooked. When they got funding to pay someone part-time I applied and got the job."

"Why have you let us all believe that you're been living it up in the night clubs?" He looked sincerely perplexed.

"You assumed that, you never asked. And I still played in the clubs and hung out with bands from time to time. I still love that too."

"But you're making steady money and...you have a *real* job."

"As opposed to the other things I did that were legal and gave me a paycheck," she said dryly.

"You know what I mean."

"What you mean is you're shocked that I was doing something respectable and responsible."

"No I—"

She raised an eyebrow at him.

"Fine, maybe that's what I meant. Sorry. I guess I bought into the whole image of you as an up-all-night party girl who was barely getting by."

"When the singing became a job and my creativity went out the window I decided that I needed to find a way to enjoy the music again."

"How'd you get hooked up with the kids' program?"

"The same roommate who taught me about gluten sensitivity."

"You have a gluten sensitivity?"

"No. She did. But it's pretty interesting stuff."

Marc shook his head and chuckled. "You're a surprising person, Seattle."

"That might be the nicest thing you've ever said to me."

"You like surprising?"

"It's better than selfish and egocentric. Which are pretty much the same thing, by the way."

"I called you selfish and egocentric?"

"Twice that I can recall at the moment." She tipped her head to the side. "You don't remember that?"

"I do. I was wondering why I was so redundant."

Now it was her turn to shake her head. "You didn't think

much of me in high school and college."

"One of those times was when you interrupted Luke's first date with Kelsey because your purse was stolen."

"Well, it was."

"You were at the mall."

"So?"

"It's not like you were alone on a dark street corner in the hood."

"I still needed a ride."

"You had lots of friends."

"Luke was closest." She had no idea if that was true. He was simply always the one she called first.

"I was two blocks away at Starbucks."

"I didn't know that."

"Luke told you that."

He had and she'd balked. "I figured you wouldn't want to come."

"I wouldn't have wanted to. But I would have done it for Luke."

"Like you did this time. And look where this has gotten you." Before she said the words she thought she was teasing him. But as they came out of her mouth, she realized that she wanted to hear him say that he didn't regret coming to pick her up. And that he also didn't regret the things that had happened between them, that he was even glad about some—or all—of it.

"Yeah. Look." He lifted a hand and dragged his thumb across her bottom lip. "But all I can do is wonder what would have happened if I'd picked you up then. Or stepped in at any point prior to Muddy Gap. Would all of this between us have happened earlier?"

She wondered the same thing. Had this chemistry, this draw, always been there?

"We didn't feel any of this before," she said softly.

"But there were lots of things in the way. We were almost never alone together, for one."

"And Luke."

Marc smiled and dropped his hand. "He was so sure he was

in love with you that I wouldn't have even imagined getting close enough to you to find out if I had feelings. And being around for all of your...interactions...with him frustrated me. I couldn't see you as anything but this thorn in his side. That he kept pushing further under his own skin."

She wrinkled her nose. "Not very complimentary."

"But it's true. He encouraged you. He liked being there for you. All the time. No matter what. Constantly."

"Okay, okay," she frowned. "I probably called him a lot in college."

"All the time."

"Daily," she conceded.

"Four times a day. At least. And you ate at least one meal together."

She opened her mouth to protest, then thought about it and admitted Marc was right. "We were friends," she said. "Friends talk."

"It makes it hard to get close to any other girl when there's one calling you all the time, though. Most don't put up with that."

"If they liked him they would have hung in there."

"How could they know if they liked him? He was always talking to you, leaving early to come see you, showing up late because he was doing something for you."

"Fine," she broke in. "I was a thorn in his side and I've prevented him from finding any happiness at all."

Marc smiled at her. "That's why I was so glad that you left and that Seattle is so far away."

"And now?"

He shrugged. "He doesn't know you anymore. It's been a long time." He paused.

Sabrina really wanted to know what he was thinking.

"It'll go one of two ways," he finally said. "He'll either realize that you don't need him like you used to and finally understand that it was never real love. Or he'll fall in love with you for different reasons."

She swallowed. Falling in love with Luke and vice versa would be perfect. If she truly wanted to be with him forever all

215

of this would be so much easier.

If she was truly madly in love with someone there would be no decision to make—she'd want to be with him, wherever he was. But the fact that Marc was the one to make her realize that didn't make things one bit easier.

Chapter Ten

"Did you know that the baby's collar bone can *break* during delivery?" Marc asked as Kat came into her office. He removed his feet from the edge of her desk. Kat glanced at her name embroidered on the left breast of her white jacket and brushed nonexistent lint off of the M.D. after it. "Yep, I knew that."

"And that the baby might have trouble breathing after it's born?"

"Knew that too." Kat laid her stethoscope on the desk and took a seat in the chair across her desk from him. "I even know how to handle that."

"Did you know that it's possible to *tear* a nerve going down into the baby's arm?"

"You are aware that I spent a ton of money and time in school, right?"

"Twenty out of every hundred babies born in the U.S. are delivered by caesarean section."

"I've assisted on two of those."

He stared at her. She seemed pretty damned casual. He'd been surfing the net for information for the past three days and there was an overwhelming number of things that could go wrong with the pregnancy and delivery.

He'd started searching online for nannies in Nashville, had then moved to doctors, which had led to several links and websites that discussed everything from ear infections to Down syndrome.

"Are there any genetic defects in her history?"

"Whose?" Kat's smile was clearly teasing. Still, she waited

for him to answer.

"Come on." He put the book, opened to the genetic disorder chapter, in front of her. "Have you done an amniocentesis?"

Kat's eyes widened. "No."

"Why not?"

"Good grief, what have you been reading?" She peered at the book. "Amnios are hardly routine. And there's no indication so far. *And* it's early, even if we were considering one. Which we're not."

"But something could go wrong."

"Something could always go wrong. Everything can be perfect up to delivery and then things can happen. Things can also happen when baby turns six months, or three years or eleven."

Marc tipped his head back and groaned. "You're killing me."

"What are you doing?" Kat asked. "Exactly?"

"I was researching nannies and doctors in Nashville. I got sucked into a bunch of websites and was clicking around and found—"

"A bunch of stuff you decided to research in real books?" she asked, indicating the textbook he'd pulled from her shelf.

"Yeah."

"Remind me what this has to do with you anyway?"

That straightened him up. "I was thinking that she's not so bad."

Kat snorted. "Nice understatement."

"What do you mean?"

"I've seen how you look at her. And vice versa."

"How do I— Vice versa?" He changed directions mid-question as her words registered.

"Yeah, how you look at her. Like she's a extra large chocolate-cherry malt."

His favorite treat. Absolutely, hands down, the thing he would forsake all other sweets for.

"And vice versa?" he repeated after he'd swallowed the lump of *Oh, no* that lodged in his throat.

Kat grinned. "She's looking at you like you're a huge plate of cheddar chili fries."

He shuddered. As a chef he was morally offended that *anyone* liked cheddar chili fries, especially the woman he—

He shut that thought down immediately. This was getting complicated.

"I thought you were doing everything just to keep her away from Luke," Kat went on.

How much did Kat know, anyway? How much, and *what*, had Sabrina told her? He couldn't tell and it was driving him nuts. "Everything like what?"

"Spending time with her, flirting, complimenting her." Kat leaned forward and pinned him with a direct stare. "Proposing to her."

"I didn't exactly propose." Though he couldn't stop thinking about the idea ever since he'd said it.

"True, 'I should probably marry you instead' is a pretty pathetic excuse for a proposal. But I figured you were kidding. Until Luke told me about your weird reaction to her being on stage the other night."

"What was weird about it?"

"He said you acted like you were pissed at him for not wanting her up there."

He swallowed again. "He wasn't being supportive."

"Maybe. But the question is why do you care so much?"

He shifted uncomfortably. There was that nagging issue of how he felt about Sabrina again. It would be so much easier if he did just want to keep her away from Luke. Of course, he did want to keep Luke away, but where it had once been for Luke's good, he was beginning to see how it would be good all the way around.

He wasn't ready to talk to anyone about that yet.

Kat's nose stud winked at him and her eye makeup was heavy and black. But within the dark eyeliner she looked at him with an unflinching, assessing gaze. "Did you say Nashville? And the word nannies?"

"Yeah." But he was thinking maybe he shouldn't have.

"Why?"

"She needs to be in Nashville, Kat. She's never been settled because she hasn't been in the place she's supposed to be."

"You think Nashville is where she's supposed to be?"

"It makes sense," he said firmly. "She's incredibly talented, music is her passion and Nashville is the place those two things can turn into something."

"Only Nashville?"

"Well, not Justice. If she's going to go she should go big."

"And you're going to help her with that?"

"She just needs a boost," he said, not meeting Kat's knowing gaze.

"And a nanny?"

"Yes. It's better than getting married because she thinks she needs help. You can fire a nanny if it doesn't work out." Though he was determined to find the perfect person.

"Good point," Kat said with a shrug. "What's she think of this? She hasn't said a word to me about Nashville."

"She made it into this big singing competition down there. But she thinks she's not going."

"And you apparently don't agree." Kat didn't sound surprised. "You're just going to put her on a plane with a one way ticket and a 'good luck'?"

He shifted in his chair remembering the last time he'd tried to put her on a plane. "She's been on stage with The Locals the past three nights."

"I've noticed they're playing there a little more often lately."

Marc refused to feel bad about that. It was a good situation for everyone. The Locals were great, especially with Sabrina, so the restaurant patrons were enjoying it, the band always liked playing and Marc loved watching Sabrina on stage. Luke was a little annoyed, but he hadn't said another word about it to Marc. He just slammed doors and stomped around more than usual.

"Anyway," he went on. "The past three nights she's been remembering how much she loves all of this. So when I tell her that I called and let the competition know she'll be there, bought her a plane ticket and got her a hotel room, she won't be upset. Or at least *as* upset."

"Right, because if she's upset she might not sleep with you again."

His jaw dropped. "She told you?"

Kat crowed, tipping back in her chair back. "No, but I knew it!"

Marc opened his mouth to reply then shook his head. "You're wicked."

"You're sleeping with her. I can't believe she kept that secret. Must mean something."

"Not sleeping with," Marc corrected. "Had sex one time. Not even in a bed. What does it mean?"

"Not even in a bed? Then where?"

"My kitchen. What does it mean?"

Kat's eyes widened. "I'm never coming to your house for dinner ever again. Yuck."

"Not on the table or anything." Marc puffed out an exasperated breath. "What does it mean?"

"Why not your bed? It's just up the stairs," Kat pointed out.

"It wasn't a well-planned-out seduction or anything." He gave up on finding out what it meant that Sabrina wasn't telling.

"Even better," Kat said with a grin. "A spontaneous, can't-take-it-anymore, explosion of passion?"

"Something like that." Marc tried hard not to think about the details of what Kat had nailed right on the head with her description. The memories of Sabrina and his kitchen would hit him at the strangest times and he wanted a repeat performance. Seriously.

Kat ran a hand through her spiky maroon hair, then leveled a sober gaze on him. "I'm guessing she's not talking because she has some feelings about it that she doesn't know how to explain."

"Yeah? Is that good?"

"Could be good or bad. She doesn't talk about her dad much either."

Marc frowned. "She told me some. Like about his past and how he wanted her to be perfect all the time."

Kat looked intrigued. "She trusts you. Took her years to tell me about her dad."

"Sabrina confided in you, though?" Marc wanted to think that Sabrina had someone on her side besides—

"Nope. Luke was there."

Uh-huh. "She didn't tell you anything?"

"Not until we were juniors in high school. I just thought she was rebellious and not interested in all those extracurricular activities. We talked and had fun, but Luke was the one who saw her hurt and vulnerable. He was there before I was, so I think she was already used to leaning on him."

Marc frowned, flexing and relaxing his fist. "Luke happened to be in the right place at the right time when she needed someone." Luke had gotten drunk after Sabrina left that night four years ago and had spilled seemingly every detail of his relationship with Sabrina.

She'd needed an escape long before she was thirteen and Luke found her hiding in his tree house. Her dad had pushed her mom as hard as he'd pushed Sabrina. She had to be perfect, she had to be involved in everything, she had to be well-respected and well-liked. Rebecca had finally had enough and divorced him. She tried to take Sabrina with her when she left Justice but Bill had all the assets, impeccable character references and a long history in a supportive town. In spite of his jail time, the court agreed that his was the more stable home environment for Sabrina and the judge gave him full custody.

Sabrina had seen Rebecca sporadically for a few years, but her mom soon remarried, had two more children and they'd drifted into rare holiday visits, phone calls and e-mail.

"I guess you could say it was right place, right time for Luke," Kat said.

"He got lucky."

"Uh-huh."

He looked up from glaring at her desk clock. "What?"

"You like her," Kat sing-songed. "You really like her."

Marc wasn't going to deny it—because that was stupid—but he was going to be very careful with what he admitted right now. "And?"

"This is good. *You* be her baby guy."

"Baby guy?" He raised an eyebrow. "I think that part's already been cast."

"I mean the guy who helps her through this whole thing. You know, the appointments, the ultrasound, the labor and delivery, the late night feedings, the diapers. Then Luke won't have to."

Marc stared at Kat. He wanted to do all of that.

Shit.

But it wouldn't matter. Sabrina was going to be in Nashville. With a nanny to help with all of that.

Though being there when the baby was born would be—

Didn't matter. It wasn't his problem, his issue, his concern.

So why couldn't he stop thinking about it?

He frowned at Kat. Why'd she have to bring that up? Luke was— Then suddenly he got it. "You have feelings for Luke."

Kat quickly ducked her head, her cheeks pink.

Holy crap. Kat Dayton was blushing.

"You do! You have feelings for Luke. Damn, girl, why didn't you say so?"

"Do. Not. Tell. Him." Kat pointed a finger at his nose. "I'll cut something off of you that's very important. I have scalpels and I know how to use them."

"Why don't *you* tell him?"

"He's hung up on Sabrina." She slumped back in her chair, looking dejected. "I thought maybe something could happen before she came home but—"

"But what difference does that make? If you two have something going on—"

"We don't," she interrupted. "The minute she showed up it was all moot anyway."

"Why? He's not really in love with her. Not the way he thinks he is. Or the way he wants to be. Or whatever." The more Marc thought about it and said it, it made sense.

"He's worried about her and wants to help her," Kat said. "That's all it takes. No matter what else he's doing, the minute she calls he jumps. I know that for a fact."

This sounded interesting. "Tell me more." He leaned back and rested his hands on his stomach.

She looked at him for a minute. Then apparently decided to share and leaned forward. "In high school there was this party at Danny Riser's house. Sabrina didn't feel good so she wasn't there but Luke and I both were. We hung out all night and talked. With no Sabrina. Then there was this moment. I knew he was going to kiss me. I almost couldn't breathe. It was going to change everything. And then she called. She wanted ice cream."

Marc knew his eyes were wide. "You liked him even back in high school?"

"The point is," she said with a frown, "the second she called, he left."

"But she was sick."

"The same thing happened in college."

"You and Luke almost kissed?"

"We *did* kiss."

Marc was loving this. "I had no idea."

"Yeah. Exactly. He never told you and it never happened again. We were in the dorm, she was at a dance, you were—" She tipped her head. "I don't know where you were."

"Probably on a date."

She smiled. "Right. I'm sure. Anyway, we were in the dorm alone, watching a movie and he turned toward me, stared at me for a second, then pulled me in and kissed me. In fact, it got pretty hot."

Marc was *loving* this. "Did you—"

"Sabrina called. She was bored at the dance and wanted Luke to come pick her up. Which of course he did immediately."

"If her date wouldn't bring her home Luke didn't really have a choice."

"She didn't even ask her date to bring her home."

Marc thought about that. "We both know that they've always had a somewhat dysfunctional relationship."

"Yeah. And now she's back so it's starting up again. Unless

you can make sure she doesn't need Luke."

"She *doesn't* need Luke."

"She doesn't *need* anyone," Kat agreed. "But neither of them believe that. And Luke doesn't have a reason to leave her alone."

"But you're in love with him," Marc pointed out. "And he's not in love with her."

"Once they're married it won't matter, will it?"

It was true. Luke would marry for life. "Are you going to help me break them up then?" he asked.

She looked at him for several seconds. "You want to break them up?"

"Yeah." That much he knew for sure.

"For Luke's sake? Or hers?" She paused. "Or your sake?"

"Maybe I want to do it for *you*."

"As long as you have a reason." She gave him a grin.

"So how do we do it?"

"I think we have to concentrate on her. She said maybe to Luke. Get her to say no."

"You think I can do that?"

"Look, I know she got knocked up by a guy who didn't even give her his real first name and took all her money but—"

Marc pushed out of the chair. "She was robbed by the guy she slept with?"

Kat hesitated, then said, "The baby's father is some scumbag con-artist who got her drunk, seduced her and then drained her accounts."

Marc closed his eyes and breathed in deep through his nose. It was official. He'd fallen for Sabrina Cassidy. He knew because in the past he would have thought it kind of funny and even fitting that she'd gotten taken advantage of when he'd seen her take advantage of Luke so many times.

But now he just really wanted to kill someone.

Namely the scumbag con-artist.

Sure, because the guy deserved it. And because he'd stolen from her and likely several other women. But also because he'd had her infatuated with him—at least—and in his bed and he'd decided to walk away. There was no amount of money worth that.

What an idiot.

"He's long gone. She reported it to the cops, but the guy was slick and knew what he was doing. Anyway, a lawyer assured her that she could safely protect the baby from ever being found by this guy."

"She went to a lawyer?"

"She knew a guy who worked in a law office and he asked someone."

"Did this guy sleep on her couch at one point in time?"

"How'd you know that?" Kat asked, genuinely surprised.

"Never mind. What were you saying about her getting knocked up?"

"I was saying that even though she got knocked up on what was essentially a one-night stand, she doesn't usually do that casually. The fact that you've had sex means something, the fact that she's talked about her dad means something. I think there's a lot here that means something. I think you could convince Sabrina that Luke isn't her only, or even her best, option."

He felt a knot in his stomach. "Maybe." The fact that he felt anxious about it probably meant that he believed her.

He could tell Sabrina that he didn't want her to marry Luke because *he* was in love with her. But that would logically mean he wanted her to be with *him*. Marry him. And she just might do it. The feelings he was having weren't completely one-sided, but even more, he could also offer her what she most wanted—stability.

Which seemed great. Except that he wanted her in Nashville. Not because he didn't want her with him, but because he needed her to be happy. Even if it wasn't with him. As long as she was going after her dream.

"So what's the plan?" Kat asked.

Nashville. Definitely.

But he had to keep her from doing something stupid with Luke before the plane could take off.

It felt strangely like he'd been in this position before.

Chapter Eleven

Sabrina shifted on the exam table, crinkling the paper she lay on, pulled the hospital gown down and sighed loudly.

If Kat thought she was putting a needle in her arm, she was nuts.

"The best thing would be an IV at this point," Kat said as she came through the door.

Sabrina glanced at her quickly. "I assume that means a needle?"

"Yes." Kat's head was bent over Sabrina's chart.

Sabrina glared at her even though Kat couldn't see it.

This was a routine OB check up. She was going to have a thousand of them. But she was nervous. She didn't know what she was doing. What if she was screwing things up already? She'd wanted to call Marc to come with her. She wanted someone to hold her hand, reassure her, ask questions that she wouldn't think of. But she couldn't impose on him like that. She knew she should have called Luke. But that didn't feel right either. Which was crazy since he had, basically, signed on for all of this. He'd asked her to marry him, knowing she was pregnant. It made sense that he would expect to be present for things like this.

But she hadn't called.

"Otherwise things look pretty good but the baby's heart rate is still high. We'll keep monitoring you for now. You—" she pointed a dark purple fingernail at Sabrina, "—need to relax."

"What is going on?"

She whipped her head toward the doorway so fast she was

almost dizzy. Marc.

Sabrina was sure her heart monitor showed a spike or two.

"She's okay. A little dehydrated. We're monitoring her and the baby," Kat said soothingly. She didn't seem surprised to see Marc.

But why did she think she had to talk soothingly to him?

"What are you doing here?" Sabrina asked.

"I asked Josie why you weren't at the restaurant yet and she told me you had a doctor's appointment."

"And you thought you should come?"

"I didn't think you would mind."

The look in his eyes made her swallow hard before she answered. He looked worried, almost hurt. As if he was prepared for her to tell him that this was none of his business.

"I don't mind at all." She was thrilled to see him—as usual. But especially here. Which was weird. Kat was her best girlfriend, her *doctor*, and yet she felt better having Marc here.

"Wish you'd told me ahead of time."

"Wish I'd known you wanted to know."

Marc looked right at her. "You're right. I've never said, 'Hey Seattle, I give a shit what happens to you and the baby, let me know if you need anything.' I didn't know I had to say it in so many words."

She swallowed at the intense look of—something—in his eyes. It was a combination of frustration and possessiveness that made her squirm and want more at the same time.

"You know what you're getting into?" Luke strolled into the room.

Marc drew himself up taller. "Yeah. I do."

"What are you doing here?" Sabrina asked, shocked to see him.

"I asked Josie where Marc was and she told me that he was at a doctor's appointment with you."

"Sabrina's fine with me being here. Right?" Marc asked, turning to her.

She nodded, unable to speak at the moment. There was a lot of tension zinging around the room suddenly.

"What do you know about pregnant women and babies?" Luke asked.

"I know what colic is. For sure." He gave Sabrina a quick half smile.

She felt a hiccup in her heart beat. She smiled back.

"Do you know about placenta previa?" Luke asked.

Marc shot a concerned look at Kat. "Is she spotting or bleeding?"

"No. Dehydrated. That's it."

Kat looked impressed and Sabrina assumed he was right about that symptom. Still, they were talking about her uterus and...stuff. "Hey, I—"

"You've been doing more studying," Kat commented to Marc.

Sabrina frowned at Kat. More studying? And what did Kat know about it?

"I've read two more books since I talked to you."

Kat smiled. "Two books in three days. Impressive."

"I thought you only read cookbooks," Luke said.

"I read what I'm interested in," Marc replied, meeting Luke's eyes.

"You're interested in *babies*," Luke clarified. "And labor, delivery, dilation, Pitocin, all that stuff?"

Marc looked at Sabrina. "Definitely."

She glanced quickly at Luke. He seemed as confused as she felt.

"She needs twenty-seven milligrams of iron a day," Luke said

"And one thousand milligrams of calcium a day," Marc returned.

Luke's eyes narrowed. "Do you know about kick counting?" he challenged.

Kick counting? Sabrina looked at Kat. "What's that?"

Her friend—and *doctor*—ignored her.

"She's just past fifteen weeks. She won't be feeling any movement yet. But the baby has fingernails now," Marc replied easily.

Sabrina looked at Kat again. "Is that true?"

Kat didn't answer.

"Does the baby have fingernails, Kat?" Her eyes were riveted on the men.

"Yeah. Shh."

She'd just been shushed by her doctor at her checkup? Even more amazing, though, her baby had fingernails. And Marc knew that.

Then she frowned. Why did Marc know that? That was what the books were about? He was studying about pregnancy and babies and—

"It can also suck its thumb," Luke said.

"That's amazing," Sabrina said. It wasn't as amazing that Luke knew it—it was like Luke to know something like that. But it was amazing that it was true.

"We need to get her out of The Camelot and off her feet more," Luke said. "Her ankles are going to start to swell."

"Then I'll buy her some support hose. There's no reason she can't be there if she wants to be."

"She doesn't need to work. She'll have whatever she needs."

Marc frowned at Luke. "I know she will."

Sabrina looked back and forth between the two men. They were both nuts. It was sweet, she supposed, that they were fighting over her. But the fact they were talking about swollen ankles and support hose kept it from being romantic—or even something she wanted to keep talking about.

"Marc. Luke. You have to—"

But they weren't listening to her.

"It's going to get harder to be on her feet as time goes on," Luke insisted.

"Then she can sing from a stool," Marc countered.

"I was talking about bartending."

"She's going to be too busy with the band to bartend much."

"Is that right?"

"They're booked three nights a week through the summer,"

Marc informed him. "Once a week with us, minimum."

"Were they booked that much with us before Sabrina joined them?"

"No. But I like her voice. And I'm perfectly capable of making decisions about the entertainment we hire." Marc looked like he was waiting for Luke to challenge that statement.

Luke stared at him for several seconds while Sabrina processed the idea that Marc had booked the band more because of her. That was also sweet.

Finally Luke asked, "Are you aware of the sexual positions pregnant women should avoid after the first trimester?"

No one even moved for a moment. That seemed to have finally tripped Marc up. He didn't reply right away and got pale. He glanced at Sabrina, then back to Luke.

Sabrina couldn't make her mouth work. Did Luke know about Marc's kitchen? And if so, why didn't he seem more upset? Or upset at all?

"Are *you*?" Marc demanded.

"Yeah." Kat was scowling at Luke. "Have you researched that?"

Luke shrugged. "No. But somebody might want to look that up."

Sabrina turned wide eyes to Kat. She looked at Sabrina. "Any position in particular you're interested in?"

Sabrina shook her head vehemently. She would Google that herself for sure.

"Standing," Marc said.

Sabrina gasped before she thought of the fact that was a sure giveaway.

Kat looked vastly amused. Sabrina didn't dare look at Luke for his reaction.

"Standing should be fine," Kat said.

"I have a whole list," Marc said. "Do you have a book I could borrow?"

Sabrina wanted to smack him.

Kat stifled a laugh. Barely. "Probably. But the only thing you—*she*—has to worry about is being on her back too long or getting her hips up in the air too far."

Marc looked at Sabrina and she couldn't look away, even though she knew she should. "Her on top, or the man behind, or on her side should all be fine then."

He'd basically announced to the man she might be marrying that they had slept together and he was intending to do it again.

She was pretty sure her blood pressure and pulse were now off the charts.

She frowned at both of them. "Time to go. You're agitating me."

"As a matter of fact," Kat said as she pointed to the monitor. "All the numbers look good."

"You're sure?" Marc asked.

Kat shrugged. "Apparently the baby isn't bothered by any of this. Probably finds it amusing. I know I do."

Kat did seem less tense as well.

Sabrina, on the other hand, was afraid she was going to have permanent frown lines. "We shouldn't talk about sex if the baby can hear us."

"How about we talk about something else?" Marc moved to perch on the bed beside her. "Like baby names. For a girl I like Abigail."

Sabrina stared at him. Names? He had an opinion on the name of her child?

Abigail was beautiful.

Luke stood looking at Marc, and Sabrina waited for him to say or do something, offer another name, argue about Abigail, something.

Instead he nodded. "Really good name." He leaned over and kissed Sabrina's head. "I'll check on you later."

She turned and watched him go. "I'll be right back." And Kat disappeared.

"Is she acting weird?" Sabrina asked.

Marc was simply watching her when she looked at him.

"How can you make a hospital gown look sexy?"

She laughed. She knew she looked the exact opposite of

sexy. "You're such a liar."

"Then why do I want to kiss you so bad?"

He leaned over and did, but it was very different from all previous kisses. It was sweet, lingering, not lustful, not like it was leading anywhere. Just a kiss of some nameless, wonderful, I-want-more-of-that emotion.

"Sorry I never told you to call me," he said softly against her mouth.

"I wanted—"

"It's okay." He stopped her with his hand over her mouth. "From here on, I want to be the one you call."

From here on? But she couldn't say it out loud.

"What if it's a boy?" she asked instead.

He laced his fingers through hers. "How about Patrick?"

Something niggled at her memory. "Why Patrick?"

"It was my dad's name."

And Abigail was his mom. It all clicked into place in her brain. Marc was offering her his parents' names. And Luke knew it—had basically agreed.

What the *hell* was going on?

"What do you think?" he asked.

She had no frickin' idea what to think. "I think I would kill for some apple juice."

He laughed and headed out for her juice. She slumped back against her pillows and squeezed her eyes shut.

It seemed apparent that Luke and Marc had lost their minds.

But she was hoping it was a bizarre dream she would soon wake up from.

Or not. It was bizarre, but kind of nice at the same time.

"We need to talk."

Sabrina felt her spine go rigid. She was crouched behind the bar putting the new shipment of liquor bottles away and she took several deep breaths before slowly straightening to where Luke could see her face.

It had been four days since the scene at Kat's office. She hadn't known what the hell to say to him, so she had just avoided him. It had worked pretty well because it seemed he was avoiding her too.

Marc hadn't. Of course. But he'd been low key compared to usual too. There hadn't been as much touching or innuendo, and they hadn't gotten naked. It was like both men were waiting for something.

She suspected it was her. Or a decision from her.

Actually, she more than suspected. She knew. They were waiting for her to make a decision. Between them. And she wasn't really sure she could do that yet. Or at all. Or ever. Because she didn't want to hurt anyone.

Luke looked different. He had really ever since she'd come home. The Luke she knew best smiled and laughed and teased and charmed all the time. Even when he was upset or frustrated he was patient and optimistic. The guy she'd known over the past three weeks in Justice was a lot more serious and didn't hide his concern and dissatisfaction as easily.

"Yeah, okay." She took a deep breath.

"Are you in love with him?"

Okay, he was going to jump right into it. She swallowed. This was Luke. She owed it to him to be totally honest. "Um, yeah, I think so."

"And you think he's in love with you too?"

"I, um—" That one tripped her up. Marc hadn't said so but surely this felt unusual to him too. "I don't know."

"Seems like something you should be really sure about."

"What does that mean?"

"It means that you can't mess around with this, Sabrina," he said, exasperated. "This isn't a band you can quit or a roommate that will move on or a song you can rewrite over and over. This isn't like being invited up on a stage once in awhile. *You* have to make some decisions and commitments here. This is important. This matters. This isn't just about you."

She stared at him. Wow. This Luke—this intense, harder Luke—was tough to get used to. It seemed clear that he wasn't here to make her feel good about herself, or to bail her out. He was here to make her face what was going on and make some difficult decisions.

"I'm not trying to mess around with things." It hurt to hear that he thought she had quit the bands and her various jobs over the last few years because she was messing around. And it bugged her that he thought she did everything she did because it was someone else's idea first.

"But you are. You're messing around and you're running out of time."

"Because you're going to propose again."

"Because you're going to have a baby."

Right. The baby. That was coming in a few months whether she had a steady job or someone to help her or any frickin' clue about her life at all. That took a lot of strength from her and her shoulders slumped. "I know."

Making decisions wasn't her forte. That was why short-term things worked best for her. Even if she chose wrong, it wasn't forever.

That was why she'd been putting this off even after realizing that she could never feel for Luke what she felt for Marc.

"So I came to tell you, no more proposals. No more convincing you," Luke said. "I'm not going to make you say no to me. For both our sakes."

Her heart squeezed. Of course he would know that was the worst part for her, imagining saying no to him. Even four years ago, she'd avoided actually saying the word. She'd asked him to come to Seattle with her, but she'd managed to not say no to his proposal.

He wouldn't ask again.

She let that realization sink in. No matter what happened with Marc, there would be no Luke as a safety net. Being without Luke would be permanent.

Then again having this baby, being a mom, was also pretty permanent.

If Marc didn't want a happily ever after with her and her child then she was going it alone. Permanently.

She swallowed hard. "Okay."

"You know," Luke said quietly. "You're still the only thing Marc and I have ever fought about."

"Marc?" Josie came into the kitchen. "Phone call for you."

He wiped his hands on his apron and held out his hand. "Marc Sterling, can I help you?"

"Hey," a male voice greeted. "This is Scott. I'm with Next Stop Nashville."

Marc froze. He'd actually been expecting this call. When he'd notified them that she would be in Nashville for the competition they'd said they would be calling with the schedule and details. But now...this was it.

"Hey, Scott."

"You were down as the contact for Sabrina Cassidy?"

"That's right." She was going to kill him.

"Okay. She is the third performer in the first round. She needs to be in Nashville at the Tennessee Theater tomorrow at four p.m. Is that going to be a problem at all?"

"None at all. She'll be there."

He'd already booked the hotel and had the plane ticket on hold. He sent the text to Kim, the only travel agent in Justice, authorizing her to go ahead and book it.

Then he went to find Sabrina.

It had been four days since the scene at Kat's office and Marc had been sticking close to her. Luke had, surprisingly, not been sticking close to her.

She was behind the bar, wiping glasses and singing Katrina and the Wave's "Walking on Sunshine". Which, considering the lack of accompaniment and acoustics, was quite good.

You had a phone call.

That was all he had to say. That wasn't hard. No big multi-syllable words. But he couldn't get it out. Instead he just watched her. Even when she turned, found him standing there and gave him a big welcoming grin. Even when she came toward him, her own smile slowly fading into a confused frown. Even when she was close enough that he could smell her hair.

"Is something wrong?" she asked.

"Not really."

"Why are you looking at me like that?"

He was pretty sure that he knew exactly how he looked. Like he wanted to carry her off to his bedroom and not let her out for the next few weeks. At least.

She was leaving and he knew he had to have her again. One more time.

"I want you."

She blinked up at him in surprise and her breathing changed immediately. "Oh."

He made a decision then and there. He stepped closer. "I want you to know that, and instead of crazy, spontaneous, should've-said-no-but-couldn't sex, I want deliberate, aware, we-both-*choose*-this sex. I want you to say yes, get in your car, drive to my house and climb the stairs to my bedroom. I want you to park your car next to mine even though people might see it."

She licked her lips, took a deep breath and said, "I see."

His heart thumped. "Say yes."

She smiled a smile that made him imagine her naked and covered in chocolate-cherry malt. "Yes."

She was in Marc's bedroom. On purpose, by choice, because they both wanted it. There was no question, there was no blaming this on something else, there were no excuses.

She wanted Marc. She loved Marc. Being with him was an easy choice to make.

"Do not remove one stitch of clothing," Marc said, toeing his shoes off and kicking them in the general direction of the closet. "I get to."

The look on his face was enough to make her breathe harder.

She barely registered the room. It was immense. The mahogany bedroom set only filled half the room.

All she could focus on was him. Everything about him. His

eyes, the exact shade of his skin, the way his khakis hugged his athletic hips, how big his feet were.

"I already took my shoes off." She crossed one foot over the other, digging her toes into the plush brown carpet.

"I know. Looking at your naked feet is making me crazy and I don't even have a foot fetish. So I get to do the rest."

She grinned and took a step forward.

"No. Stay there. I'm trying to get under control before I touch you," he said.

She clenched her fists. She wanted him out of control, hot for her, barely able to think. She could admit that. "Maybe I could—"

"Stay. There," he ground out. "We've had fast and hot and crazy. I want to go slow this time but it's gonna take some effort on my part." He stripped out of the navy blue polo, revealing a soft, white T-shirt. "I want to touch every inch of you, taste every inch of you..." He pulled the T-shirt off.

Sabrina stared. He was so gorgeous. The muscles in his shoulders, chest and abdomen were well defined. Light brown hair fanned softly across his pecs and then led in a silky trail to the fly of his pants. She wanted to touch all of it.

She shifted, feeling warmer and damper by the minute. "Everything you do to me, I get to do to you," she said softly. She squeezed her knees together, making herself stay put, simply looking and studying him, memorizing the heat in his gaze, the flexing of his muscles, the deep gravel of his voice.

This man wanted her. He was turned on by her. He was here because of and for her at this moment and she wanted to draw it all out.

This was big. Inexplicably big. Scary important. A first she never wanted to forget.

"I can absolutely be okay with that," he replied huskily. "In fact, with that rule, I just added two or three items to the list of things I'm going to do."

She smiled. This was sex with Marc. This was how it should be. Fun, flirty, sexy, sweet.

"Bring it on."

The half smile was the epitome of sexy and she clenched

her fists tighter, resisting the urge to touch him. She wanted him out of control, but she also wanted this to be what *he* wanted. He wanted slow. She could do slow.

Probably.

He left his pants on and finally stepped forward.

"I need to see you," he said softly. He reached for the collar of the shirt she wore unbuttoned over the simple cotton tank top. He peeled the shirt off her shoulders, down her arms and tossed it behind him. Then he pulled the tank top off and over her head.

He stared down at her bra.

She looked down too. "What?" she finally asked.

"The lavender one. From Mushy Marsh."

"Muddy Gap," she corrected. "You remember?"

"Damn right. This isn't the first painfully hard erection you've caused."

Her eyes flew to the object of his comment then back to his face. "Yeah?"

"Oh, yeah."

She pressed close. "Love knowing that."

"This is what I wanted to do even then." He reached behind her and flicked the bra hooks open.

She let the bra fall from her arms, her nipples puckering immediately under his gaze. He lifted a hand and cupped her left breast, brushing the stiff point with his thumb.

Shots of fire streaked from her nipples to her gut to her clit. She wanted his hands all over, all at once, right now. "Marc," she moaned.

He played with the other nipple at the same time, rolling and tugging gently until her legs felt weak.

"More," she whispered.

"This is going to get serious," he warned playfully.

"Maybe I'd better lie down."

"Good idea." He walked her back to the edge of the bed, but caught the waistband of her jeans with a hooked index finger before she could sit. "I have a little more work to do here first."

He slowly slid her jeans over her hips, dropping to his

knees in front of her as he skimmed them down her legs and then pulled them free when she lifted first one foot then the other. He tossed them to the side and as they landed a small tube fell out. He reached for it, then raised his eyebrows at her when he saw what it was. "Cinnamon is my favorite flavor."

"Really? I had no idea."

"Yep." He flipped the top of the edible body lotion open, squeezed some onto his finger and then painted a cinnamon-scented stripe down her inner thigh.

His lips met the skin just above her knee, then his tongue licked up along the line of lotion.

She moaned, then asked breathlessly, "How's it taste?"

His tongue stopped an inch short of the elastic band of her panties. "Good. But I think I'm about to have a new favorite flavor." He pressed a kiss against the center of her panties.

She felt her knees wobble.

"I've thought of these more than once." He pulled the edge of the lavender panties down and pressed his lips to the Taz tattoo. "You've sure caused a whirlwind in my life."

"Good," she breathed. It couldn't be one-sided. It wouldn't be fair to feel the way she did for him without some return of emotion. She wanted him. But this was more than sex.

He turned her with his big hands on her hips and put his lips against the Caution sign tattoo as well. "I'm not feeling particularly cautious," he admitted.

"I'll keep you safe."

"I think I'm a goner no matter what, Seattle."

She started to ask him what he meant but he slipped lavender silk over her hips, leaving her bare. She stepped out of the panties and he turned her again.

"I knew what to expect from what I've felt," he said, looking at the narrow strip of hair that ran down the middle of her mound to point directly to her clit. "But this is even prettier than I imagined."

On his knees as he was he was eye level with her most intimate spot. But rather than feel vulnerable, she felt hot. He was looking at her like he'd never seen a woman before and while she knew that was far from the truth, she liked to think that this was different for him too.

He ran a fingertip down and over the stripe of hair. He stopped short of her sweet spot and she moaned. He traced the path twice more before Sabrina finally couldn't take it and put one foot up on the bed.

Marc sucked in a quick breath through his nose and she watched him lick his lips. "Subtle, Seattle. Very subtle."

"I hope you can take a hint."

"You mean like this?" Finally his finger touched her clitoris.

She jerked in response. "Yeah," she choked. "Something like that."

He swirled his finger around the nub, then slid lower, his middle finger sliding along her damp cleft. She watched him watching his finger. When the pad of his finger was at her entrance, she widened her stance and bent her knee slightly, moving her body against his finger.

He chuckled softly. "Got that hint too."

"You sure?"

He raised his eyes to hers as his finger slid into her. Her breath caught as he filled her.

"Pretty sure," he said mildly, adding a second finger, still holding her gaze with his.

She concentrated on staying upright on wobbly legs and breathing. She wanted more and yet was already on the verge of an orgasm.

He stroked in and out deep twice, then circled her clit again with wet fingers. Waves of pleasure washed over her. She supposed an orgasm right now would be okay. She had no doubt Marc could give her another later on.

"You want this right now?" he asked, almost reading her mind.

She let her head fall back, pulling on his fingers with her inner muscles as he slid home again. "I can't say that I would object."

The next thing she knew, he had two fingers deep and he spread his opposite hand on her right butt cheek, pressing her forward. Then she felt his tongue flick against her clit.

She grabbed his head with one hand, gripping his hair

harder than she meant to. But that was all that kept her from falling over. He didn't let up even with the tugging on his hair. He licked and pumped his fingers in and out as she felt the coil of desire tightening and tightening.

Finally he sucked rather than licked, hooked his finger just right and gripped her ass.

She went over the peak, coming hard, gasping his name.

He didn't let go of her immediately. Instead he nudged her back until she sat on the mattress, his fingers sliding free.

"Definitely a new favorite flavor." He stood at the bottom of the bed, looking at her in amazement. "I could do that again and again and never have enough."

"I wouldn't fight you off," she said with a chuckle.

He gave her a cocky grin.

"Take your pants off, Marc."

He continued to watch her as he unbuttoned, unzipped and shucked out of his khakis. He wore boxers. Quite obviously tented by a massive erection.

"More," she urged.

He slid the boxers down and let them drop.

She'd felt his cock with her hands and inside of her, but she hadn't had a chance to really look at him. She sat up on the bed, the position putting her mouth nearly on level with his erection.

Without hinting at what she intended, she leaned forward and licked the head.

His hands tangled in her hair. "God, Seattle."

She licked again, then sucked the head into her mouth, swirling her tongue around the tip.

He pressed close then pulled out. "Later. Definitely," he said gruffly, looking at her mouth. "But I need this. Now."

He pushed her gently and she dropped back to prop on her elbows. She watched him, loving the look of his hands on his cock. "Stroke it for me."

His eyebrows shot up. But he did. His fist sliding up and down his length three times.

"Let me." She started to sit up but he stepped between her

knees.

"Not now. I have to be inside you."

She wasn't about to argue with that.

His knees bumped the mattress and he leaned to grasp her hips, pulling her down until her butt was nearly off the end. Then he stood up and hooked her knees over his elbows. "I love this view," he said, looking down her body to where she was spread open.

She also looked as he pressed forward, sliding slowly, deliciously into her.

She gasped as he groaned.

When he was as deep as he could go, he paused. Then he slid out, excruciatingly slowly.

He plunged again, then pulled out. Each thrust slow, deliberate, with both their eyes on where he disappeared into her, then reappeared slick and wet.

Each time he went deep Sabrina caught her breath. He filled her completely, stretching her, making her muscles massage his length, reluctantly letting him go each time.

Finally, the fire began burning hotter and the thrusts became harder and closer together.

"Dammit," he said with clenched jaw. "I wanted this to go on for about a month, but I'm not gonna last."

"Good." She wiggled and reached around her own thigh to cup his balls.

He thrust hard and suddenly. "Ah," he groaned. "I love this with you."

That was enough to make her muscles begin contracting around him. She stroked him again, loving the effect. He pumped harder, deep enough that she felt tremors in her core.

"Come with me, Seattle," he panted.

She moved her hand from him to her clitoris, circling the slick nub. He watched her fingers, thrusting faster.

Then he lifted his gaze to hers and as their eyes locked he whispered, "Sabrina."

And the waves of her climax crashed over her.

She watched his face as he reacted to her vaginal muscles

milking him. A moment later he came hard inside of her, pumping until the last shiver quieted.

He continued to look in her eyes as he finally pulled out and let her legs down. They were shaky as she pushed herself up the mattress where she could lay comfortably.

Marc climbed up onto the bed beside her and ran his hand through her hair, then down her arm. She curled into him.

"By the way, I intend to have you on top and then like we just did again before we leave this house, so if you need to rest or stretch or eat or whatever, better get to it."

She laughed, running her hands up and down his chest. "And then we can start on the positions I want."

He grinned at her. "What do you want to start with?"

"You behind."

His eyebrows shot up. "You on hands and knees?"

"Or bent over the back of a chair," she said eyeing the big easy chair near the window.

He stared at her. Then started chuckling. Then laughing. "You just might be the perfect woman."

She snuggled close. "From you, that's saying a lot." The guy who'd once believed her to be the ultimate evil now thought she was perfect. She liked the sound of it. Even if he was full of crap and it was only post-coital bliss, she still really liked the sound of that.

Chapter Twelve

Marc ran his hand from the base of her head to the back of her knee, appreciating every inch in between. She was on her stomach, her cheek resting on her forearms, face turned to him. She wasn't asleep but she was pretty damned mellow.

He'd be the same way if he could get past the knot of tension in his gut.

He wanted her again. To ride him, to moan and beg, to put her mouth around him again. But he had to tell her about Nashville.

"You hungry?" he asked.

Food was always his fallback. When he didn't know what to say, or do, or how to help someone, he'd cook. Food was great for comfort, for reward, as a thank you, for celebration, for grief and for happiness. It made a whole host of things better and he was better at making it than most. Therefore, he reasoned that he was better at comforting and rewarding people than most.

He wasn't sure if he was comforting, rewarding or simply distracting Sabrina, but no matter which it was, food seemed the best answer.

"For something you're going to make? Always." She rolled and sat up on the edge of the bed in one fluid movement.

Her words made him grin—it was always nice to be appreciated—and her naked back made him hard. "Cover up or we won't get far," he growled, rolling in the opposite direction even as his body felt a definite pull toward her.

She gave him a naughty smile over one shoulder. "My stomach is only one part of my body I'd like you to take care of."

He groaned but made himself pull running shorts on over his already growing erection. "I want enough calories in you so you can keep up," he told her.

He watched her pull her shorts and shirt on without bra or panties. He hadn't noticed before—he'd been far too distracted by the physical need roaring through him—but her stomach wasn't completely flat anymore. She didn't look pregnant exactly, but she had a roundness that hadn't ever been there before. Having never seen her breasts before Wyoming he wasn't sure if they were heavier, but from what he'd read, they would be by now.

"What's wrong?" she asked, looking over at him.

I want you and your baby and your everything.

But he didn't say that. He wanted to watch her tummy grow, wanted to be able to compare day to day how her body changed. He wanted to watch her change too, as motherhood would surely add to her personality. He was curious how she would react when her child started walking, or when he or she first learned to read. He wanted to tease her and laugh with her and support her and tell her she was amazing.

But all he said was, "I'm starving."

She let it go and followed him down to the kitchen where she pulled herself up to sit on the counter while he got busy.

They'd had amazing hot sex right there in that kitchen but all Marc could think was how much he was going to love cooking for her. She'd eaten at The Camelot, of course, and he'd cooked for his roommates in college, including Luke, which meant Sabrina had been there frequently. But this would be different. He'd be cooking specifically for her. To please her.

He started the angel hair pasta boiling and gathered the ingredients for a red sauce with shrimp. He wanted to put the conversation off until after she ate. Stupidly. He wanted her to smile about him and something he'd done for her before they started arguing about Nashville.

They didn't say much for a few minutes, but he was acutely aware of her eyes on him, how her bare feet swung, how deep her breaths were, how hard her nipples were under her shirt.

When he finally set a plate on the center island, she slid to the floor. "Holy crap. I want to move in."

His eyebrows shot up. "Yeah?"

"Great food and amazing sex?" she asked. "Oh, yeah."

She took a bite and sighed in appreciation. Before he could say, *Let's go get your bags*, he said, "I took a phone message for you earlier at The Camelot."

"Really?" She took another bite and he paused to watch her savor it. "Who from?" she asked after she swallowed.

"Scott."

She looked confused. "Scott who?"

Marc suddenly had no appetite. He pushed his plate back. It was too bad. He liked this dish a lot. "He's with Next Stop Nashville."

She swallowed her bite of food and said, "I've been meaning to call them, I just—"

"You haven't called them yet to say you weren't coming?" She wanted to go. He knew it.

"Not yet."

"Have you checked the website?" He'd seen how tempted she'd seemed by his laptop the other night.

She didn't look up. "Just once. Or twice."

It was very confusing to have half of his heart thrilled that she was interested in the whole thing while the other half clenched with the realization that she was willing to leave after all.

"But why'd he call you?" she asked, lifting her head to look at him.

"Because I put myself down as the contact when I called to confirm that you were coming."

"You called them?"

"After I assumed you'd called to say no."

"But— Wow."

He took a deep breath. He wanted her to know that she was amazing and others thought so too. He wanted to be excited. He was but...he didn't want to lose her. Sabrina belonged in Nashville, he knew that, but he could admit that there was a part of him that would love to keep her with him, whatever it took, forever. Finally, he understood Luke wanting to keep her even if her heart wasn't fully in it. Having even part of Sabrina's heart was tempting.

It was ironic. For years it had driven him crazy that Luke couldn't shake her. Now, as hard as Marc had tried to keep them apart, he'd ended up feeling the same way.

He loved her. And because of that he couldn't keep her. Loving her meant wanting her happy. Which meant he had to let her go. If she stayed, he'd never know if she would eventually want to go, or if she was wishing for more, or if she was regretting staying. He couldn't live with that. He couldn't live with her being anything less than everything she could be, as happy and fulfilled as possible. Marc knew that Luke's hatred for her music meant that it wasn't true love that he felt for her. But true love was exactly what Marc felt, because he loved what the music did to and for her, and he wanted her to have it. No matter what that meant for him.

"You have to be there by four p.m. tomorrow."

"There's no way I can be in Nashville by four p.m. tomorrow."

"Actually you have a nine fifty-two flight out of Alliance tomorrow morning. You'll go through Denver and be in Nashville in plenty of time."

She was staring at him like she'd never seen him before. "What are you talking about?"

"I made all the arrangements."

"I'm— I can't. I'm having a baby, remember?"

"Being pregnant doesn't affect your vocal chords. That's been quite clear to everyone over the past few days. You don't have to give anything up. In fact, you have a chance at an even better, bigger, life."

Marc felt like he was having a heart attack. His chest was tight and his heart hurt.

She had to do this and he, evidently, had to make her.

Instead of holding onto her as tight as he could—like Luke had tried to—Marc wanted to make her go. That had to be better than watching her stay and knowing she wished she'd gone.

"I thought that—" Her gaze dropped to her plate, then came back up to his face. "I thought something was happening here. With us."

This was it. He'd known it would come to this. Of course she thought something was happening with them. Because it was. He was in love with her. And he was pretty sure she felt the same way.

If he told her he was in love with her and wanted to be a father to her child, she would settle with him. He knew that. And it was really tempting. He wanted her, there was no doubt in his mind. But telling her that, giving her that stability, would mean she would never go to Nashville.

And she'd always be missing something.

He couldn't handle that.

She'd been brave enough to leave before, to try, to dream. But there was one thing she hadn't fully done on her own—she had to see that she could come out on top. All by herself.

She was going to have to go to Nashville without him.

"We've had some amazing sex, I'll give you that," he said with a fake cocky smile.

She frowned. "Yes we have." She paused, as if waiting for him to insert something else. When he didn't she said, "That's it?"

Of course it wasn't it and he was going to have to lie his ass off.

"Well, we've had some laughs too. I love flirting with you, hanging out with you. But I get it, Seattle. This isn't where you belong. Don't worry. It's not like I was thinking this was long term."

There was a sour taste in his mouth and he doubted his ability to truly pull this off. He needed to get off of the topic of his feelings for her or he was definitely going to cave.

Something had been bugging him for a while about her singing career—or lack of it—so he went there instead. "What's with Seattle anyway?" he asked. "Why'd you go that way?"

She looked puzzled. "What way?"

"You sing country. Why go west? Why not Nashville from the beginning? Or even Texas, for God's sake?"

"The band I left with wasn't country."

"But you only stayed with them for a year. What about after that?"

She dropped her eyes back to her plate. "I was settled."

"You've never been settled, Sabrina." He knew the use of her name instead of his nickname got her attention. "You haven't had a steady job, a steady band, a steady roommate, a steady guy. What are you looking for?"

She met his eyes again. "I don't know."

"What do you want?"

She pressed her lips together. Then said, "A place that feels like home should feel."

Marc silently cursed. He knew exactly what home felt like. He'd been lucky enough to have two. And time in between to truly appreciate having them.

She should have had it too. She'd had her dad, a house, a hometown. But it had never been real or lasting or deep. So she'd gone looking.

"You have to keep looking until you find what you want, where you should be."

She shook her head and sat up straighter. "I'm good here. And I'm going to be a mom and now it's about making a home for my child."

She was right. But he also knew, from experience, that wherever she was would be home for that child. Wherever the love was, was home.

Marc's hand hit the counter. "You're going to Nashville."

"No."

"You're going to do everything you can to make this happen," he said pointing a finger at her nose.

"I—"

"You can't stay here," he finally said. "You know that." She had to know that. She had to feel it in her gut. And her heart.

"I want—"

He was desperate. All she had to do was blurt out that she was in love with him and he'd be a goner. He'd propose and whisk her off the church tomorrow and then they'd both be stuck wondering *what if?* for the rest of their lives.

This was going to hurt—both of them—but it was necessary. "Listen," he said, able to look at her and lie only because he did truly love her more than anything. "There's no reason to stay now. Kat's checked you over, you have a spot in the competition, some money. It's time to go."

"So upstairs earlier was—"

What I'm going to think about every night for the rest of my life. He managed to shrug. "Fun. I told you that you're the best I've ever had. That's the truth." The whole truth. "Why would I pass up something you were so willing to give? Shit, Seattle, give me a little credit for being that smart." He sounded like a total dick. He didn't like himself at all at the moment.

She looked like she felt the same. "And what about all the baby stuff? You learning all that stuff about the pregnancy and everything?"

"I couldn't let you think Luke was some big hero. Hell, anyone who can read can learn that stuff. I had to show you that he wasn't doing anything special." He was definitely a huge dick. He'd punch himself if he could. But he couldn't tell her the truth—that he wanted to know everything about all she was going through. It had nothing to do with one-upping Luke, or making him look bad, or making Marc look good. It had been pure curiosity and interest. Period.

Sabrina's expression was a combination of hurt, shock and anger. He was really glad there were no rolling pins lying around. He had no doubt she'd threaten to use it, and it wouldn't turn out quite as well as last time had.

"And telling me that I should name the baby Patrick? Or Abigail?"

Her voice broke on his mother's name and Marc had to suck in a quick breath. Fuck. Hurting her was like carving out his own heart.

Somehow—he had no idea how—he managed another shrug. "Had to trump whatever Luke was going to come up with."

Luke had been the farthest thing from his mind when he'd offered his parents' names up as possibilities. He'd love nothing more than to have Sabrina's daughter named after his mom.

God, he had to get this over with or he was going to be on his knees begging her to let him be part of her life, to stay, to give up everything for him.

She studied him without a word. Then she nodded, lay her fork down and took a deep breath. The next thing he knew, a fistful of angel hair pasta and red sauce hit him square in the chest.

"You might want to make a note of not keeping hard things, like apples or coconuts, on this counter if you're going to keep being such an asshole."

Then she turned, padded to the door in her bare feet and pulled it open. She stepped into the evening and shut the door behind her. He heard her car start a moment later.

That was when he let himself unclench the hold he had on the edge of the island and take a deep breath. In spite of the red-hot fire poker that seemed to have been jammed through his heart.

Because he realized that she wouldn't be in his kitchen to throw things at him anymore anyway.

Sabrina was amazed by how much it hurt.

She had her suitcase open, a few things thrown in, but she couldn't concentrate on packing. She had no idea about the weather in Tennessee, hadn't thought about how long she'd be gone, or what she should wear.

If only she could be angry. Or excited to go to Nashville. Or not care where she lived one way or the other as she had over the past four years.

Until a few weeks ago, the idea of an all-expenses paid trip to Nashville for several days with fellow music-junkies, whether she was performing or not, would have been a thrill. She would have begged for a ride to the airport. Even when she'd gotten the letter from Next Stop Nashville she'd considered going. In fact, she hadn't really stopped considering it.

But now there were a whole bunch of things making Justice more appealing.

Now there were things that Justice had that Nashville didn't.

And she was so beyond angry. So beyond hurt.

She hadn't wanted to believe the things he'd been saying to her, but he'd kept going. He knew he was hurting her and he'd kept going. He wanted her to leave. Maybe for a lot of reasons. Maybe just one. Maybe because of Luke. Maybe not.

But it was clear that he wanted her gone. Badly enough to pay for everything she needed to get gone. Far away gone.

Sure the competition was just a few days and there were no guarantees from it, but maybe he was hoping she'd win, or even just get a taste for the Nashville life and be addicted.

That definitely could have happened a year or two ago.

Now she wasn't so sure.

Sabrina realized that she should have stuck with the idea that Marc Sterling was a cocky bastard. That would have kept her from liking him, kept her from sleeping with him and kept her from falling for him.

Probably.

He'd tried to put her on a plane before. She wasn't sure why she was surprised he was doing it again.

Okay, the sex thing had made her think he might have changed his mind about her. But he'd said himself that he didn't have to like her to want to see her naked. She shouldn't have forgotten that line. Even if he did like her, which she rather thought he did, it didn't mean that wanting to see her naked equaled *stay here forever*.

Hell, she was the one who had accused Luke of jumping to conclusions from the time they'd slept together. Now she'd done the same thing.

She'd been weaving romantic fantasies about families and forever while Marc had been just killing time—in bed with her—right up until the perfect moment to get rid of her.

It wasn't like she could claim to be a victim though. The first time she'd gone to his house basically knowing what would happen. The second time he'd had her drive her car to his house and climb the stairs, knowing exactly what was going to happen.

Yep, there was no way she could claim that he'd manipulated her into sex.

Except that he kind of had. Maybe not into sex, but into saying no to Luke, into turning down the stability she needed, into making bad decisions. Again.

He'd come to Kat's office, he'd seemed concerned, he'd been reading baby books, for God's sake. It had all been part of his plan? To make her doubt Luke? To make her want something else? To make her want him?

Because how could she possibly marry Luke if she was in love with his best friend?

She dropped to sit on the edge of the bed.

His plan had worked brilliantly.

The bastard.

How could she possibly think about ever having dinner with another man, sleeping with another man, fighting with another man—not to mention marrying another man—when she was in love with Marc?

How indeed?

She flopped back on the bed, eyes squeezed tight. She was in love with Marc.

And he was trying to send her to Nashville. For good.

She didn't want to go. Sure, her heart rate kicked up a notch, maybe two, with the idea of being on a real Nashville stage. Okay, so a play list of songs had already formed in her mind, in spite of her being certain she wasn't going. She really didn't want to go.

Because her mind and heart had accepted Justice.

She couldn't go, get shot down, and come back and start over again convincing herself that she was good here, happy here, content here.

That was the hard part and she was past it. Why start over again?

"What's going on?" Kat strode in, blood pressure cuff and stethoscope in hand. "I saw your car was here instead of at work."

Sabrina opened her eyes but otherwise refused to move.

"I have a problem with my heart."

Kat took her blood pressure and listened to her heart. "That all checks out, hon. What are you feeling?"

"I don't think you can hear this heart problem with a stethoscope."

That's when the tears started.

Kat didn't say a word or ask a single question until Sabrina's tears slowed and she could take a deep breath.

"Is it Luke?" Kat's voice sounded funny but Sabrina couldn't push herself up to see her friend's face.

"No. Marc."

"What'd he do now?"

"Bought me a plane ticket to Nashville so I can be in a singing competition."

"And you're upset about that because..."

"He shouldn't want me to go."

"It's only for a few days, right?"

"He's practically got a U-Haul parked outside!" Sabrina exclaimed. "He's convinced this is my big break and I'm never coming back."

"That's sweet," Kat offered.

"Yes," Sabrina agreed. "If we were friends and this was just a sign he believed in me, yes."

"But you're not friends?"

"No."

"If he's not your friend he's—" Kat prompted.

"The asshole I fell in love with." Sabrina put her forearm over her eyes.

Kat sat in complete—probably stunned—silence.

Finally Sabrina couldn't stand it and said, "He's also the asshole who would do anything to keep me away from Luke, including showing me all the things I won't have with Luke and making me want them."

Kat still said nothing. Sabrina moved her arm and rolled to face her friend. Kat was staring at the comforter on the bed, a strange little smile on her face.

"Say something," Sabrina demanded.

"You're in love with Marc."

"I'm not happy about it."

"Still…"

"Yes," Sabrina moaned. "Yes. But I don't like him much."

"Does Luke know?"

"About Nashville?" Sabrina asked.

"About Marc."

"What about Marc?"

"That you're in love with him?"

"Yes. But I'm not," Sabrina said stubbornly. "Not anymore. He's a jerk. He doesn't want me? Well, he doesn't deserve me. The sex was just to show me what I wouldn't have with Luke? Fine, that's over. In fact…" she trailed off as she searched for her cell phone. "I'm calling Luke right now. I'm going to tell him I was an idiot and of course I'll marry him. Right away. Tomorrow."

That would show Marc.

Of course she knew marrying someone for revenge on someone else was crazy, but that definitely was not the only reason she was marrying Luke. He was all of the things she'd known before and he could offer all of the things that had made him the perfect choice before Marc decided to mess it all up.

"Um, no, you're not." Kat grabbed Sabrina's phone before she could. "You're in love with another man."

"Who can't wait to get rid of me," Sabrina pointed out. "Nothing is going to happen with me and Marc."

Kat quirked an eyebrow at her. She specifically pierced that one because she could raise it like that.

"Nothing *else*," Sabrina conceded.

"Bree, you *love* someone else."

"I'll get over it." She was sure she would. Probably. Someday.

"But—"

"It doesn't change the fact that Luke and I can make a great life together. That my child deserves a father like Luke. That Luke wants a wife and child. That we get along great, care about each other and can both have what we need this way."

But her stomach felt upset as she said it. Yes, they could

make a great life—that would always be missing something.

Kat crossed her arms. "You're not marrying Luke."

"Kat!" Sabrina couldn't believe it. "Give me my phone."

"No way. Luke deserves better than that and you know it. You're panicking. Once you've thought about it and calmed down a little you'll realize that Luke's not the answer to this. And just to make sure, I'm going over there to point that out to him."

"Fine," Sabrina said stubbornly. "You'll see. Luke will agree with me. He doesn't think I should go to Nashville either and he'll be mad that Marc did all of this."

"We'll see." Kat turned on her heel and left the room.

Holy crap! Sabrina scrambled to the edge of the bed and pushed to her feet. Kat was really going to do it.

She started after Kat. She couldn't let Kat talk to Luke about why he shouldn't marry her. For one thing, he might listen. He was already upset about her and Marc. If someone he trusted and respected and who knew everything, like Kat, tried to talk him out of it, it might work. Kat was quite logical and well-spoken. This would not go well for Sabrina.

She still didn't have underwear or shoes on but she headed down the stairs and pulled the front door open as soon as Kat shut it. She was at her car, fumbling with her keys as Kat backed out of the drive.

Sabrina followed her BFF—on the verge of being her *former* BFF—to The Camelot and parked right by the front door while Kat pulled into an actual spot. She yanked open the door and ran past Josie and toward Luke's office. She almost overshot his doorway and grabbed the doorjamb just in time to hear his cell phone ringing.

Kat.

He looked up as she barged in, his phone in hand.

"Sabrina? What's wrong?"

Panting she shook her head and clutched her chest with one hand and pointed at his cell with the other. "Don't. Answer. That."

"It's Kat." He lifted the phone to his ear.

Sabrina lunged at him, knocking the phone away. "I need

to talk to you."

He frowned. "What is going on?"

She was a wreck. She was broken-hearted, panicked, alone. She'd taken yet another risk based on emotions—and had failed. Luke was the one person she'd always been able to depend on. He was her safety net. He wouldn't break her heart.

That was reason enough right there to be with him.

She was tired of heartbreak. Tired of trying to make it with her music only to be told she wasn't quite good enough. Tired of getting her hopes up only to be told that she wasn't quite what they were looking for. She'd get a taste of what it could be like, enough to make her dream, but that was all it ever turned into. Just like with Marc. She'd had a taste of being with him—his humor, his sweetness, his touch—only to find it was just a dream.

With Luke that would never happen. She'd never be *almost* or *not quite* good enough. She was exactly what he was looking for. He thought she was wonderful, he wanted her. Forever. There would be no more trying and failing.

"Yes," she said.

"Yes?"

"Yes, I'll marry you. Tomorrow. Let's find a Justice of the Peace."

Surprise registered on Luke's face first and he started to shake his head. Just one shake but she saw it and panicked.

She stepped close. "Yes. Yes. It's perfect. We know each other. We trust each other. We will never be hurt or let down because we know what to expect. It won't drive me crazy that you love *The Price Is Right* because I already know you'll watch every day. It won't annoy you that I never finish a can of soda because you'll be expecting it. It will be great. No fights, no tears, no jealousy."

No passion, a voice taunted. But she ignored it—because without passion there would be no hurt feelings, no heartbreak.

"Marry me, Luke."

Marc let himself in through the back kitchen door of The

Camelot, hoping to go unnoticed. He was severely hung over, having used a bottle of scotch to try to deal with his feelings for Sabrina.

He'd simply not gone back to work after Sabrina left his house—unprecedented for him—and had ignored both his home and cell phone. A text to Luke saying *I'm sick* was enough to keep anyone from knocking on his door. But now it was Friday morning and Sabina would be getting on a plane to Nashville, so he didn't have to worry about running into her, or avoiding her. It was time to get back to work.

"What are you doing here?"

Marc winced as Josie's voice seemed to slam into his sore brain. "I work here."

She glanced at the clock. "Seriously, Marc you'll never make it." She peered closely at him. "Are you drunk?"

"Not anymore. Make what?" He never scheduled meetings or vendor appointments on Fridays. It was one of their busiest nights.

"The wedding. What are you going to do?"

"What wedding?"

But he knew exactly what wedding.

No.

"Luke and Sabrina's wedding." Josie clearly thought Marc had lost his mind.

She had no idea.

Marc closed his eyes and reached into his pocket for his cell phone. As it powered on he opened his eyes, cursed scotch, cursed Muddy Gap, Wyoming and cursed the fact that people could go to a Justice of the Peace to get married. That had to be what was going on.

He'd driven all that way, battled a thousand emotions, done incredibly stupid things and Luke was still going to marry Sabrina.

He had four voice messages and six texts from Kat.

Nothing from Luke. Nothing from Sabrina.

The texts started with *call me*, then *911*, then *where r u?* and finally *ur an idiot*. The voice messages were similar but included more details about what was happening and how big an idiot he really was.

"They're in Alliance at the Courthouse. Surprise elopement. Get your ass over there."

Surprise elopement. Oh, hell no.

He tore out of the parking lot, wide-awake and completely lucid. He glanced at the dashboard clock. It was seven forty-eight in the morning. Surely the Justice of the Peace didn't work this early. It was almost an hour drive to Alliance. He pushed harder on the accelerator and pressed his speed dial number three for Kat. As it rang he thought about Sabrina. Did she want this? No. She just thought she did. Luke was safe, Luke was settled, Luke made a pretty good-looking home. Except that it wasn't hers.

Marc kept his message to Kat short and sweet. *Stall them.*

Chapter Thirteen

Sabrina couldn't deny the butterflies. In fact, they were going to make her very sick, very soon.

Which didn't make sense. This was the right thing to do.

The sick to her stomach thing would pass. Because this was the right thing to do.

She hoped that if she kept repeating it, it would be true.

It *was* true. It had to be.

Luke wanted a life with her, wanted her baby. There was love. It wasn't mad, passionate love, but it was there. That would be enough.

She hoped.

And she'd get over Marc. Eventually. Maybe.

She hoped.

But the butterflies swooped again taking her back to her days of morning sickness. Crud. Not the way to feel on her wedding day.

She pressed her hand against her belly, willing it to calm. She assumed there was a garbage can behind the judge's desk, but to use it she'd have to get past Luke and the administrative assistant they'd dragged in as a witness.

The light yellow sundress was as close to a white dress as she'd been able to find. She hadn't spoken to Kat since her friend had threatened to talk Luke out of the marriage and so didn't have a girlfriend to dress shop with. And it didn't seem like something she should do alone. The sundress wasn't especially dressy, but Luke wore tan khakis and a pale blue button-up shirt so she didn't think he cared she wasn't in heels.

Her clothes were getting harder to fit into every day and she was grateful the dress had been a bit billowy—meaning too big—to start with.

She smoothed the front of the dress and looked around the room.

If they could get on with it and get it over with then she'd quit thinking about it and the butterflies would go away and she'd quit feeling like puking.

But Luke was out in the hallway on his phone. For the second time.

The Judge was sitting behind his desk reading something from the stack of papers in front of him and the admin looked terribly bored. The office hadn't opened until eight-thirty and with Luke's phone calls it was now eight fifty-six. She knew because every time the judge checked his watch, she glanced at the wall clock.

What possible emergency a restaurateur needed to deal with this early in the morning was beyond her, but apparently Marc was nowhere to be found—ever since yesterday afternoon—so Luke was the guy. She refused to think or wonder or worry about Marc.

"Sorry about that." Luke re-entered the chamber with a smile. "Just a few, um, issues."

"That Marc couldn't handle?" She almost couldn't believe she'd said his name without crying or choking.

"He's not there."

She scowled at the brass desk lamp in front of her. As far as Marc knew she was at the airport preparing to get on a plane. To Nashville. Out of Luke's life.

Out of his life too.

She squared her shoulders. If he thought he was going to be invited to their place for barbecues, he was crazy. "Let's go," she said resolutely.

Sleeping with Marc had been a dumb thing to do. Trusting him, falling for him, had been completely stupid and irresponsible. Well, she was done with all of that. She was going to start doing the right thing, for the right reasons. Responsible and logical were her new favorite adjectives. It was about damned time too.

Marrying Luke made sense. It was good for her and her child and could be good for him too. It was going to be fine.

Fine.

What a great word to describe what should be the most important relationship in her life.

She was about to start giggling hysterically when the judge finally pushed his heavier-than-average frame away from his desk and out of his chair.

"Let's get started. Luke Hamilton, do you take this woman, Sabrina Cassidy, to be your lawfully wedded wife?"

Luke wouldn't look at her. He shifted his weight from one foot to the other and cleared his throat. "I do," he finally managed.

The judge turned to look at her. The butterflies dive-bombed and she literally had to swallow twice to keep from lunging for the wastebasket.

"Sabrina Cassidy do you—"

Oh, God. She couldn't do this. She loved Luke but she *loved* Marc. How could she live with Luke and see Marc all the time and not shrivel up from the wanting and needing, but never having?

"—take this man, Luke Hamilton—"

She felt a little faint. She had run away from Luke before. Now she was going to actually reject him. Out loud. In front of other people. But she couldn't marry him.

"—to be your lawfully wedded husband?"

She took a deep breath, said a little prayer and opened her mouth. "I—"

"Oh, *hell* no." The growl came as the office door bounced off the inner wall.

Everyone turned at once.

Sabrina's heart knew who it was—and thudded accordingly—even before she saw him.

Marc looked pissed. And disheveled. And bloodshot.

She was thrilled. He was here to—

"What are you doing here?" Luke asked. But he certainly didn't demand it, or bellow it, or act all that shocked or displeased.

"Sabrina has a plane to catch." Marc started toward her.

The dangerous glint in his eyes made her blood hum rather than freeze as was probably more common for hunted prey. In fact, she took a step toward him.

"She didn't mention that," Luke said calmly.

"Marc," she started.

"Don't."

His voice was low, full of warning, his eyes directly on her. He stooped as he got near and before she knew it he had her scooped up in his arms.

"Marc, you can't—"

"Watch me." He turned and headed out the door.

The last thing Sabrina saw over Marc's shoulder was Luke's grin.

"What are you doing?" Sabrina demanded as they headed through the atrium of the courthouse. "Are you insane?" She kicked her legs but Marc's hold was firm.

"Knock it off. You're causing a scene."

"I'm—" She stopped as they passed a security guard. She'd successfully done that to him once before. But she didn't really want to get away this time.

He was literally carrying her away from Luke, preventing their marriage. That had been his intention all along. Since Wyoming. But if she fought him, it would be fighting to go back in and become Luke's wife.

In Marc's arms she realized that she couldn't do that.

He set her on her feet next to the curb outside the courthouse two minutes later. Then he stood looking down at her, a mixture of emotions on his face.

Finally she asked, "What?"

"You deserve a real wedding dress. And a church."

Crap. When he said stuff like that it was hard to be mad.

"It was spur of the moment."

"I know. It shouldn't be. When you mean it, it should

be...intentional."

Or deliberate, she thought. That word again. And if she was imagining the look in his eye she was going to commit herself to the insane asylum.

"You're right," she said softly.

"You're *not* marrying Luke today."

"Obviously," she said dryly.

He didn't smile. "Go to Nashville. Then, when or if you come back and you still want to marry him, I won't interfere."

His words sucked the air from her lungs. It wasn't about keeping her away from his best friend?

"Why?" she asked.

"Because I want you to have..." He trailed off and swallowed.

"What?" She stepped closer. "What do you want me to have?"

"Anything you want," he said huskily.

"Maybe what I want is here."

"I would love that. But you won't know for sure unless you go." He stepped back from her. "You have to know that you're *choosing* whatever it is. Not settling because you didn't have a choice."

She pressed her lips together. She understood. If she came back it had to because she *wanted* to come back to Justice. Not the way she'd come back from Seattle. Coming home then had been a last resort, the only option. If she came back from Nashville it would be because she chose it over all the other possibilities.

"I might not advance in the competition," she said.

"You'd better pull out all the stops."

She just watched him, memorizing his face, his scent, the feel of him with her.

"You'll have to take a cab to the airport. I can't watch you leave."

She felt her eyes widen. "You trust me to get on the plane?"

"I do."

The two words sent a shock through her. The man she

loved was saying *I do* to her today after all.

Finally she nodded. "Okay." She couldn't say goodbye to him at the airport anyway. It was bad enough now.

He gave her an envelope and pushed her into the backseat of a cab sitting at the curb. "Knock 'em dead, Seattle," were his last words.

She felt the tears well up as the cab pulled away. She tore into the envelope hoping for a love letter. Instead it was the print out of her flight itinerary, hotel information and five hundred dollars. She realized she didn't even have a toothbrush with her—much as he'd found her in Wyoming.

Chapter Fourteen

It only took Marc one day to figure out he couldn't live without her.

"Luke, can I have a minute?" he asked from Luke's office doorway.

Luke was at his desk, his head bent over paperwork. "Yeah, come on in." He didn't look up. "I wanted to talk to you too."

"Let me go first. Brad charges by the hour."

Luke looked up then. "Brad?" He saw Brad Conner, their attorney, standing with Marc. "What's going on?"

"I have some things I'd like to go over with you."

Luke set his pen down and leaned back, looking wary. "Things like what?"

Marc took a seat in one of the chairs in front of Luke's desk and Brad took the other. "I'd like you to buy me out."

"Buy you out?" Luke looked from one man to the other. "What are you talking about?"

"I want out of The Camelot. I assumed that you'd rather buy my half than take on another partner."

"I don't want another partner," Luke said.

Marc nodded. He'd known that but it was an option that should be presented. He hated this. He loved this restaurant, loved that they'd done it together, loved what it had become. But it was here and Sabrina was in Nashville. There really was no decision to be made.

"But I don't want to buy you out either," Luke said.

Marc sighed. "I know. But it's the only option. I'm leaving Justice. I don't know for how long. I need to have this settled before I go."

"You're going to Nashville?"

Marc was surprised by the calm question. "Yes."

"She's winning then?"

She'd only made it past the first round at this point, but she was in the lead and Marc knew she'd go all the way. "Yes."

"And you're glad about that?" Challenge glinted in Luke's eyes.

Marc shifted in his chair, trying to hold his temper, which was very close to the surface when it came to Luke, Sabrina and her music. "Yeah, I'm glad. It makes her happy."

Luke nodded. "It does. More importantly, her being happy makes *you* happy."

Suspicious, Mark said, "Absolutely."

"In fact, you'd go to great lengths to make her happy."

Marc narrowed his eyes. "Absolutely."

"She asked you to come?"

That was a good question. She hadn't but Marc couldn't forget the look on her face at the curb in front of the courthouse. She loved him, he knew it. She wouldn't mind him showing up in Nashville.

"No. But I'm going anyway."

"I can't believe you let her go."

Marc came to his feet. "I'm not going to stand in her way, Luke. How I feel doesn't matter. It's about her. Shut the hell up about making her stay here."

"I'm not talking about her staying. It's about *you* staying."

Marc's anger fizzled like a match blown out. "What are you talking about?"

"Why didn't it occur to you to go with her right away?"

"Because—" He stumbled on that one. It had occurred to him. He finally shrugged. "This is home. Where I belong."

Luke paused and leaned forward, arms on his desk. "We'll still be here when you come back. This is your home, your family, no matter where you are. I know that's the most important thing to you. But we're going to be here. You can go. Expand your family."

Marc stared at the man who he considered a brother. Luke had always known him better than anyone but he was stunned to find Luke knew something that Marc hadn't even realized until Sabrina showed up and made him want something more. He'd felt anchored to Justice because he was afraid to go. He'd lost one family, he didn't want to lose another, to leave them when they meant the world to him.

But he knew it was true. They would be there, loving him, supporting him, no matter what.

Was that why it hadn't occurred to him to go with her? That they could be together regardless of where she needed to be?

"So you think she should be with me?"

"Of course."

Marc slumped into his chair. "How long have you felt this way?"

"Since the hospital."

"Because you realized I was taking it seriously with the books and all?"

"Because she's never looked at me the way she looked at you."

Marc didn't know what to say to that, other than, "We didn't mean for it to happen, to hurt you. I really did think, at first, that I was just keeping you apart for your own good."

"Yeah. I know. That's why I haven't flattened you for going after her."

They sat, not quite able to smile, but at least more comfortable together than they had been for several days.

"Can we let Brad leave?" Luke asked.

The other man sat watching them both with a bemused expression.

"What about The Camelot, the kitchen, while I'm gone? I have no idea when I might be back and then I don't know if it will be to stay," Marc said. This was all very new and he felt vulnerable. He was going out into the world without a plan, without a safety net. Yes, his family would still be here, but he was going to have to make his way.

Thank goodness he'd have Sabrina.

269

"We'll get a chef, but there's no reason you can't be a co-owner and not be within the city limits of Justice twenty-four seven."

Marc was amazed as he processed what Luke was giving him.

Then something occurred to Marc. He scowled at Luke.

"What if I hadn't showed up at the courthouse?"

Luke shifted in his chair and cleared his throat. "I would have done it."

Marc stared at him. "You would have married her. Even knowing that I'm in love with her?"

"She deserves a guy who will fight for her. Even fight me. The one who would do anything for her. If you would have let her marry me then you're not the guy."

Incredibly defensive, possessive and jealous, Marc growled, "I *am* the guy."

"Which is why you're going to do the one thing no one else has ever done." Luke slid a piece of paper across the desk to Marc. "Go after her."

It was a seat confirmation on the next flight out. In Marc's name.

"Damn, she's good." Derek was the lead guitar player for the band accompanying Sabrina tonight.

"She's the one to beat tonight," Brian, the drummer, confirmed. "She's number two. Barely. Behind Sabrina after last night."

Sabrina tried to ignore the hitch in her breathing when he said that. She was in first place. For now, anyway. It was still hard to believe. But as the guys said, the woman on stage, Kristine Simons, was fantastic. She'd been on Sabrina's heels throughout the competition.

Still, she was having a great time. They'd been tied going in last night until she'd sung "Falling Hard"—the song she'd finished in Justice. It had been met with huge praise and she was now in the number one spot.

But it was close.

"What are you doin' tonight?" Derek asked. "You need another big performance."

Obviously. It was the finale. The winner would be decided tonight.

"How about Martina McBride?" Brian suggested. "You've got the pipes for it."

It was a good suggestion. She could rock Martina McBride. She also had another original she could pull out. "Coming Back" was perfect for her voice and had gotten the band in Seattle some attention and play on a local radio station.

But it wasn't enough.

She watched the woman on stage. She would win if Sabrina did Martina or even "Coming Back". Sabrina knew it. She would have a solid second, some cash, some attention. The competition was huge and radio and recording execs were in the audience tonight. The winner was guaranteed a deal, but that didn't mean the rest wouldn't get anything at all.

And she could be okay with second place.

She missed Marc. And Justice. And The Camelot, The Locals. All of it. But mostly Marc.

Being away had helped her see and feel things for what they really were.

She didn't believe that he'd done it all just to keep Luke away. Especially after seeing him at the courthouse. The look in his eyes, the insistence that she come to Nashville, it had been more than that. She couldn't say how she knew exactly, but she did.

She was ready to go home.

And that morning she'd felt the baby move. It was more of a flutter, more like nervous butterflies getting out of hand, but it was there and she'd known exactly what it was.

Everything had completely changed with that. Until then, the baby had been real in the sense that her life had changed completely and someone was depending on her in a way no one ever had before. But now it was *real* in the sense that when he or she moved it physically affected her.

And emotionally affected her. When she performed she wanted and needed physical release. With this, she needed an emotional one.

She wanted someone to talk to, someone to hug, someone who would be as amazed as she was. This was only the beginning too. It only got more amazing from here. Not just the pregnancy but the whole parenthood adventure.

She wanted to share that—have that emotional release—with someone.

With Marc.

Luke would have been there, Kat would be excited as a pseudo-aunt. Her dad might even step up as a grandfather. But she wanted Marc for so much more. Because she had a feeling he wanted it too. Vacations and lazy Sunday mornings, New Year's Eve, sickness, health, richer, poorer, better or worse.

She had to win this competition so she could convince him that she *chose* him.

"I have a new song for tonight," she announced to the guys.

"How new?" Derek asked.

"Wrote it on the plane on the way down here." About Marc.

His eyes widened and he gave her a grin. "What's it called?"

"'Anything You Want'."

"Is it a winner?"

"You bet your ass it is."

Marc Sterling was madly in love with Sabrina Cassidy. That was the only explanation as to why he was standing in the parking lot of the Tennessee Theater in Nashville at one o'clock in the morning.

He'd seen her last performance and had been blown away. Of course he was only one of the many who had been. She'd done an original, with just her and her guitar.

He hadn't expected to hear *their* story in the song, however.

He had expected her to win the whole damned thing. Which she did.

It seemed that all of Nashville filed past him before he finally saw her emerge from a side door with three other performers.

She drew nearer, engrossed in conversation with the tall blonde on her right, oblivious to Marc's presence. When she was close enough to hear him he said, "Hey, Seattle."

She whipped her head in his direction, freezing mid-stride. She looked beautiful and stunned.

"Marc?"

"I missed you."

She said something to the other singers that Marc couldn't hear. Then she turned to Marc as the rest headed in the opposite direction.

The parking area was well lit with neon and tall streetlights, and he could see her expression clearly. She still looked shocked, but happy to see him and he relaxed.

"I wanted to—" he started, but she rose on tiptoe and pulled his head down to kiss him. And she *really* kissed him.

He sank his fingers into her hair and angled his head to taste her fully. God, he'd missed her. He brought her hips to his and she pressed against him, clearly as eager as he was to be as close as they could get. She walked him back until he was against the side of the closest firm surface—the huge RV behind him. Then she looped her arms around his neck and boosted herself up until her legs were around his waist and she was against the hard erection only she could produce so quickly. He was more than willing to help keep her there and he put both hands under her butt to hold her up.

When they finally needed air, he blinked at her. "Post-performance horniness?"

"I've-been-without-you-for-three-days horniness." She gave him a sexy smile. "I missed you too."

"You're not mad I stuffed you into that cab?"

"I've forgiven you."

"Because I was right to make you come to Nashville?" He knew he was and he did want her to believe that, but it would also be admitting that leaving Justice was right for her. He had mixed feelings about that, but he always would. Thank God he knew that being together and being together in Justice were two different things.

"Because you did it because you care about me." She

looked at him for a few seconds. "Right?"

"That's a hell of an understatement, Seattle."

The smile she gave him could only be described as dazzling and he knew that he'd do almost anything to see it again and again.

"I think we might have a problem," he said then.

"Hmm?" Her lips were against his neck. "Too many clothes?"

He laughed and squeezed her ass. "I'm serious."

She lifted her head and took a breath. "What problem?"

"I can't be without you like this again."

Her eyes widened. She pressed her lips together. "I felt the baby move," she finally said softly. There was a glow in her eyes he hadn't seen before.

It took him a second to process but a slow warmth spread through him. The baby was good, the baby was moving, growing, communicating with Sabrina. And she was excited about it. "Wow." His eyes dropped to her stomach. When he looked back into her eyes she was teary. "I want to feel that."

One tear slid off her lower lashes. "If you marry me you can feel it every day. And so much more."

Surprise and pleasure in equal parts shot through him. "I was going to ask you."

She grinned. "I should probably be single for a while so I don't seem like one of those women who thinks she always needs a man around, but I'm seriously in love with you."

Another shot of adrenaline pulsed through him. "You're not going to be single. Ever again."

She wiggled against him. "Yay," she said quietly.

"Inside. Now." There were other things that couldn't wait either.

He set her on her feet and reached for the door to the RV behind him.

"Inside?" she repeated as he nudged her forward.

"I bought you—us—an RV. Like five hours ago."

She stepped through the door like Alice into Wonderland. "You did *what?*"

"I wanted you to really understand that I'm in this with you, wherever you are. This way when you're on the road performing, we can be together. I made sure the bed is big." He nudged her forward again.

She turned suddenly and put her hands flat on his chest. "*What* are you talking about?"

"If you're going all over performing, I'm going to be there."

She frowned up at him. "How are you going to make a living?"

"Luke and I agreed I would keep my share of The Camelot and we'd hire a new chef. If there are down times with your travel I'll work, but I don't have to be there to own it. I'm also going to scout new places for a potential second Camelot and if you're in Nashville a lot, maybe there's a small town down the road that—"

She covered his mouth with her hand. "I'm not traveling all over the country performing, Marc."

He moved her hand. "You won."

She shook her head, still frowning in confusion. "I won. But I'm not traveling."

"You are not going to give this up, Seattle. I'm here with you, wherever you go. We're together. You can have it all."

"All I want is in Justice," she said solemnly. "Honestly. Performing the last few nights has given me a good taste for what it would be like if I made it. I don't want this, Marc. I love singing for Justice, a crowd I know. It's a whole different level of appreciation. And I love The Locals. They are talented but they keep it in perspective. These guys down here are already talking about T-shirts and a logo and it exhausts me. I want to be home at night. Yes, in bed with you—" She ran her hand over his chest. "But also on our couch watching TV and having breakfast in our kitchen and sitting on our porch and then serving and entertaining our customers at our restaurant. I want to have birthday and anniversary parties there with people who care..." She trailed off, her voice thick.

Marc wanted to stop her, assure her that wherever they were together was home, but he knew she wanted to finish.

She took a deep breath. "You were right, Marc. I've never

been settled. But it's because I've never been *home*. That place where you're loved exactly as you are even when you're not your best. That place where you want to be your best—and where that's actually possible. I was looking for a *place,* then a career, but it's *you*. It's the life we can make together. It's all the things that means—extended family and special occasions and jobs and babies and the every day stuff too. It's you and me together." Tears filled her eyes.

"It's ironic that I found my home on my way home. That Justice is where all of that was all along. But I think that everything over the past four years had to happen for me to recognize you when the time was right."

He loved this moment. This was *the* moment of his life. But he had to say...

"So no more proposals to or from Luke."

She smiled. "Promise."

He was completely confident in her answer when he asked, "So I'm it, huh? What you want? Forever?"

She slipped her arms around his waist and gave him the smile he would be seeing—and loving—for the rest of his life. "I thought you'd have learned by now that I'm tough to get rid of."

"That you are. Thank God," he said before bending to kiss her.

They were mostly undressed when it occurred to him to ask, "But what happens with the win?"

She unhooked her bra and he nearly lost the entire train of thought.

"I got first place and an offer to travel with Brandon Long, an up and coming country star."

Her hands went to his underwear. He sucked in a quick breath but managed to ask, "And you turned it down?"

She ran her hand up and down his length. "I told the big shots that I had a whole bunch of songs that would be great for Brandon."

He closed his eyes as her hand circled him and stroked. "That's enough for you? Really?"

"Definitely. I get to write whatever I want. Brandon said he'll listen to anything I send him and right now he's looking for a lot of material for a new album. I could sell him five or six songs. I'll get credits on his albums. Others will hear the songs and possibly come to me."

"Awesome." The music deal *and* her touch. Before she could kneel and take him in her mouth he picked her up and tossed her on the bed.

"We better not get this dirty," she teased. "Since we're not keeping it."

He climbed onto the bed beside her and stripped her panties off. "Who says we're not keeping it? I'm going to want to check Brandon Long out when he tours with this new album and this thing is made for family vacations to Yellowstone and the Grand Canyon. Abigail definitely needs to see the Grand Canyon."

Her eyes filled again even as she smiled at him. "So does Patrick."

He felt a little sting behind his eyelids too. "Right."

"I like the way you think," she said.

"Oh, you're gonna like the way I do a lot of things."

And he set about showing her one right then and there.

About the Author

Erin Nicholas has been reading and writing romantic fiction since her mother gave her a romance novel in high school and she discovered happily-ever-after suddenly went a little beyond glass slippers and fairy godmothers! She lives in the Midwest with her husband who only wants to read the sex scenes in her books, her kids who will *never* read the sex scenes in her books, and family and friends who say they're shocked by the sex scenes in her books (yeah, right!).

For more information about Erin and her books, visit:
www.ErinNicholas.com (Twitter and Facebook links!)
http://ninenaughtynovelists.blogspot.com/
http://groups.yahoo.com/group/ErinNicholas/

SAMHAIN
PUBLISHING

It's all about the story...

Romance

HORROR

www.samhainpublishing.com

CPSIA information can be obtained at www.ICGtesting.com
Printed in the USA
BVOW011251140312

285173BV00003B/7/P